# The Bee Hunters
## A Tale Of Adventure

*by*

Gustave Aimard

Double 9
BOOKS

# The Bee Hunters
## A Tale Of Adventure
### by Gustave Aimard

Copyright © 2023

All Rights reserved.

ISBN: 978-93-61155-69-7

**Published by**

# DOUBLE 9 BOOKS
2/13-B, Ansari Road
Daryaganj, New Delhi – 110002
info@double9books.com
www.double9books.com
Tel. 011-40042856

This book is under public domain

# ABOUT THE AUTHOR

Gustave Aimard wrote multiple volumes about Latin America and the American frontier. Oliver Aimard was born in Paris. As he previously stated, he was the offspring of two married individuals, "but not to each other". His father, François Sébastiani de la Porta (1775-1851), was a commander in Napoleon's army and a representative of the Louis Philippe government. Sebastiani was married to the Duchess of Coigny. In 1806, the couple had a daughter, Alatrice-Rosalba Fanny. The mother died shortly after she was born. Fanny was reared by her grandmother, Duchess of Coigny. Aimard was placed as a baby with a family that were paid to raise him. By the age of nine or twelve, he was sent off on a herring boat. Later, about 1838, he served briefly with the French Navy. After one more trip to America (when he claims he was adopted into a Comanche tribe). Aimard returned to Paris in 1847, the same year his half-sister, Duchess de Choiseul-Pralin, was cruelly killed by her noble husband. Reconciliation or acknowledgement by his biological family did not occur. After serving briefly in the Garde Mobil, Aimard returned to the Americas.

# CONTENTS

**CHAPTER I**
A MEETING IN THE FAR WEST ........................................................ 7

**CHAPTER II**
IN THE FOREST ................................................................................ 19

**CHAPTER III**
THE CALLI ........................................................................................ 31

**CHAPTER IV**
SUPERFICIAL REMARKS ................................................................ 41

**CHAPTER V**
CONFIDENTIAL CHAT .................................................................... 51

**CHAPTER VI**
THE JOURNEY .................................................................................. 62

**CHAPTER VII**
THE SKIRMISH ................................................................................. 72

**CHAPTER VIII**
THE PUEBLO (THE TOWN) ............................................................. 82

**CHAPTER IX**
DOÑA HERMOSA ............................................................................. 94

**CHAPTER X**
EL AS DE COPAS (THE ACE OF HEARTS) .................................... 105

**CHAPTER XI**
THE RANCHO ................................................................................... 115

**CHAPTER XII**
THE REDSKINS ................................................................................ 125

**CHAPTER XIII**
THE MIDNIGHT MEETING ............................................................. 135

**CHAPTER XIV**
DON ESTEVAN DIAZ ............................................................ 144

**CHAPTER XV**
DON GUZMAN DE RIBERA ............................................... 151

**CHAPTER XVI**
THE POST HOUSE IN THE PAMPAS.................................... 165

**CHAPTER XVII**
A DELICATE FEDERAL ATTENTION................................. 179

**CHAPTER XVIII**
TREACHERY ...................................................................... 189

**CHAPTER XIX**
THE END OF THE STORY .................................................. 199

# CHAPTER I
# A MEETING IN THE FAR WEST

Since the discovery of the goldfields in California and on the Fraser River, North America has entered into a phase of such active transformation, civilisation has advanced with such giant strides, that only one region is still extant—a region of which very little is known—where the poet, or the dreamer who delights in surrounding himself with the glories of nature, can revel in the grandeur and majesty, which are the great characteristics of the mysterious savannahs.

It is the only country, nowadays, where such men can sate themselves with the contemplation of those immense oceans of alternate verdure and sand, which spread themselves out in striking contrast, yet wonderful harmony,—expanding, boundless, solemn, silent, and threatening, under the eye of the omnipotent Creator.

This region, in which the sound of the squatter's axe has not yet roused the slumbering echoes, is called the Far West.

Here the Indians still reign as masters, tracing paths on rapid mustangs, as untamed as their riders, through the vast solitudes, whose mysteries are known only to themselves; hunting the bison and wild horse, waging war with each other, or pursuing with deadly enmity, the white hunters and trappers daring enough to venture into this last formidable refuge of the redskins.

On the 27th July, 1858, about three hours before sunset, a cavalier, mounted on a magnificent mustang, was carelessly following the banks of the Rio Bermejo, a tributary of the Rio Grande del Norte, into which it falls after a course of from seventy to eighty leagues across the desert.

This cavalier, clad in the leather dress worn by Mexican hunters, was, as far as one could judge, a man not more than thirty years of age, of tall and well-knit frame, and graceful in manner and action. His face was proud and determined; and his hardy features, stamped with an expression of frankness and good nature, inspired, at first sight, respect and sympathy.

His blue eyes, soft and mild as a woman's; the thick curls of blonde hair, which escaped in masses from under the brim of his cap of vicuña skin, and wantoned in disorder on his shoulders; the sallowish white of his skin, very different from the olive tint, approaching to bronze, peculiar to the Mexicans,—all these would lead one to surmise that he had not first seen the light under the hot sun of Spanish America.

This man, who was to all appearance so peaceable and so little to be dreaded, concealed, under a slightly effeminate exterior, a courage which nothing could daunt, nor even startle: the delicate and almost diaphanous skin of his white hands, with their rosy nails, served as a covering to nerves of steel.

At the moment of which we speak this personage seemed to be half-asleep in his saddle, and allowed his mustang to choose his own pace; and the beast, profiting by a liberty to which he was not accustomed, nibbled off with the tips of his lips the blades of sun-dried grass he met with on his road.

The place where our cavalier found himself was a plain of tolerable extent, cut into two nearly equal parts by the Rio Bermejo, whose banks were steep, and here and there strewn with bare, gray rocks.

This plain was enclosed between two chains of hills, rising to right and left in successive undulations, until they formed at the horizon high peaks covered with snow, on which the purple splendours of sunset were playing.

However, in spite of the real or pretended somnolence of the cavalier, his eyes half opened occasionally and, without turning his head, he cast a searching glance around him, but betrayed no symptom of apprehension, which nevertheless would have been quite pardonable in a district where the jaguar is the least formidable of man's enemies.

The traveller, or hunter,—for as yet we do not know who he is,—continued his road at a pace which became more and more slow and careless; he was on the point of passing at about a hundred yards' distance from a rock which rose like a solitary watchtower on the bank of the Rio Bermejo, when, from behind the mass, where he had probably lain in ambuscade, there half emerged a man, armed with an American rifle.

This individual for a moment examined the traveller with the minutest attention: then, levelling his rifle, he pressed the trigger, and fired.

The cavalier, bounding in his saddle, and uttering a suppressed scream, flung up his arms, lost his stirrups, and rolled on the turf, where, after a few convulsive movements, he remained motionless.

The horse, in alarm, reared, lashed out wildly with his heels, and started off at full speed in the direction of the woods scattered over the hills, in the midst of which he soon disappeared.

Having thus cleverly knocked over his man, the assassin dropped the butt of his weapon on the ground, and, doffing his cap of vicuña skin, dried his forehead, while he murmured expressions of gratified vanity.

"¡Canarios! This time I don't think my marauding friend will come to life again; I must have broken his backbone for him. What a glorious shot! What will those fools say who wanted to make me believe at the venta that he was a sorcerer, who could not be hit without putting a silver ball into my rifle, if they could see him now, stretched out in that way? Capital! I have loyally earned my hundred piastres. It's not bad luck. I had lots of trouble in succeeding. May the holy Virgin be blessed for the protection she has deigned to grant me! I will take care not to be ungrateful to her for it."

All the time he was muttering thus, the worthy fellow was reloading his rifle with the most scrupulous care.

"Well," continued he, seating himself on a clod of turf, "I am knocked up with having had to watch so long. Suppose I were to go and convince myself of his death? By Heaven, no; he might still be breathing, and treat me to a thrust of the knife. I'm no such fool. I prefer sitting here in peace, and smoking a cigarette. If, within an hour, he has not stirred, all will be over, and then I'll run the risk. And indeed I'm in no sort of hurry," he added, with a sinister smile.

Upon that, with an air of the greatest coolness, he took the tobacco from his pouch, twisted a *pajillo* (straw cigarette), lit it, and commenced smoking with immense *sangfroid*, never ceasing to watch, out of the corner of his eye, the corpse lying a few yards from him.

Let us profit by this moment of respite to make the reader a little better acquainted with this interesting personage.

He was a man a little below the average height, but the breadth of his shoulders and bigness of his limbs showed him to be endowed with immense muscular power; his forehead was low and receding like that of a wild beast; his nose, long and hooked, bent down over a mouth immense in size, but with thin lips, and garnished with long pointed and irregular teeth; gray eyes, with squinting pupils, stamped his physiognomy with a sinister expression.

The man was dressed in a hunter's garb, similar to that of the cavalier. *Calzoneras* (loose trousers) of leather, bound about at the hips with a *faja*, or sash of silk, and falling as low as the knee, were fastened under *botas vaqueras* (heavy boots), intended to preserve the legs. A kind of half-jacket, half-blouse, also of leather, covered the upper part of his body, which garment, open in front like a shirt, had sleeves reaching to the elbow; a *machete* or straight sword, passed without sheath through an iron ring, hung on his left hip; and a game bag, apparently well supplied was slung to his right side by a strip of bison hide worn across the shoulder; a *zarapé*, or Indian blanket, motley with brilliant colours, lay on the earth beside him.

In the meanwhile time was passing; an hour and a half had already elapsed without our friend, who smoked cigarette after cigarette, appearing to be able to decide upon going to convince himself of the death of him on whom he had treacherously drawn trigger from behind the rock.

During all this time, the cavalier, after he fell, had preserved the most complete immobility; attentively watched by the assassin, the latter had not been able to perceive the slightest motion. The *zopilotes* (turkey buzzards) and the condors, in all probability attracted by the scent of the corpse, were beginning to circle in wide rings over it, uttering their rough and discordant cries; the sun, on the point of disappearing, had assumed the shape of a globe of fire on the edge of the horizon. It became necessary to act.

The assassin rose, greatly against his will.

"Pooh!" he murmured, "The man must be dead enough by this time, or if not his soul has turned to ashes in his heart. Let's go and look. Nevertheless, as prudence is the mother of safety, let us be prudent."

And in accordance with this reasoning, he drew from his garter the sharp-pointed knife which every Mexican carries for the purpose of cutting the thong if an enemy happens to cast the lasso round his neck. Having tried the spring of the blade against a stone, and convinced himself that the point was not broken, he made up his mind, at last, to approach the body, still lying motionless on the spot where it had fallen. But in the American deserts there is an axiom the justice of which is acknowledged by all. It is this: That the shortest road from one point to another is a curve. Our friend took good care to put it in practice on this occasion. Instead of advancing straight to the object of his visit, he made a long circuit, drawing nearer little by little, stealing along softly, stopping at intervals to examine the body, and ready to fly at the slightest movement he might see, and with his knife ready to strike.

But these precautions were useless; the corpse preserved the immobility of a statue, and our man stopped almost within reach without discovering a single thing to betray an atom of life in the unhappy wretch stretched upon the ground before him.

The murderer crossed his arms over his chest, and contemplated the body, whose face was turned to the ground.

"By my faith, he is dead indeed. It is a pity; for he was a formidable fellow. I should never have dared to attack him face to face. But a man must stick to his word. I had been paid; I was bound to fulfil my engagement. Curious! I see no blood! Pooh! It is a case of internal bleeding. So much the better for him, for his sufferings will have been less. However, to make doubly sure, I'll plant my knife between his two shoulders: in that way I shall be sure of my bird, although there is no danger of his coming to life again. You see, one must not deceive those who pay us; a man must stick to his word."

After this soliloquy he knelt down, bent over the body, supporting himself by one hand on its shoulders, and lifted his knife; but suddenly, by a movement of unexampled rapidity, the supposed corpse rose with a bound like a jaguar, and oversetting the stupefied assassin, seized him by the throat, pinned him to the earth, planted his knee on his chest, and deprived him of his knife before his brains could render an account of what was happening.

"Hulloa, *compadre!*" (comrade) said the cavalier in a jeering tone; "One moment, if you please, *¡cuerpo de Cristo!*"

All this passed in much less time than we have taken to write it.

However, sudden and unexpected as the attack had been, the other was too much accustomed to strange vicissitudes in somewhat similar situations not to recover his presence of mind almost immediately.

"Well, comrade," resumed the cavalier, "what have you got to say to all this?"

"I?" replied the other, with a sneer; "*¡Caray!* I say the game has been well played."

"Then it is one you are acquainted with?"

"A little," was the modest reply.

"I have been a little sharper than you."

"Yes, sharper; yet I certainly thought I had killed you. Curious," he continued, as if talking to himself, "the others were right; it is I who have been a fool. I will take a silver ball next time; it is surer."

"What are you saying?"

"Nothing."

"Pardon me, you did say something."

"Are you very anxious to know?"

"Apparently, since I have asked the question."

"Very well. I said I would take a silver bullet next time."

"What for?"

"Why, to kill you."

"To kill me? Go to; you are a fool! Do you fancy I will let you escape?"

"I do not fancy anything of the kind, the more so as you could not do anything worse."

"Because you would kill me?"

"By Heavens! Yes, as soon as possible."

"Then you hate me?"

"I? Not the least in the world."

"Well, then, if not, what is your motive?"

"Confound it! A man must stick to his word."

The cavalier cast a long look upon him, shaking his head the while with a thoughtful air.

"H'm," said he, at last, "promise me not to attempt to escape if I leave you free for a time."

"I promise, with so much the more pleasure, since I am obliged to confess that I find myself in a most fatiguing posture, and am very anxious to change it."

"Rise," said the cavalier, helping him up.

The other did not wait for the mandate to be repeated: in an instant he was on his legs.

"Ah," he replied, with a grunt of satisfaction, "liberty is a blessing!"

"Is it not? Now shall we talk a little?"

"I desire nothing better, *caballero*. I can only be the gainer by your conversation," replied the other, bowing, with an insinuating smile.

The two enemies placed themselves side by side, as if nothing extraordinary had happened between them.

This is one of the distinctive traits of Mexican character: murder amongst these people has grown so thoroughly into a habit, that it never astonishes anyone; and it often happens that the man just escaped falling a victim to an ambuscade, does not scruple to press the hand extended by his would-be assassin, foreseeing that someday or other he too will be called on to play in his turn the part of murderer.

In the present circumstances it was certainly not this consideration which induced the cavalier to act as he was doing. He had a powerful motive, with which we shall become acquainted presently; for, in spite of his feigned indifference, it was only with a sentiment of lively disgust that he seated himself beside the bandit.

As to the latter, we feel ourselves bound in justice to state that he had only one feeling of regret—the shame of having missed his blow; but he promised himself, *in petto*, to take his revenge as soon as possible, and this time to take such sure precautions that he must succeed.

"What are you thinking of?" demanded the cavalier, all of a sudden.

"I? On my honour, nothing," was the ingenuous reply.

"You would deceive me. I know what you are thinking of at this very moment."

"Oh, as for that, permit me to tell you—"

"You were thinking of killing me," said the cavalier, interrupting him abruptly.

The other returned no answer; he contented himself with muttering between his teeth—

"What a devil! He reads the most hidden thoughts. One is not safe beside him."

"Will you answer honestly, and frankly, the questions I am about to put to you?" resumed the cavalier, after a time.

"Yes; as well as lies in my power."

"That is to say, just so far as your interest does not lead you to lie."

"Confound it, señor, no one likes to make war upon oneself! No one ought to force me to speak ill of myself."

"You are right. Who are you?"

"Señor," replied the other, raising himself proudly, "I have the honour to be a Mexican, My mother was an Opata Indian; my father a *caballero* (gentleman) of Guadalupe."

"Very well; but I learn nothing from this about yourself."

"Alas, señor!" was the reply, given in that whining tone the Mexicans know so well how to adopt, "I have been unfortunate."

"Oh, you have met with misfortunes! Well, pardon me once more. You have forgotten to mention your name."

"It is a very obscure one, señor; but since you desire to know it, here it is: I am called Tonillo el Zapote—at your service, señor."

"Thanks, Señor Zapote. Now proceed; I am listening."

"I have followed many trades in my day. I have been by turns *lepero* (vagabond), muleteer, husbandman, soldier. Unhappily, I am of a quick temper: when I am in a passion, my hand is very ready."

"And heavy," said the cavalier, with a smile.

"It is all the same; so much so, that I have had the misfortune to *bleed* five or six individuals who had the imprudence to pick a quarrel with me. The *Juez de letras* (magistrate) was annoyed; and under the pretence that I was guilty of six murders, he asserted I deserved the garotte; so, seeing my fellow citizens misapprehended me—that society would not appreciate me at my real value—I took refuge in the desert, and turned hunter."

"Of men?" interrupted the cavalier in a tone of sarcasm.

"By Heavens! Señor, times are hard: the Gringos pay twenty dollars for a scalp. It is a pretty sum; and, on my honour, particularly so when want presses. But I never have recourse to these means except in the direst extremity."

"It is well. And now tell me, do you know me?"

"Very well by report; personally, not at all."

"Have you any reasons for hating me?"

"I have already the honour to tell you—none."

"In that case, why have you attempted to assassinate me?"

"I, señor?" cried he, showing signs of the utmost astonishment; "I assassinate you? Never!",

"What, fool!" exclaimed the cavalier, lowering his brows, "Dare you maintain such an imposture? Four times have I served as a target to your rifle. You have drawn trigger upon me this very day, and—"

"Oh! By your leave, señor," said El Zapote with warmth, "that is quite a different thing. True, I fired at you; it is even likely I shall fire at you again; but never, as I hoped for Paradise, have I dreamed of assassinating you. For shame!—I, a *caballero*! How could you form so bad an opinion of me, señor?"

"Then what was your intention in firing at me?"

"To kill you, señor; nothing more."

"Then in this case murder is not assassination?"

"Not in the slightest degree, señor; this was business."

"What! Business?—The rogue will make me go mad, upon my soul!"

"By Heaven, señor, an honest man must stick to his word."

"If it is to kill me?"

"Exactly so," answered El Zapote. "You can understand that, under the conditions, I was compelled to keep my engagement."

There was a moment of silence; evidently the reasoning did not seem so conclusive to the cavalier as to the *lepero*.

Then said the former:

"Enough; let us have done with this."

"I ask no better of your seigneurie."

"You acknowledge, I suppose, that you are in my power?"

"It would be difficult to assert the contrary."

"Good! As, according to your own confession you have fired on me with the evident intention of killing me—"

"I cannot deny it, señor."

"In killing you, now you are in my power, I should only be making use of reprisals?"

"That is perfectly true, *caballero*, I must even confess that you could not possibly have a stronger reason for doing so."

His companion gazed at him in surprise.

"Then you are content to die?" said he.

"Let us understand each other," replied the *lepero* with avidity. "I am not at all content. On the contrary, I only know that I am a thorough gambler, that is all. I played; I lost; I have to pay. It is reasonable."

The cavalier seemed to reflect.

"And if, instead of planting my knife in your throat, even as you yourself acknowledge I have the right to do—"

El Zapote made a sign of assent.

"I were to restore you to liberty," continued the cavalier, "leaving you the power of acting according to your own impulse?"

The bandit shook his head sorrowfully.

"I repeat," he said, "that I would kill you. A man must stick to his word. I cannot betray the confidence of my employers; it would ruin my reputation."

The cavalier burst out laughing.

"I suppose you have been well paid for this undertaking?" said he.

"Not a great deal; but want makes many things be done. I have received a hundred piastres."

"No more?" exclaimed the stranger, with a gesture of disdain; "It is very little; I thought myself worth more than that."

"A great deal more, particularly as the undertaking was difficult; but next time I will take a silver bullet."

"You are an idiot, comrade. You will not kill me the next, any more than you did the other times. Think of what has occurred up to today. I have already heard your balls whistle four times about my ears: that annoyed me. At last I wished to find out who you were: you see I have succeeded."

"It is the truth. Now, after all, were you not aware of my being close to you?"

The cavalier shrugged his shoulders.

"I will not even demand of you," he said, "the name of him who has ordered you to compass my death. Here, take your knife, and begone. I despise you too much to fear you. Adieu!"

Speaking thus, the cavalier rose, and dismissed the bandit with a gesture full of majesty and disdain.

The *lepero* remained an instant motionless, then bowed profoundly before his generous adversary.

"Thanks, your worship," said he, in a voice exhibiting some emotion; "you are better than I. Never mind; I will prove to you that I am not the scoundrel you fancy me, and that there is still something within me which has not been utterly corrupted."

The cavalier's only answer was to turn his back upon him, with a shrug of the shoulders.

The *lepero* gazed after his retiring form with a look of which his savage features would have seemed incapable: a mixture of sorrow and gratitude impressed on his countenance a stamp very different to their customary expression.

"He does not believe me," he muttered—we have already seen that he had a decided taste for soliloquy—"he does not believe me. Why, indeed, should he trust my words? It is sad; but an honest man must stick to his word, and I will prove to him that he does not yet know me. Let me begone."

Comforting himself with these words, the bandit returned to the rock behind which he had originally hidden; there he picked up his rifle, then from the other side of the rock he brought his horse, which he had concealed in a hollow, replaced the bridle, and departed at a gallop, after casting a glance behind him, and murmuring, in a tone of sincere admiration:

"¡Caray! What a tremendous fellow! What natural power! What a pity it would be to knock him over like an antelope, from behind a bush! ¡Viva Dios! That shall not happen, if I can hinder it, on the honour of a Zapote."

He forded the Rio Bermejo, and speedily disappeared amongst the tall grasses that bordered the opposite bank.

As soon as the unknown had assured himself of the lepero's departure, he began to calculate the time by the enormously lengthened shadows of the trees; and, after looking about him attentively, gave a whistle, sharp and prolonged, which, although restrained, was nevertheless repeated by all the echoes of the river, so powerful was its tone.

At the end of a few seconds a distant neighing made itself audible, followed almost immediately after by the sound of precipitate galloping, resembling the rolling of distant thunder.

Little by little the sound grew nearer, the branches crashed, the underwood was violently dashed aside, and the unknown's mustang made his appearance on the skirt of a wood at a little distance.

When there, the noble animal paused, snuffed the air vigorously, turning his head and neck in all directions; then starting off, with a thousand capers he made the best of his way, till he halted before his master, and gazed upon him with eyes full of intelligence.

The latter patted him gently, talking to him in a caressing voice; then, having made quite sure that the lepero was gone, and that he was assuredly alone, he readjusted the trappings of his horse, which had become slightly disordered, vaulted into the saddle and in his turn departed.

But instead of continuing to follow the course of the Rio Bermejo, he turned his back upon it, and rode in the direction of the mountains.

The bearing of the unknown had undergone a complete change; it was no longer the man whom we formerly presented to our readers, half asleep, swaying in the saddle, and leaving his horse to wander at leisure. No; now he held himself firm and upright on his mustang, with limbs closely pressing its flanks; his face was overcast with dark shades of thought; his glances wandered about as if they would pierce the mysteries of the thick forest with which he was surrounded; with head slightly bent forward, he listened with strained attention to the most trifling noise; and his rifle, placed across the saddlebow, had the lock exactly under his right hand, in such a fashion that he could fire instantaneously, if circumstances required.

One might have said, so suddenly had the man changed, that the strange scene to which we have just introduced our reader was for him only one of those thousand accidents, without consequences, to which his desert life exposed him, but that now he was preparing to battle with dangers which might really prove serious.

# CHAPTER II
# IN THE FOREST

The unknown had struck into a dense forest, the last skirts of which dwindled away close to the banks of the Rio Bermejo.

American forests have little resemblance to those of the Old World: in the former, the trees shoot up hap-hazard, crossing and interlacing each other, and sometimes leaving large spaces completely open, strewn with dead trees, uprooted, and piled on each other in the strangest manner.

Some trees, partially or wholly withered, show in their hollow remnants of the strong and fruitful soil; others, equally ancient, are supported by the entangled creepers, which, in process of time, have almost attained the size of their former props—the diversity of foliage forming here the most agreeable contrast; others, concealing within their hollow trunks a hotbed, formed from the remains of their leaves and half-dead branches, which has promoted the germination of the seed that fell from them, seem to promise an indemnification for the loss of the parent trees in the saplings they nourish.

One could imagine that nature had determined to put beyond the ravages of time some of these old trees, when sinking under the weight of ages, by clothing them in a mantle of gray moss, which hangs in long festoons from the topmost branches to the ground. This moss, called *barbe d'Espagnol*, gives to the trees a most fantastic aspect.

The ground of these forests, formed from the remains of trees falling, in successive generations, for centuries, is most eccentric: sometimes raising itself in the shape of a mountain, to descend suddenly into a muddy swamp, peopled by hideous alligators wallowing in the green slime, and by millions of mosquitoes swarming amidst the fetid vapours exhaled, sometimes extending itself endlessly in plains of a monotony and regularity truly depressing.

Rivers, without a name, traverse these unknown deserts, bearing nothing on their silent waters save the black swans, which let themselves carelessly float down the currents; while rosy flamingoes, posted along the banks, fish philosophically for their dinners, with eyes half-closed and sanctimonious air.

Even where the view seems most contracted, sudden clearings sometimes open out prospects picturesque in the extreme and deliciously fortuitous.

Incessant noises, nameless sounds, make themselves heard without a break in these mysterious regions—the grand voices of the solitude—the solemn hymn of the invisible world, created by the Almighty.

In the bosom of these redoubtable forests the wild beasts and reptiles, which abound in Mexico, find refuge; here and there one meets with paths incessantly trodden for centuries by jaguars and bisons, and which, after countless meanderings, all debouch on unknown drinking holes.

Woe to the daring mortal who, without a guide ventures to tempt the inextricable mazes of these immense seas of verdure! After ineffable tortures, he succumbs, and falls a prey to the savage beasts. How many hardy pioneers have died thus, without the possibility of the veil being lifted which shrouds their miserable end! Their blanched bones, discovered at the foot of some tree, alone can teach those who come upon them that on that spot men have died, a prey to infinite suffering, and that the same fate, perchance, awaits the finders.

The stranger must have been the constant guest of the forest into which he had so audaciously plunged at the moment when the sun, quitting the horizon, had left the earth to darkness—darkness rendered still denser in the covert, in which the light even at midday could only struggle in at intervals through the tufted branches.

Bending a little forward, eye and ear on the watch, the unknown advanced as rapidly as the nature of the ground under his horse's hoofs would let him, following unhesitatingly the capricious deviations of a wild animal's path, whose traces were scarcely discoverable amidst the tall grasses which strove continually to efface it.

He had already ridden for several hours without having slackened the pace of his horse, plunging deeper and deeper into the forest.

He had forded several rivers, scaled many a steep ravine, hearing at a short distance, on right and left, the hoarse growlings of the jaguar and the mocking wailing of the tiger cat, which seemed to follow him with their menacing yells.

Taking no heed of roar or tumult, he continued his route, although the forest assumed a more dreary aspect at every step.

The bushes and trees of low growth had disappeared, to make room for gigantic mahogany trees, century old cork trees, and the acajou, whose sombre branches formed a vaulted roof of green eighty feet above his head. The path had grown wider, and stretched, in a gentle incline, towards a hillock of moderate height, entirely free from trees.

Arrived at the base of the hillock, the stranger halted; then, without dismounting, cast a searching glance on all around.

The stillness of death pervaded everything; the howling of the wild beasts was lost in the distance; no noise was audible, save that caused by a slender stream of water, which, trickling through the crevices of a rock, fell from a height of three or four yards into a natural basin.

The sky, of the deepest blue, was spangled with an infinite number of brilliant stars; and the moon, sailing amidst a sea of whitish clouds, cast her silvery rays in profusion on the hillock, whose sides, fantastically lighted up, formed a striking contrast with the rest of the landscape, merged, as it was, in the deepest obscurity.

During several minutes the unknown remained motionless as a statue, listening to the faintest sound, ready to fire at the slightest appearance of danger.

Convinced, at last, that all around was peaceful, and that nothing unusual disturbed the silence of the solitude, he prepared to dismount, when suddenly his horse threw up his head, laid back his ears, and snorted loudly.

A moment more, and a violent crashing was heard among the underwood; a noble moose deer rose from amidst the bushes, and, bounding to within a short distance from the cavalier, rapidly traversed the path, tossing his antlers in terror, and vanished in the darkness.

For a time the noise of its headlong course resounded over the dry leaves, crushed under its feet in the constantly increasing speed of its flight.

The cavalier, with a scarcely perceptible motion of the hand, backed his horse gradually to the foot of the hillock, with his head always turned in the direction of the forest, like a vidette who retires before a superior force.

As soon as he reached the spot he had selected, the unknown leaped lightly to the ground; and, making a rampart of his horse's body, levelled his rifle, steadied the barrel across the saddle, and waited patiently.

He had not to wait long: after a while the tread of several persons was heard approaching his place of ambush.

Most likely the unknown had already divined who these persons might be, even before he saw them; for he quitted his temporary shelter, passed his arm through his horse's reins, and, uncocking his rifle, let the butt drop on the ground, with every symptom of complete security, while a smile of indefinable expression played about his lips.

At last the branches parted, and five persons appeared on the scene.

Of these five persons, four were men; two of them supported the tottering form of a woman, whom they almost carried in their arms. And, what was most wonderful in these regions, the strangers, whom it was easy to recognise as white men by their dress and the colour of their skin, had no horses with them.

They continued to advance without being aware of the presence of the unknown, who, still motionless, marked their approach with mingled pity and sadness.

Suddenly one of the strangers happened to lift his eyes.

"Praise be to God!" cried he, in Mexican, with lively satisfaction; "We are saved. Here is a human being at last."

The five stopped. The one who had first observed the unknown came rapidly towards him, and exclaimed, with a graceful inclination:

"Caballero, I entreat you to grant, what is seldom refused in the wilderness, aid and protection."

The unknown, before he replied, threw a searching look at the speaker.

The latter was a man of some fifty years; his manner was polished, his features noble, although his hair was growing white about his temples; his figure, upright and compact, had no more bent an inch, nor his black eyes lost a particle of their fire, than if he had been only thirty. His rich dress and the ease of his manner clearly proved him to belong to the highest grade of Mexican society.

"You have committed two grave errors in as many minutes, caballero," answered the unknown: "the first, in approaching me without precaution; the second, in demanding aid and protection without knowing who I am."

"I do not understand you, señor," replied the stranger, with astonishment. "Do not all men owe mutual assistance to each other?"

"In the civilised world it may be so," said the unknown, with a sneer; "but in the wilderness, the sight of a man always forebodes danger: we are savages here."

The stranger recoiled in astonishment.

"And thus," said be, "you would leave your fellow creatures to perish in these horrible solitudes without stretching forth a hand to help them?"

"My fellow creatures!" cried the unknown, with biting irony; "My fellow creatures are the wild beasts of the prairie. What have I in common with you men of towns and cities, natural enemies of every being that breathes the pure air of liberty? There is nothing in common between you and me. Begone, and weary me no more."

"Be it so," was the stranger's haughty answer. "I would not importune you much longer; were it only a question of myself, I would not have uttered a single prayer to you. Life is not so dear to me, that I should seek to prolong it on terms repugnant to my honour; but it is not a question of myself alone; here is a female, still almost a child, my daughter who is in want of prompt assistance, and will die if it is not rendered."

The unknown made no reply; he had turned away, as if reluctant to carry on any further conversation.

The stranger slowly rejoined his companions, who had halted at the edge of the forest.

"Well?" he asked uneasily.

"The señorita has fainted," sorrowfully replied one of the men.

The stranger uttered an exclamation of grief. He remained for some moments fixing his eyes on the girl, with an indescribable expression of despair.

All of a sudden he turned abruptly, and rushed towards the unknown.

The latter had mounted, and was on the point of retiring.

"Stop!" called the stranger.

"What is it you want with me?" replied the unknown once more. Then he added fiercely, "Let me begone; and thank God that our unforeseen meeting in this forest has not been productive of graver consequences to you."

The menace contained in these enigmatical words disturbed the stranger in spite of himself. However, he would not be discouraged.

"It is impossible," he resumed vehemently, "that you can be as cruel as you wish us to believe. You are too young for all feeling to have died out of your heart."

The unknown laughed strangely.

"I have no heart," he said.

"I implore you, in the name of your mother, not to abandon us!"

"I have no mother."

"Then I beseech you in the name of the being you love most upon earth, whoever that may be."

"I love no one."

"No one?" repeated the stranger, shuddering; "Then I pity you, for you must be most unhappy."

The unknown trembled; a feverish glow stole over his face; but soon recovering himself, he exclaimed:

"Now let me go."

"No; not before I learn who you are."

"Who I am! Have I not already told you? A wild beast; a being with only the semblance of humanity, with a hatred towards all men which nothing can ever appease. Pray to God you may never again encounter me on your path. I am like the raven—the sight of me foretells evil. Adieu!"

"Adieu!" murmured the stranger; "And may God have mercy on you, and not visit your cruelty upon you!"

Just at this moment a voice, feeble, but in its sad modulations sweet and melodious as the notes of the *centzontle*, the American nightingale, rose through the stillness.

"My father, my dear father!" it uttered. "Where are you? Do not abandon me."

"I am here, I am here," exclaimed the stranger tenderly, as he turned quickly to run to her who thus called him.

A cloud passed over the face of the unknown at the sound of these melodious accents; his blue eye flashed like the lightning. He placed his hand on his heart, trembling as if he had received an electric shock.

After a short hesitation, he forced his horse to make a sudden bound forward, and placing his hand on the stranger's shoulder:

"Whose voice is that?" he asked in singular accents.

"The voice of my daughter, who is dying, and calls me."

"Dying?" stammered the unknown, strangely moved. "She!"

"My father, my father!" repeated the girl in a voice which grew weaker and weaker.

The unknown raised himself to his full height; his face assumed an expression of indomitable energy.

"She shall not die!" said he in a low voice. "Come!"

They rejoined the group.

The young girl was stretched upon the ground, with her eyes closed, her face pale as a corpse; the feeble gasps of her breathing alone evincing that life had not completely left her.

The persons surrounding her watched her in profound sadness, while tears rolled silently down their bronzed cheeks.

"Oh!" cried the father, falling on his knees beside the young girl, seizing her hand and covering it with kisses, while his face was inundated with tears; "My fortune—my life—to him who will save my cherished child!"

The unknown had dismounted, and observed the girl with sombre and pensive eye. At last, after several minutes of this mute contemplation, he turned towards the stranger.

"What ails this girl?" he asked abruptly.

"Alas! An incurable ailment: she has been bitten by a grass snake."

The unknown frowned till his eyebrows nearly met together.

"Then she is lost indeed," said his deep voice.

"Lost! O Heavens! My daughter, my dearest daughter!"

"Yes; unless—" then, arousing himself: "How long is it since she was bitten?"

"Scarcely an hour."

The face of the unknown lighted up. He remained silent for a moment, during which the bystanders anxiously bent towards him, awaiting with impatience the opinion he would probably pronounce.

"Scarcely an hour?" said he at last. "Then she may be saved."

The stranger uttered a sigh of joy.

"You will answer for it?" he cried.

"I?" returned the unknown, shrugging; his shoulders; "I will answer for nothing, except that I will attempt impossibilities for the chance of restoring her to you."

"Oh, save her, save her!" eagerly exclaimed the father; "And, whoever you may be, I will bless you."

"It matters not to me what you may do. I do not try to save this girl for your sake; and, whatever may be the motives inducing me, I exempt you from all feelings of gratitude."

"You may possibly harbour such thoughts; but for myself—"

"Enough," rudely broke in the unknown; "we have already lost too much time in idle words; let us make haste, if we would not be too late."

All were silent.

The unknown looked around.

We have already said that the strangers had halted at the edge of the forest; over their heads the last trees of the covert expanded their mighty branches.

Approaching the trees, the unknown examined them carefully, apparently in search of something he could not find.

All of a sudden, he uttered a cry of joy; and, unsheathing the long knife fastened to his right knee, he cut a branch from a creeper, and returned to the strangers, who were anxiously watching his proceedings.

"Here," said he to one of the party, who looked like a *peon* (a serf), "strip all the leaves from this branch, and pound them. Be quick; every second is worth a century to her whom we wish to save."

The *peon* set himself actively to the allotted task.

Then the unknown turned to the father:

"In what part of the body has this child been bitten?"

"A little below the left ankle."

"Has she much courage?"

"Why do you ask?"

"Answer! Time presses."

"The poor child is quite worn out; she is very weak."

"Then we must hesitate no longer; the operation must be performed."

"An operation!" cried the stranger, affrighted.

"Would you rather she should die?"

"Is this operation indispensable?"

"It is: we have already lost too much time."

"Then perform it. God grant you may succeed!"

The girl's leg was horribly swollen; the part round the serpent's bite, terribly tumefied, was already taking a greenish hue.

"Alas," muttered the unknown, "there is not a moment to spare. Hold the child so that she cannot stir while I perform the operation."

In these last words the voice of the unknown had assumed such an accent of command, that the strangers obeyed without hesitation.

The former seated himself on the ground, took the limb of the girl upon his knee, and made his preparations. Luckily the moon shone at this moment so clearly, that her vivid rays flooded the landscape, and everything was almost as visible as in broad daylight.

When the girl had first felt the bite, she had immediately, and happily for herself, torn off her silk stocking. The unknown grasped the blade of his knife an inch from the point, and, lowering his brow with terrible determination, buried the point in the wound, and made a cruciform incision about six lines deep, and more than an inch long.

The poor child must have felt terrible anguish; for she gave utterance to a dreadful scream, and twisted herself about nervously.

"Hold her tight, *cuerpo de Cristo!*" shouted the unknown in a voice of thunder, while with admirable coolness and skill he pressed the lips of the wound, so as to force out the black and decomposing blood it contained; "And now the leaves—the leaves!"

The *peon* ran up.

The unknown took the leaves, parted asunder the lips of the wound, and gently, carefully expressed their juice on the palpitating flesh. Making a kind of plaster of the same leaves, he applied it to the wound, tied it down firmly with a bandage, placed the foot carefully on the ground, and rose.

As soon as a certain quantity of the sap of the creeper had fallen upon the wound, the girl had seemed to experience a sensation of great relief; the nervous spasms began to abate; she closed her eyes; and finally she leaned back without attempting to struggle any longer with the persons who held her in their arms.

"You may leave her now," whispered the unknown; "she is asleep."

In fact, the regular though feeble breathing of the patient proved her to be plunged in a profound slumber.

"God be praised!" exclaimed the poor father, clasping his hands in ecstasy; "Then she is really saved?"

"She is," answered the unknown leisurely; "bating unforeseen accidents, she has nothing more to fear."

"But what is the extraordinary remedy you have employed to obtain such a happy result?"

The unknown smiled with disdain, and did not seem willing to reply; however, after a short hesitation, yielding perhaps to that secret vanity which induces us all to make a parade of our wisdom, he decided upon giving the information demanded.

"The pettiest things astonish you fellows who dwell in cities," said he ironically; "the man who has passed his whole life in the wilderness knows many things of which the inhabitants of your brilliant towns are ignorant, although, with the sole aim of humiliating, they take pleasure in parading their false science before us poor savages. Nature hides not the secret of her mysterious harmonics from him who ceaselessly pries into the darkness of night and the brightness of day, with a patience beyond proof, without suffering himself to be discouraged by failure. The sublime Architect, when he had created this immense universe, did not let it fall from his omnipotent hands until it had been made perfect, nor till the amount of good should counterbalance everywhere the amount of evil—placing, so to say, the antidote side by side with the poison."

The stranger listened with increasing surprise to the words of this man, whose real character was an enigma to him, and who at every moment showed himself in lights diametrically opposed, and under forms entirely distinct.

"But," continued the unknown, "pride and presumption make man blind. Accustomed to make all things bear upon himself, imagining that all existence has been specially created for his convenience, he takes no pains to study the secrets of nature further than they seem to have a direct influence on his personal welfare, not caring to make inquiry into her simplest actions. So, for instance, the region in which we now are, being low and marshy, is naturally infested with reptiles, which are so much the more dangerous and to be dreaded, because they are half-calcined and rendered furious by the rays of a torrid sun. Therefore provident nature has produced in abundance throughout these same regions a creeper called *mikania*—the one I have just used—which is an infallible remedy for the bites of serpents."

"I cannot doubt it, after having witnessed its efficacy; but how were the virtues of this creeper discovered?" said the stranger, involuntarily interested in the highest degree.

"A hunter of the woods," continued the unknown, with a certain self-complacency, "observed that the black falcon, better known as the *guaco*, a bird which feeds chiefly upon reptiles, takes special delight in exterminating serpents. This hunter had also observed that if, during the struggle, the serpent contrived to wound the *guaco*, the latter immediately retired from the combat, and flying to the *mikania*, tore off a few leaves, which it bruised in its beak. It afterwards returned to the fight more resolute than ever, until it had vanquished its redoubtable enemy. The hunter was an astute man, and of great experience; one who knew that animals, being devoid of reason, are more especially under the providence of God, and that all their actions proceed from laws laid down at the beginning. After mature reflection, he resolved to test his experience upon himself."

"And did he execute his project?" cried the stranger.

"He did. He let a coral snake bite him, the deadliest of all; but, thanks to the *mikania*, the bite proved as harmless to him as the prick of a thorn. That is the manner in which this precious remedy was discovered. But," added the unknown, suddenly changing his tone, "I have complied with your wishes in bringing help to your daughter; she is safe. Adieu! I may stay no longer."

"You must not go before you have told me your name."

"What good will this pertinacity do you?"

"I wish to embalm the name in my memory as that of a man to whom I have vowed a gratitude which will only end with my life."

"You are mad!" rudely answered the unknown. "It is useless to pronounce to you a name which you will very likely learn but too soon."

"Let it be so; I will not persist, nor ask the reasons which compel you to act thus. I will not seek to learn it in despite of you; but, if you refuse to teach me your name, you cannot prevent my making you acquainted with my own—I am called Don Pedro de Luna. Although until today I have never penetrated thus far into the prairies, my residence is not very far off. I am proprietor of the Hacienda de las Norias de San Antonio, close to the frontiers of the Despoblado, near the *embouchure* of the Rio San Pedro."

"I know the Hacienda de las Norias de San Antonio. Its owner ought to belong to the happy ones of earth, according to the opinion of those who dwell in cities. So much the better: if it does belong to you, I do not envy riches with which I should not know what to do. Now, you have nothing more to say, have you? Well, then, adieu!"

"What! Adieu! You will leave us?"

"Certainly; do you think I intend to remain all night with you?"

"I hoped, at least, you would not leave unfinished the work you have undertaken."

"I do not understand you; caballero."

"Will you abandon us thus? Will you leave my daughter in her present state, lost in the wilderness, without the means of escape,—in the depths of this forest, which has been so nearly fatal to her?"

The unknown frowned several times, then cast a stolen look on the girl. A violent struggle seemed to commence in his bosom; he remained silent for several minutes, uncertain how to decide. At last he raised his head.

"Listen," said he in a constrained voice; "I have never learnt to lie. At a short distance I have a *jacal* (hovel), as you would call the miserable *calli* (cottage) which shelters me; but, believe me, it is better for you to remain here than to follow me there."

"And why?" said the stranger, surprised.

"I have no explanation to give you, and I will not lie. I only repeat: believe me, and remain here. Nevertheless, if you persist in following me, I will not oppose it; I will be your faithful guide."

"Danger menace us under your roof? I will not stop on such an hypothesis: hospitality is sacred in the prairies."

"Perhaps so; I will neither answer yes nor no. Do you decide; only make your resolve quickly, for I am in haste to have the matter decided."

Don Pedro de Luna threw a sorrowful look at his daughter; then addressing the unknown—

"Whatever may happen," said he, "I will follow you. My daughter cannot stay here; you have done too much for her not to wish to save her. I confide in you; show me the way."

"Agreed," replied the unknown laconically. "I have warned you; take care you are on your guard."

# CHAPTER III
## THE CALLI

Much as the unknown had hesitated in offering shelter to Don Pedro de Luna and his daughter,—and we know in what terms the offer had been finally made,—he showed himself equally anxious, as soon as his decision was made, to quit that part of the forest where the scene passed which we have recorded in our preceding chapter. His eyes wandered about continually with a disquietude he took no pains to conceal. He turned his head repeatedly towards the hillock, as if he expected to see some horrible apparition suddenly rising from its summit.

In the state the girl was in, to awaken her would have been to commit a grave imprudence, seriously compromising her health. In accordance with orders delivered in a dry tone by the unknown, the *peones* of Don Pedro, and the *hacendero* himself, hastened to cut down some branches, in order to fashion a litter, which they covered with dry leaves. Over these they spread their *zarapés*, of which they deprived themselves in order to make a softer couch for their young mistress.

These preparations finished, the girl was raised with great precaution, and gently placed upon the litter.

Of the three men who accompanied Don Pedro, two were *peones*, or domestic Indians; the third was the *capataz* (bailiff) of the *hacendero*.

The *capataz* was an individual of about five feet eight, with broad shoulders, and legs bowed by the constant habit of riding. He was extraordinarily thin; but one could truly say of him, he was nothing but muscle and sinew. His strength was wonderful. This man, called Luciano Pedralva, was devoted, body and soul, to his master, whom, and his family, he and his had served for nearly two centuries.

His features, bronzed by the vicissitudes of the weather, although not striking, had an expression of intelligence and astuteness, to which his eyes, black and well opened, added an appearance of energy and courage beyond the common. Don Pedro de Luna had the greatest confidence in this man, whom he considered more in the light of a friend than a servitor.

When the girl had been placed upon the litter, the *peones* lifted it; while Don Pedro and the *capataz* placed themselves one on the right, the other on the left of the patient, in order to guard her from the branches of trees and creepers.

At a mute sign from the unknown, who had remounted, the little troop leisurely began its march.

Instead of reentering the forest, the unknown continued to advance towards the hillock, the base of which was speedily attained. A narrow pathway serpentined along its side in an incline sufficiently gentle. The little troop entered upon it without hesitation.

They ascended in this manner fur some minutes, following ten or a dozen yards behind the unknown, who rode on in front by himself. Suddenly, on arriving at an angle of the road, round which their guide had already disappeared, a whistle rent the air, so sharp that the Mexicans halted involuntarily, not knowing whether to advance or retreat.

"What is the meaning of this?" murmured Don Pedro anxiously.

"Treachery, without a doubt," said the *capataz* casting his eyes searchingly around.

But all remained quiet about them; no change was perceptible in the landscape, which looked as lonely as ever.

Nevertheless, in a few minutes, more whistling, similar to the first they had heard, was audible in different directions at the same lime, answering evidently to a signal which had been made.

At that moment the unknown reappeared; his face pale, his gestures constrained, and a prey to the most vivid emotion.

"It is you who have willed this," said he; "I wash my hands of what may happen."

"Tell us, at all events, what peril threatens us," replied Don Pedro, in agitation.

"Ah!" said the other, in a voice of subdued passion,

"Do I know it myself? And what would it aid you to know? Would you be the less lost for that? You refused to believe me. Now, pray to God to help you; for never danger threatened you more terrible than that which hangs over your head!"

"But why these perpetual reservations? Be frank; we are men, *vive Dios*, and, great as the peril may be, we shall know how to meet it bravely."

"You are mad! Can one man oppose a hundred? You will fall, I tell you; but it is to yourself alone you must address your reproaches; it is yourself who have persisted in braving the *Tigercat* in his lair."

"Alas," cried the *hacendero* in accents of horror, "what name is that you have uttered?"

"The name of the man in whose clutches you are at this very moment."

"What! the Tigercat? That redoubtable bandit, whose numberless crimes have shocked the land for so long; that man who seems endowed with a diabolical power to accomplish the atrocious deeds with which he incessantly sullies himself;—is that monster near us?"

"He is; and I warn you to be prudent, for perhaps he hears you at this moment, although invisible to your eyes and mine."

"What do I care?" energetically exclaimed Don Pedro. "Away with caution, since we are once in the power of this demon; he is a man devoid of pity, and my life is no longer my own."

"What do you know about it, Señor Don Pedro de Luna?" answered a mocking voice.

The *hacendero* trembled, and recoiled a step, uttering a stifled cry.

The Tigercat, bounding with the agility of the animal from which he took his name, had leaped upon the summit of an elevated rock which overhung the pathway some distance off, and now dropped lightly on the ground two paces from Don Pedro.

There was an instant of terrible silence. The two men, thus placed face to face, their eyes flashing, their lips compressed with rage, examined each other with ardent curiosity. It was the first time the *hacendero* had seen the terrible partisan, the fame of whose thirst for blood had reached the most ignorant villagers in the land, and who for thirty years had spread terror over the Mexican frontiers.

We will give, in a few words, the portrait of this man, who is destined to play an important part in our history.

The Tigercat was a species of Colossus, six feet high; his broad shoulders and limbs, from which the muscles stood out in marble rigidity, showed that, though long past the prime of life, his strength still existed in all its integrity; his long locks, white as the snows on Coatepec, fell in disorder on his shoulders, and mingled with the grizzly beard that covered his breast. His forehead was broad and open; he had the eye of the eagle, under the brows of the lion; his whole person offered, in a word, a complete type of the man of the desert,—grand, strong, majestic, and implacable. Although his skin was stained by every inclemency of weather till it had almost acquired the colour of brick, it was nevertheless easy to recognise, in the clearly defined lines of his face, that this man belonged to the race of whites.

His dress lay midway between that of the Mexican and of the redskin; for although he wore the *zarapé*, his mitasses, in two pieces, worked with hairs attached here and there, and his moccasins of different colours, embroidered with porcupine quills and ornamented with glass beads and hawks' bells, showed his preference for the Indians, to whose customs, by the by, he seemed to have entirely adapted his mode of life.

A large scalping knife, a hatchet, a bullet bag, and powder horn, were slung from a girdle of wild beast's skin, drawn tightly above his hips.

One thing must not be forgotten, — a singularity in a white man, — a white-headed eagle's plume was placed above his right ear, as if this man arrogated to himself the dignity of chief of an Indian tribe.

Lastly, he held in his hand a magnificent American rifle, damaskeened, and most skilfully inlaid with silver.

Such is the physical portrait of the man to whom white hunters and redskins had given the name of Tigercat; a name he deserved in every respect, if hearsay had not belied him, and if only half the stories reported of him were true.

As to the character of this strange being, we will abstain from dwelling upon it for the present. We are persuaded the scenes which follow will enable us to appreciate it correctly.

Although struck with surprise at the apparition — as sudden as it was unexpected — of the dreaded freebooter, Don Pedro was not long in recalling his presence of mind.

"You appear to know me much better than I know you," replied he coolly; "but if half the things I have heard reported about you be true, I can only expect, on your part, treatment similar to that which all unhappy persons encounter who fall into your hands."

The Tigercat smiled sarcastically.

"And do you not dread this treatment?" he asked.

"For myself, personally, no!" answered Don Pedro disdainfully.

"But," continued the freebooter, with a glance towards the wounded lady, "for the young girl?"

The *hacendero* trembled; a livid pallor overspread his features.

"You cannot mean what you are saying," was his answer; "for the honour of humanity, I will not think so. The Apaches themselves, fierce as they are, feel their rage vanish before the feebleness of woman."

"Have I not among the dwellers in cities the reputation of being fiercer than the fierce Apaches,—even than the very beasts?"

"Let us end this," replied Don Pedro haughtily; "since I have been fool enough, in spite of repeated warnings, to place myself in your hands, dispose of me as you think fit; but deliver me from the torture I undergo in conversing with you."

The Tigercat frowned; he struck the ground forcibly with the butt of his rifle, muttering some unintelligible words; but, by an extreme effort of his will, his features instantaneously resumed their habitual imperturbability, every trace of emotion vanished from his voice, and he answered, in the calmest tone:

"In beginning the conversation, about which you seem to care so little, *caballero*, I said to you, 'What do you know about it?'"

"Well?" said the *hacendero*, surprised and overcome, in spite of his efforts, by the strange change in the dreaded speaker.

"Well," replied the latter, "I repeat the phrase, not, as you may suppose, in mockery, but simply to elicit your frank opinion of me."

"That opinion can be of little value to you, I presume."

"More than you may imagine. But why these words? Answer me!"

The *hacendero* remained mute for a time. The Tigercat, his eyes fixed steadily upon him, watched him attentively.

As to the hunter who had been almost forced to consent to serve Don Pedro de Luna as guide, his astonishment was extreme. Believing himself to be thoroughly acquainted with the character of the freebooter, he could not understand the scene at all, and inwardly asked himself what this feigned courtesy of the Tigercat would end in.

Don Pedro himself argued quite differently on the bandit's sentiments; right or wrong, he fancied he had perceived an accent of sad sincerity in the tone in which the last words had been addressed to him.

"Since you absolutely desire it," said he, "I will reply frankly: I believe your heart to be not so cruel as you would have it supposed; and I imagine that this conviction, which you inwardly possess, makes you extremely unhappy; for, notwithstanding the barbarous acts with which they reproach you, other crimes have entered your thoughts, before the execution of which you have recoiled, in spite of the pitiless ferocity they attribute to you."

The Tigercat seemed about to speak.

"Do not interrupt me," continued the *hacendero* hastily; "I know that I am treading upon a volcano; but you have my promise to speak frankly, and, willing or not willing, you must hear me to the end. Most of mankind are the architects of their own fortunes in this world; you have not escaped the common lot. Gifted with an energetic character, with vivid passions, you have not sought to overcome these passions; you have suffered yourself to be overcome by them, and thus, fall after fall, you have reached that depth in which you are now lost; and yet all good feeling is not utterly dead in you."

A smile of contempt flickered over the lips of the old man.

"Do not smile at me," the *hacendero* went on; "the very question you have put proves my assertion. Leading in the wilderness the life of the plundering savage, hating society, which has cast you off, you still hanker after the opinion the world forms of you. And why? Because that sentiment of justice, which God has planted in the hearts of all, revolts in you at the universal reprobation heaped upon your name. It has roused your shame. The man who can still be ashamed of himself, criminal as he may be, is very close to repentance; for the voice that cries aloud in his heart is the voice of awakening remorse."

Although Don Pedro had ceased speaking for some time, the Tigercat still seemed to be listening to his words; but suddenly lifting his head proudly, he cast a mocking glance around him, and burst into a laugh, dry and hard as that which Goethe ascribes to Mephistopheles.

This laugh cut the *hacendero* to the heart. He comprehended that the evil instincts of the freebooter had resumed their sway over the better thoughts which, for a moment, had seemed to assert their mastery.

After this bout of laughter, the countenance of the Tigercat resumed its usual rigid immobility.

"Good!" cried he in a tone of apparent glee, which did by no means deceive Don Pedro; "I expected a sermon, and find I was not mistaken. Well, at the risk of sinking in your estimation,—or, to speak more truly, in order to flatter your self-esteem by leaving you in the belief that you judge my feelings correctly,—I decree that you and your followers return to your Hacienda de las Norias de San Antonio, not only without the loss of a hair, but even as partakers of my hospitality. Does not this decision astonish you? You were far from expecting it."

"Not so; it is exactly what I anticipated."

"Indeed!" said he, with astonishment; "Then if I offer you the hospitality of my *calli*, you will accept it?"

"And why not, if the offer is made in good faith?"

"Then come without fear; I pledge you my word that you nor yours need fear any injury on my part."

"I follow you," said Don Pedro.

But the unknown had watched with increasing anxiety the erratic course of this conversation, and advancing abruptly in front of, and extending his arms towards, the *hacendero*—

"Stop, as you value your life!" he cried in a voice trembling with secret emotion. "Stop! Do not let yourself be deceived by the assumed benevolence of this man; he is spreading a snare for you; his offer conceals a treason."

The Tigercat drew himself up to his full height, stared disdainfully at the speaker, and replied, in an accent of supreme majesty:

"Your senses wander, boy; this man runs no risk in confiding in me. Granted that there are many things I do not respect in this world, still there is at least one which I have always respected, and have suffered no one to doubt,—my word,—my word, which I have given to this *caballero*. Come! Let us pass; the young woman whom you have succoured so opportunely is not yet out of danger; her state demands attentions which are beyond your power to afford."

The unknown trembled; his dark-blue eyes flashed, his lips parted as if to answer; but he remained silent, and retired a few paces, knitting his brow in concentrated passion.

"Moreover," imperturbably continued the freebooter, "whatever force may lie at your disposal in other parts of the wilderness, you know that here I am all-powerful, and that here my will is law. Leave me to act as I please. Do not force me to measures I should abhor; for if I raised but a finger I could tame your fool's pride."

"I know," said the young man, "that I am powerless; but beware how you treat these strangers, who placed themselves under my protection; for I shall know how to take my revenge."

"Yes, yes," said the Tigercat drearily; "I know you would not hesitate to revenge yourself even on me, if you fancied you had a cause. But I care not; I am master here."

"I shall follow you even into your haunt; think not I intend to desert these strangers now they are in your hands."

"As you please; I do not forbid you to accompany them; on the contrary, I should regret your leaving them."

The unknown held his peace, smiling disdainfully.

"Come," resumed the Tigercat, turning to the *hacendero*.

The troop began again to ascend the hillock, following in the footsteps of the old freebooter, close to whom rode their former guide.

After some turnings and windings in the path, of more or less abruptness, some of which caused the Mexicans no little difficulty, the Tigercat turned towards the *hacendero*, and addressed him in a voice perfectly free from embarrassment:

"I beg you to excuse my guiding you over such villainous roads; unfortunately they are the only ones leading to my dwelling. It is at hand; in a few minutes we shall be there."

"But I see no traces of habitation," replied Don Pedro, vainly, scanning the country in all directions.

"True," said the Tigercat, with a smile; "nevertheless, we are hardly an hundred paces from the end of our journey; and I can assure you the abode to which I am leading you would harbour a hundred times our present numbers."

"I have not much idea where this dwelling is to be found, unless it be subterranean, as I begin to suspect."

"You have almost guessed it. The place I inhabit, if not subterranean in the strict sense of the word, is at least a dwelling covered by the ground. Few have entered it to leave it again safe and sound, as you shall."

"So much the worse," retorted roundly the *hacendero*; "so much the worse for them—and for you."

The Tigercat frowned, but immediately replied, in the light and careless tone he had affected for the last few minutes:

"Look you, I will clear up this mystery. Listen; the story is interesting enough. When the Aztecs quitted Azlin, which signifies 'the country of herons,' to conquer Anahuac, or 'the country between the waters,' their peregrinations were long, extending over several centuries. Disheartened at times by long travel, they halted, founded cities, in which they installed themselves as if they never intended to abandon the place they had chosen; and, perhaps with the object of leaving behind them ineffaceable traces of their passage through the wild countries they traversed, they constructed pyramids. Hence the numerous ruins littering the soil of Mexico, and the *teocalis* one meets with occasionally,—last and mournful vestiges of a people that has disappeared. These *teocalis* built on a system of incredible solidity far from crumbling under the strenuous embrace of time, have ended in becoming a part of the ground which supported them, and so completely, that there is often difficulty in recognising them. I can give you no better proof of my assertion than what you have now before you. The elevation you are now ascending is not, as you might suppose, a hill caused by some perturbation of the earth,—it is an Aztec *teocali*."

"A *teocali!*" exclaimed Don Pedro, in astonishment.

"It is, indeed," continued the freebooter; "but so many centuries have elapsed since the day it was built, that, thanks to the vegetable matter incessantly conveyed by the winds, nature has apparently resumed her rights, and the Aztec watchtower has become a green hill. You are doubtless aware that the *teocalis* are hollow?"

"I am aware of it," answered the *hacendero*.

"It is in the interior of this one I have fixed my dwelling. See, we have reached it. Allow me to show you the way into it."

In fact, the travellers had arrived at a kind of coarse portal—a Cyclopean construction—which gave admittance to a subterranean building, in which a profound obscurity prevailed, forbidding any estimate of its dimensions.

The Tigercat stopped, and gave a peculiar whistle. Immediately a dazzling light broke forth from the interior, and illuminated it in all its vastness.

"Let us enter," said the freebooter, preceding his companions.

Without hesitation Don Pedro prepared to follow, after making a sign to his attendants, warning them to conceal their rising fears.

For a moment the unknown found himself, so to speak, alone with the *hacendero*, and bending swiftly down, whispered softly in his ear, "Be prudent; you are entering the tiger's den."

Saying this, he rapidly left them, as he feared the freebooter might perceive that he was giving a last word of warning to the stranger.

But, good or bad, the advice came too late: hesitation would have been folly, for flight was impossible.

On all sides, on every jutting rock, appeared as by enchantment, the dark shadows of a host of persons, who had started up around the strangers without their understanding whence they came, so stealthy had been their approach.

The Mexicans entered, then, although not without feelings of dread, into the terrible cavern, whose mouth opened yawning before them. The building was vast, the walls were lofty.

After proceeding for about ten minutes, the Mexicans found themselves in a species of rotunda, in the centre of which a huge brazier was flaming; four long corridors crossed the rotunda at right angles. The Tigercat, still followed by the travellers, entered one of these. He stopped on reaching a door formed of a reed hurdle.

"Make yourselves at home," said he; "your lodgings consists of two chambers, which have no communication with the rest of the cave. By my orders you will be supplied with food, with wood to make a fire, and torches of ocote to give you light."

"I thank you for these attentions," replied Don Pedro. "I had little reason to expect them."

"And why not? Do you think that I do not know how to practise Mexican hospitality, in its fullest extent, whenever it suits me?"

"Sir!" said the *hacendero*, with a gesture of deprecation.

"Silence!" said the bandit, interrupting him; "You are my guests for the night. Sleep in peace; nothing shall disturb your rest. In an hour I will send you a potion for the lady to drink. We shall meet again tomorrow." And, bowing with an ease and courtesy little expected by Don Pedro from such a man, the Tigercat took his leave and quitted the chamber.

For a few seconds the step resounded under the dark vault of the corridor; then it was silenced. The travellers were alone, and the *hacendero* determined to investigate the chambers prepared for them.

# CHAPTER IV
## SUPERFICIAL REMARKS

The *haciendas* of Spanish America were never feudal tenures, whatever certain badly informed authors may assert, but simply large agricultural holdings, as their name clearly indicates.

These *haciendas*, scattered over Mexico at great distances from each other, and surrounded by vast stretches of country, for the greater part uninhabited, are generally situated on the top of abruptly rising hills, in positions easy of defence.

As the *hacienda*, properly so called,—*i.e.* the habitation of the proprietor of the estate,—forms the nucleus of the colony, and, in addition to the barns and stables, contains also the out houses, the lodgings of the *peones*, and, above all, the chapel, its walls are high, massive, and surrounded by a ditch, so as to put it out of danger from a *coup-de-main*.

These numerous *haciendas* frequently maintain from six to seven hundred individuals of all trades, the lands belonging to a farm of this description being often of greater extent than a whole province in France.

They are the wholesale breeding places of the wild horses and cattle that graze at freedom in the prairies, watched over at a distance by *peones vaqueros* as untamed as themselves.

The Hacienda de las Norias de San Antonio—*i.e.* St. Anthony's Wells— rose gracefully from the summit of a hill covered with thick groves of mahogany, Peru trees and *mesquites*, forming a belt of evergreen foliage, the palish green of which contrasted agreeably with the dead white of the lofty walls, crowned with *almenas*, a kind of battlement intended to announce the nobility of the proprietor of the holding.

In fact, Don Pedro de Luna was what is called a *cristiano viejo* (old Christian), and descended in a direct line from the first Spanish conquerors, without a single drop of Indian blood having been infused into the veins of his ancestors. So, although after the Declaration of Independence the ancient customs began to fall into disuse, Don Pedro de Luna was proud of his nobility, and clung to the *almenas* as marks of distinction which only noblemen were allowed to adopt in the time of the Spanish rule.

Since the period when, in the suite of that genial adventurer, Fernando Cortez, a Lopez de Luna had first put foot in America, the fortunes of this family, very poor and much reduced at that time—for Don Lopez literally possessed nothing but his cloak and sword,—the fortunes of this family, we say, had taken an incredible flight upwards, and entered on a career of prosperity that nothing in time's course could trammel. Thus Don Pedro de Luna, the actual representative of this ancient house, was in the enjoyment of wealth, the amount of which it would certainly have puzzled him to state,—wealth which had been increased still more by the property of Don Antonio de Luna, his elder brother, who had disappeared more than twenty-five years after events to which we shall have to revert, and who it was supposed had perished miserably in the mysterious wilderness in the neighbourhood of the *hacienda*. It was likely that he had fallen a victim to the horrible pangs of hunger, or more probably into the hands of the Apaches, those implacable enemies of the whites, on whom they ceaselessly wage an inveterate war.

In short Don Pedro was the sole representative of his name, and his fortune was immense. No one who has not visited the interior of Mexico can figure to himself the riches buried in these almost unknown regions, where certain land owners, if they would only take the trouble to put their affairs in order, would find themselves five or six times more wealthy than the greatest capitalists of the old world.

Now, although everything seemed to smile on the opulent *hacendero*, and although, to the world that looks beyond the surface, he seemed to enjoy, with every appearance of reason, an unalloyed happiness, nevertheless the deep wrinkles channelled in the forehead of Don Pedro, the mournful severity of his face, and his gaze often turned to heaven with an expression of sombre despair, might give rise to the surmise that the life all thought so happy was secretly agitated by a profound sorrow, which the years, as they rolled on, augmented instead of solacing.

And what was the sorrow? What storms had troubled the course of a life so calm on the surface?

The Mexicans are the most forgetful people on earth. This certainly arises from the nature of their climate, which is incessantly distracted by the most frightful cataclysms. The Mexican, whose life is passed on a volcano, who feels the soil incessantly trembling under his feet, only cares to live for today. For him yesterday no longer exists; tomorrow he may never see the sun rise; today is his all, for today is his own.

The inhabitants of the Hacienda de las Norias, incessantly exposed to the inroads of their redoubtable neighbours the redskins, constantly occupied in defending themselves from their attacks and depredations, were still more forgetful than the rest of their countrymen of a past in which they took no interest.

The secret of Don Pedro's grief, if really such a secret existed, was, therefore, confined pretty nearly to his own breast; and as he never complained,—never made allusion to the earlier years of his life, —surmise was impossible, and the ignorance of everyone on the subject complete.

One single being had the privilege of smoothing the anxious brow of the *hacendero*, and of bringing a languid and fleeting smile to his lips.

It was his daughter. Doña Hermosa at sixteen was dazzlingly beautiful. The jet black arches of her brow, finely traced as with a pencil, enhanced the beauty of a forehead not too high and of a creamy white. Her large eyes, blue and pensive, contrasted harmoniously with hair of ebon hue, which curled about the delicate neck, and on which the sweet jasmines died away with pleasure.

Short, like all Spanish women of her race, her figure was slender but well knit. No smaller feet had ever pressed in the dance the greensward of Mexico; no more delicate hand ever ransacked the dahlias of a garden. Her walk, easy, like that of all Creoles, was a serpentine and undulating motion, full of grace and of *salero*, as they say in Andalusia.

This exquisite girl scattered mirth and joy over the *hacienda*, whose echoes from morning to night repeated lovingly the melodious modulations of her pellucid notes, the pure and fresh qualities of which made the birds die of envy as they hid themselves under the foliage of the *puerta* (open court).

Don Pedro idolised his daughter; he felt for her that passionate and boundless affection the immense power of which can only be understood by those who are fathers in the true sense of the word.

Hermosa, brought up at the *hacienda*, had only paid a few short visits, at long intervals, to the great centers of the Mexican Confederation. Their manners were entirely strange to her. Accustomed to lead the free and untrammelled life of a bird, and to express her thoughts aloud, her frankness and innocent simplicity were extreme, while her sweetness of temper made her adored by all the inhabitants of the *hacienda*, over whose welfare she watched with constant care.

Nevertheless, owing to the peculiar kind of education she had received,—exposed on this distant frontier to the frequent sound of the frightful war whoop of the redskins, and to be present during horrible scenes of carnage,—she had accustomed herself from an early age to look perils in the face, if not coldly, at all events with a courage and strength of mind scarcely to be expected in so delicate a child.

In conclusion, the influence she exercised over all who approached her was incomprehensible: it was impossible to know her without loving her, or without feeling a wish to lay down one's life for her.

On several occasions, in the attacks made on the *hacienda* by those ferocious plunderers of the desert the Apaches and Comanches, some wounded Indians had fallen into the hands of the Mexicans. Doña Hermosa, far from suffering these wretches to be maltreated, had ordered every care to be taken of them, and restored them to liberty as soon as their wounds were healed.

From this course of action it resulted that the redskins by degrees renounced their attacks upon the *hacienda*, and that the girl, attended by only one man—with whom we shall soon make the reader acquainted— unconcernedly took long rides in the wilderness, and often, carried away by the ardour of the chase, rambled off to a great distance from the *hacienda;* while the Indians who saw her pass not only abstained from injuring her, but laid no obstacles in her way. On the contrary, these primitive beings, having conceived a superstitious veneration for her, contrived, while remaining out of sight themselves, to remove from her path any dangers she might otherwise have encountered.

The redskins, with that natural tone of poetry which distinguishes them, had called her "the White Butterfly," so light and fragile did she seem to them as she bounded like a frightened fawn through the tall prairie grasses, which hardly bent under her weight.

One of her most favourite resting places in these excursions was a *rancho*, (a farm) seven or eight miles from the *hacienda*. The *rancho*, built in a charming situation and surrounded by fields well looked after and carefully cultivated, was inhabited by a woman of fifty and her son, a tall and handsome man of twenty-five or twenty-six with a proud eye and a warm heart, named Estevan Diaz. Na Manuela, as they called the old woman, and Estevan had an affection for the girl which knew no bounds. Manuela had nursed Hermosa when an infant, and the foster mother almost looked upon her young mistress as her own child, so deep was the love she bore her. The woman belonged to a class of domestics, now unhappily extinct in Europe, who form, as it were a part of the family, and are looked upon by their masters more as friends than servants.

It was under Estevan's escort that Hermosa took those long rides of which we spoke above. These continual *têtes-à-têtes* between a girl of sixteen and a man of twenty-five, which in our hypocritical and prudish world would be considered compromising, seemed very natural to the inhabitants of the *hacienda*. They knew the profound respect and loyal affection which bound Estevan to his mistress, whom he had dandled on his knees when a child, and whose first steps he had supported. Hermosa, who was as laughing, playful, and teasing as most girls of her age, took very great pleasure in being with Estevan, whom she could torment and plague to her heart's delight without his ever attempting to turn restive at the capricious vagaries of his young mistress. Did he not endure all her caprices with a patience beyond praise?

Don Pedro manifested an affectionate esteem for Manuela and her son. He had great confidence in both, and for the last two years had entrusted Estevan with the important post of *major-domo*—a post he shared, as far as the land was concerned, with Luciano Pedralva, who, however, was placed under his orders.

Thus Estevan Diaz and his mother were, next to the proprietor, the persons of greatest account at the *hacienda*, where they were treated with infinite respect, not only on account of the post they occupied, but also for the sake of their character, which was duly appreciated by all.

The Mexican *hacenderos*, whose properties are of immense extent, have a practice at certain times of the year of making a progress through their estates, in order to cast over their holding that "eye of the master" which, according to the favourite saying in Southern America, makes the crops ripen and the cattle fatten. Don Pedro never failed to undertake these tours, on which he was anxiously expected by the inferior persons in his employ, and by the *peones* of the *haciendas*, to whom the casual presence of their master brought some temporary alleviation of their miserable lives.

In Mexico slavery, abolished in principle by the Declaration of Independence, no longer exists by right; but it exists *de facto* through the whole extent of the Confederation; and the following is the adroit manner in which the law is eluded by the rich owners of the soil:— Every *hacienda* necessarily employs a great number of individuals as *peones, vaqueros, tigreros,* (herdsmen, hunters), &c. All these people are *Indios mansos,* or civilized Indians—that is to say, they have been baptised, and practise, after their own fashion, a religion they will not take the trouble to understand, and which they mix up with most absurd and ridiculous customs derived from their old creeds.

Brutalised by misery, the *peones* hire themselves, at very moderate wages, to the *hacenderos*, for the sake of satisfying their two chief vices,— gambling and drunkenness. But as Indians are the most thriftless beings in creation, their petty wages never suffice to feed and clothe them; and every day they are liable to die of hunger, if they cannot contrive to procure the ordinary necessaries of life from some source independent of their pay. It is when they have reached this climax that the rich proprietors trap them.

The *capataz* and *major-domo* keep in every *hacienda*, by order of their master, stores filled with clothing, arms, household utensils, and so forth, which are open to the *peones*, who pawn their labour for the needful articles advanced to them; the prices of the articles being always ten times their value.

It follows, from this simple combination, that the poor devils of *peones* not only never touch an infinitesimal fraction of the nominal wages allotted to them, but find themselves always on the debit side of the *hacendero's* balance sheet; and in a few months owe sums they could not possibly pay off in a lifetime. As the law is positive in these cases, the *peones* are compelled to remain in the service of their masters until, by their labour, this debt is liquidated. Unfortunately for them, their necessities are so imperious at all times, their position so precarious, that, after a life spent in incessant toil, the *peones* die insolvent. They have lived as slaves, fatally, *adscripti glebæ*, shamelessly worked, without mercy, down to their latest sigh, by men whom their sweat and their labour have enriched tenfold.

Doña Hermosa, good natured, as girls usually are when brought up in the bosom of their families, generally accompanied her father in these annual progresses, and pleased herself by leaving bounteous marks of her welcome visit with the poor *peones*.

This year, as in the preceding ones, she had attended Don Pedro de Luna, signalizing her visit to each *rancho* by relieving, in some way or other, the infirm, the old, and the children.

About forty-eight hours before the day on which our story commences, Don Pedro had left a silver mine he was working some leagues off in the desert, and set off for Las Norias de San Antonio. When he had got within twenty leagues of the *hacienda*, he felt convinced that his escort was not needed so near his own property, and sent forward Don Estevan and the armed retainers to announce his return, keeping with him only the *capataz*, Luciano Pedralva, and three or four *peones*.

Don Estevan had tried to dissuade his master from remaining in the desert almost single-handed, pointing out to him that the Indian frontiers were infested by freebooters and marauders of the vilest kind, who, skulking among the thickets, would be upon the watch for an opportunity of attacking his little band; but, by a singular fatality, Don Pedro, convinced that he had nothing to fear from these vagabonds, who had never exhibited signs of hostility towards him, had insisted on the *major-domo's* departure, and the latter had been forced to obey, although with reluctance.

The escort rode off; the *hacendero* quietly continued his road, chatting with his daughter, and laughing at the sinister presentiments clouding the face of the *major-domo* when he took leave of his master.

The day slipped away without anything happening to confirm the misgivings of Don Estevan; no accident interrupting the monotonous regularity of the march; no suspicious sign excited the fears of the travellers. The desert was at peace; as far as the eye could reach, nothing was to be seen but some straggling herds of elks and antelopes, browsing on the tall and tufted grasses of the prairie.

At sunset Don Pedro and his companions had reached the outskirts of an immense virgin forest, part of which they would have to cross to reach the *hacienda*, now about a dozen leagues off.

The *hacendero* resolved to encamp for the night at the edge of the covert, hoping to reach Las Norias early on the morrow, before the great heat of the day set in.

In a short time everything was arranged; a hut of branches was put together for Doña Hermosa; fires were lit, and the horses securely tethered, to prevent their straying during the night.

The travellers supped gaily; after which everyone laid down to sleep as comfortably as he could manage.

However, the *capataz*, a man trained to Indian artifices, thought it prudent not to neglect a single precaution to secure the repose of his companions. He placed a sentry, to whom he recommended the utmost vigilance, and saddled his horse, with the intention of making a reconnaissance round the camp.

Don Pedro, already half asleep, raised his head, and asked Don Luciano what he intended to do. When the *capataz* had explained, the *hacendero* burst out laughing, and peremptorily ordered him to leave his horse to feed in peace, and to lay himself down by the fire, in order to be ready to resume the journey at break of day. The *capataz* shook his head, but obeyed; he could not understand the conduct of his master, who was usually so prudent and circumspect.

The truth was, that Don Pedro, impelled by one of those inexplicable fatalities which, without apparent reason, often make the most intelligent blind, was convinced that he had nothing to fear so near his home, and almost on his own territory, from the rovers and marauders of the frontiers, who would think twice before they attacked a man of his importance, having the means in his power to make them pay dearly for any attempt upon his person. Nevertheless, the *capataz*, agitated by a secret uneasiness, which kept him awake in spite of his efforts to sleep, determined to keep good watch during the night, notwithstanding the injunctions of his master.

As soon as he saw Don Pedro decidedly asleep, he rose softly, took his rifle, and crept stealthily towards the forest to reconnoitre; but he had scarcely quitted the circle of light formed by the watch fire, and advanced a few paces into the covert, than he was suddenly and rudely seized by invisible hands, thrown on the ground, gagged, and bound with cords; and with such expedition, that he could neither use his arms nor utter a cry of warning to his companions.

But, in strange contrariety to the tragical usages of the prairie, the persons who had so abruptly mastered the *capataz* subjected him to no ill usage, contenting themselves with binding him firmly, so as to put the possibility of the slightest resistance out of the question, and leaving him stretched upon the ground.

"My poor mistress!" sighed the worthy fellow as he fell, without indulging a thought for himself.

He remained in this position for a length of time, listening greedily to every sound in the desert, expecting every instant to hear cries of distress from Don Pedro and Doña Hermosa. But not a cry was heard: nothing disturbed the calm of the wilderness, over which the silence of death seemed brooding.

At last, after twenty or twenty-five minutes, someone threw a *zarapé* over his face, most likely with the intention of preventing any recognition of his assailants; he was lifted from the ground with a certain degree of precaution, and two men carried him in their arms to some considerable distance.

The situation became more complicated every moment. In vain the *capataz* racked his mind to divine the intentions of his captors. The latter uttered not a word, and glided over the ground with light and noiseless steps, as if they were spectres. The generality of Mexicans are fatalists. The *capataz*, recognizing the futility of a struggle, philosophically consoled himself for what had happened, and patiently awaited the result of this singular scene.

He had not long to wait for the issue. His unknown captors, having probably reached the intended spot, halted and laid the *capataz* on the ground, after which everything round him grew calm and silent again.

At the end of several minutes he determined on an attempt to recover his liberty, and made a desperate effort to break his bonds. But here again a fresh surprise was reserved for him: the cords which bound him, and which were so fast a minute before, broke after a slight resistance.

The *capataz's* first impulse was to lift the *zarapé* which covered his face, and free himself from the gag. He next looked about him to reconnoitre, and to find out what had become of his companions, and uttered a cry of astonishment and fright on seeing Doña Hermosa, her father, and the *peones* stretched on the ground close by, gagged as he had been, and their heads muffled in *zarapés*.

The *capataz* hastened to the relief of his mistress and Don Pedro, after which he severed the cords which bound the *peones*.

The place to which the travellers had been transported by their invisible aggressors was completely dissimilar to the site chosen for the camp. They were in the midst of a thick forest, where at an immense height above their heads, the gigantic trees formed a green vault, almost impenetrable to the light of day. The horses and baggage of the travellers had vanished. Their position was frightful, deserted as they were in the virgin forest without provisions or horses. Every hope of safety was gone, and a terrible death, after horrible sufferings stared them in the face.

It is impossible to describe the despair of Don Pedro. He acknowledged, when it was too late, the folly of his conduct. He fixed his weeping eyes on his daughter with an expression of unspeakable tenderness and sorrow, accusing himself as the sole cause of the evil that had overwhelmed them. Doña Hermosa was the only one who did not give way to despair in these critical circumstances. After trying to raise the courage of her father by tender and consoling words, she was the first to speak of quitting the place and endeavouring to find the road they had lost.

The courage which sparkled in the eye of the daughter reanimated the energy of her father and the rest. If she did not succeed in reviving hope in their breasts, at all events she aroused in them sufficient spirit to encounter the necessary struggle before them. The final words of this young creature put a stop to all hesitation, and completed the happy reaction she had excited in their minds.

"Our friends," said she, "on finding we do not arrive, will suspect our misfortune, and devote themselves immediately to a search for us. Don

Estevan, to whom all the secrets of the wilderness are known, will infallibly recover our trail. Our position, therefore, is far from desperate. Let us not abandon ourselves, if we do not wish God to abandon us. Let us go: soon I hope we shall find our way out of the forest, and see the sun once more."

So they began their march.

Unfortunately it is impossible to find the right direction in a virgin forest, unless we are well acquainted with the localities,—the forests, where all the trees are alike, where there is no visible horizon, and where the only available knowledge is the instinct of the brute, not the reason of man. Thus the travellers wandered at random the whole day long, always turning, without knowing it, in the same circle, travelling far without advancing, and vainly seeking to find a road which was not in existence.

Don Pedro endeavoured to discover a reason why the men who had stolen their horses should have abandoned them in this inextricable labyrinth; why they had been thus callously condemned to an agonising death; and who the enemy might be who had cruelly conceived a plan of such atrocious revenge. But the *hacendero* racked his brains in vain for even a surmise. His mind suggested no one on whom suspicion could rest as the probable author of this unqualified crime.

All the morning the travellers continued their devious course: the sun went down, the day gave way to night, and they were still toiling on, wandering mechanically without any fixed direction, now to the right, now to the left; struggling on more in the endeavour to escape from their thoughts by physical fatigue, than in the hope of emerging from the forest— their horrible prison.

Doña Hermosa uttered no complaint. Cool and resolute, she pushed forward with a firm step, encouraging her companions by voice and gesture, and still finding spirit enough to chide and shame them for their want of perseverance.

All of a sudden she uttered a cry of pain. She had been bitten by a snake. This fresh misfortune, which should have apparently completed the travellers' despair, on the contrary, excited them to such a pitch, that they forgot all else, except how to think for and to save her whom they called their guardian angel.

But human strength has limits, beyond which it may not go. The travellers, overcome by fatigue and their poignant emotions during their wanderings, and convinced, besides, of the inutility of their efforts, were on the point of yielding to their despair, when God placed them suddenly face to face with the hunter.

# CHAPTER V
## CONFIDENTIAL CHAT

After conducting his guests to the compartment of the *teocali* which he had appointed for them, the Tigercat retraced his steps, and turned in the direction of a sufficiently ample excavation, which served for his own particular abode.

The old man walked at a slow pace, with his head raised, and his brow wrinkled under the tension of mighty thoughts. The flame of the torch he held in his right hand played capriciously over his countenance, revealing a strange expression on his features, where hate, joy, and uneasiness reflected themselves by turns.

When he arrived at his *cuarto* (bedchamber),—if it is right to give the name chamber to a kind of hole ten feet square by seven feet high, which contained as furniture a few skulls of the bison dispersed here and there, with a handful of maize-straw negligently thrown into a corner, and serving, no doubt, as couch for the inhabitants of this sorry refuge,—the Tigercat fixed his *ocote* torch in a bracket of iron made fast to the wall, crossed his arms on his breast, lifted his eyes with an air of defiance, and muttered the words:

"At last!"

Doubtless these words summed up in his thoughts a long series of dark and bold combinations.

After pronouncing these words, the old man cast a searching glance around him, as if he dreaded having been overheard. A mocking smile passed across his pale lips; he sat down on a bison's skull, and, burying his face in his hands, plunged into profound meditation.

A long time elapsed before he changed his position. At last, a slight noise fell on his ear: he lifted his head with a start, and turned towards the entrance to his cell.

"Come in!" he shouted. "I have waited for you with impatience."

"I think not!" replied a powerful voice; and the young hunter appeared at the threshold, where he stopped, holding his head erect, and looking proud and daring.

A shade crossed the forehead of the Tigercat.

"Ah, ha!" cried he, with pretended gaiety. "In truth, I was not expecting you, *muchacho* (boy); but never mind; you are welcome."

"Is that wish truly in your thoughts at this moment?" sneered the other.

"And why should it not be in my thoughts? Am I in the habit of disguising them?"

"It is a useful habit under particular circumstances."

"A truth I do not deny; but not in this case. Come in; sit down, and let us talk."

"I comply," answered the hunter, taking a few steps forward, "particularly as I have to demand an explanation from you."

The Tigercat frowned, and replied, with rising and ill-suppressed anger:

"Is it to me you speak thus? Have you forgotten who I am?"

"I forget nothing that I ought to remember," concisely replied the other.

"Boy! Have you forgotten that I am your father?"

"My father! Who will prove it?"

"You are over-venturesome," cried the old man in ire.

"After all," said the hunter scornfully, "it is nothing to me whether you be my father or not. What does it matter? Have you not told me a thousand times over, that bonds of relationship do not exist in nature; that they are only a factitious sentiment, invented by human egotism for the profit of the petty exigencies of debased society? Here, we are only two men, equals in strength and courage; of whom the one comes to demand from the other a clear and unvarnished explanation."

While the hunter was speaking, the old man fixed upon him a look which flashed fire from under his half-closed eyelids. When he ceased, the Tigercat smiled ironically.

"The wolf's cub feels he is cutting his teeth, and wants to bite his fosterer."

"He will devour him without hesitation, if it be needful," fiercely replied the hunter, as he let the butt end of the heavy rifle he carried in his hand fall violently on the ground.

Instead of being lashed into a fury by a menace uttered so peremptorily, the Tigercat suddenly became calm. His austere features lighted up with an expression of good nature which rarely visited them. Clapping his large hands together gaily, he exclaimed, with an air of lively satisfaction:

"Well roared, my lion's whelp! *¡Vive Dios!* You deserve your name, Stoneheart! The more I see of you, the more I love you. I am proud of you, *muchacho;* for you are my handiwork, and I congratulate myself on my success in producing so complete a monster. Go on as you have begun, my son: I prophesy, you will go far."

The tone in which these words were pronounced by the Tigercat clearly proved that they were in reality the unreserved expression of his thoughts.

Stoneheart—for at last we know the name of this man—listened to his father with a shrug of his shoulders, and an affectation of disdain. When the latter ceased, the son replied as follows:

"Will you listen to me or not?"

"Certainly, my darling child. Speak! Tell me what frets you."

"Seek not to dupe me, gray-haired demon. I know your hellish malignity, and your unmatchable knavery."

"You are complimentary, *muchacho.*"

"Answer frankly and categorically the questions I will put to you!"

"Bah, Bah! Go on, go on. What are you afraid of?"

"Of nothing, I tell you; but my time is short: I have no leisure to follow you through all the Indian circumlocutions it may be your pleasure to invent. That is why I listen to nothing but the plain truth."

"I cannot bind myself to that until I hear the questions you wish to put."

"Take heed, father! If you deceive me, I shall find it out, and then—"

"And then?" repeated the old man mockingly.

"May the devil take my soul, if I do not plant my bowie knife between your two shoulders."

"You forget that two can play at that game."

"So much the better; it will be a strife and I prefer it."

"You are not fastidious. But proceed; speak, or may the pestilence stifle you! I am listening. I, too, have no more time to lose than you."

Stoneheart, who up to this moment had been standing erect in the middle of the cell, seated himself on a bison's skull, and rested his rifle across his knees.

"Did you not expect to see Zopilote when I burst into your cell?"

"I did expect Zopilote: you have guessed it, *muchacho.*"

"Having finished, with his assistance, the ruffianly deeds of yesterday and today, you two are anxious to concoct the treason you meditate tomorrow."

"On my soul, *muchacho*, you are incomprehensible!"

"The devil I am! Then your apprehension is dull today."

"Perhaps it is: but oblige me by explaining your meaning."

"I will; however, attempt no denial: only a few minutes ago I learned the whole story through the gossiping of the very men who were with you."

"If you know all, why do you come here to question me?"

"In the first place, to ascertain if they spoke truly."

"They could not speak more truly: you see, I am frank."

"Then you really did surprise these travellers in their sleep?"

"Yes, *muchacho*, like a litter of prairie dogs in their earth."

"You stole their horses and baggage?"

"In good truth, I did all that."

"Afterwards, you had them carried into the thick of the forest, to die a frightful death?"

"I did have them carried to the forest; but not, as you pretend to believe, for the purpose of leaving them to starve."

"For what other purpose, then? I cannot suppose it was with the intention of effacing all traces of the robbery. You care little about such precautions, and do not stick at a knife thrust."

"Admirably reasoned, *muchacho*. I had no intention to do these travellers the least harm in the world."

"Then what did you want from them? I cannot understand your conduct. It is marvellous."

"Confess that it mystifies you, my son."

"It does; but will you explain?"

"That depends upon circumstances. But now promise, in your turn, to answer a single question."

"One? I will answer it. Ask; I am listening."

"What do you think of Doña Hermosa? Has she not beautiful eyes! One would think she had stolen a piece of the sky, they are so blue."

At this home-thrust Stoneheart recoiled; a sudden flush tinted his features.

"Why do you ask me?" said he hesitatingly.

"What does that matter? Answer, as you have promised."

"I have scarcely looked at her," he replied, with increasing embarrassment.

"You lie, my son: you have looked at her often enough; or young men in these days are changed from what they were in my time—which I can hardly believe." "Well, then, I have; and I care not who knows it," said Stoneheart, in a voice in which embarrassment was mingled with ill humour. "I have looked at Doña Hermosa, if that is her name, and have found her beautiful. Are you satisfied?"

"Almost. Has this charming creature had no other effect upon you?"

"I am not bound to answer you, father: that is a second question."

"You are right; nevertheless, I know what your reply would be. I can dispense with it."

Stoneheart turned away his head to escape the searching look of the Tigercat.

"But now," said he, after a momentary silence, "let us return to your explanation."

"You are an ingrate, who will not understand. Have you not already discovered that all this business has been undertaken for your sake alone?"

Stoneheart started with surprise.

"For my sake? Is there anything in common between this girl and me? You are laughing at me!"

"Not in the least; on the contrary, I am speaking seriously."

"Even if you do, I confess I am still in the dark."

"Aha! You are laughing now at my expense. Throughout the whole of this comedy I assign you a capital part to play: I make you interesting; I introduce you as the deliverer; are you still in the dark?"

"I myself assumed the character which you say you assigned me; I adopted it myself, alone, without any interference of yours."

"Do you believe that, my son?" said the bandit, with a grin.

Stoneheart, not thinking it necessary to insist on this point, answered:

"I will admit that you may have arranged all that happened; but what are your intentions towards the travellers now they are in the *teocali?*"

"On my honour, *muchacho*, I confess that it is not settled yet; it depends entirely on yourself."

"On me?" stammered the other.

"Yes; on my honour. Reflect; decide what you wish me to do: I give you my word that I will conform to your wishes."

"Will you swear so, father,—solemnly swear?"

"Oh, yes. You see, I am very accommodating."

"It is exactly this pliancy, so foreign to your character and habits, which makes me tremble."

"Folly! What more unjust suspicion! It happens one day that I remember I am man; that it is my duty to succour my fellow creatures: and you give me no credit for it!"

"*¡Caspita!* How could it be otherwise? Your intrigues are so dark, the means you employ are so utterly at variance with common usage in similar cases, that, in spite of my knowledge of your character, the real object of your machinations perpetually eludes me."

The visage of the Tigercat lighted up once more with a smile of triumph; but he repressed it immediately, and assumed a look of paternal benevolence.

"In spite of all you say," he answered, "my object in this case is so plain that a child might see it."

"Then I must be an idiot, for I cannot divine it; on which account, I must beg you to explain your wishes frankly."

"To make you adore the little one, *¡vive Cristo!*"

"Me!" exclaimed the hunter, astounded at the proposition, and purple with blushes.

"And whom else, if not you?—unless it were myself."

"No, no," said the other, shaking his head mournfully; "that is impossible: everything separates us. You have forgotten who she is; you have forgotten what I am—I, Stoneheart, the man whose name, pronounced to an inhabitant of the borders, makes him thrill with terror. No; it is the dream of a fool: a love like that would be monstrous. I repeat, it is impossible."

The Tigercat coolly shrugged his shoulders.

"My son," said he, "you have yet much to learn concerning that many-sided being, that graceful compound of angel and devil, that whimsical mixture of all good qualities and all vices, the world calls woman. Be quite sure, my son, that since the time of mother Eve, woman has never changed; there are the same treasons, the same perfidies, still the same feline nature of the tiger, mingled with the no less tortuous ways of the serpent. Woman must be quelled by the bold, or she will busy herself with the hope of quelling him; she will always despise the man for whom, in her secret heart, she feels no fear, and for whom she entertains no involuntary respect. Your chances of winning the heart of Hermosa, and installing yourself therein as master, are numberless; you are proscribed, and your name is a name of terror. Oh, my boy, love lives upon contrasts, knows no disparities, and despises the barrier raised by human vanity. The man most sure to succeed with a woman is precisely the only one whom, in the eyes of the world, she ought to repel the most."

"Enough of this theme!" cried the hunter violently; "Your horrible theories have already troubled my soul, and harrowed my heart. Let us stop this conversation, of which I am weary. Again, I ask, what are your intentions towards your prisoners?"

"I repeat, that it depends entirely upon yourself; they are in your hands."

"If that be the case, they shall not stay long in your hideous lair; tomorrow, at daybreak, they shall go."

"Just what I wish, my son."

"I myself will be their guide. You will restore everything you have taken from them—horses and baggage."

"You shall restore them yourself; you can easily invent a story for returning what belongs to them which shall not compromise me."

"Compromise you!" sneered Stoneheart.

"By our Lady," replied the Tigercat, with a hideous smile, "I stick to the only good deed of my life; I will not lose the credit of it."

"Then all is agreed between us; you will not break your word to me?"

"Rest in peace; I will not break it."

"Then, good-bye, till tomorrow. I go to make everything ready."

"Good night, my son. Do not take that trouble; I take it upon myself."

And the two men separated.

The Tigercat listened attentively to the sound of his son's footsteps as they died away in the distance. When silence was completely re-established, he shook his head more than once with a preoccupied air.

"Love makes him shrewd," he murmured in a suppressed voice. "I will not leave him leisure to divine my plans, or, at the moment it is within my reach, he would frustrate the vengeance I have been so many years in preparing."

Instead of retiring to his couch, the old man seized the torch, and went forth from his cell.

In the meanwhile, in spite of the fears naturally caused by their precarious position in the midst of people whose ferocious looks and brutal manners spoke little in their favour, the travellers had passed the night in tranquillity. No sound of evil augury had disturbed their repose; and, worn out by fatigue, and wearied with the various emotions of this day of misfortunes, after a short conversation, they settled themselves to sleep.

Doña Hermosa, on waking at daybreak, found herself perfectly free from the sufferings of the preceding day. Thanks to the remedy applied by the hunter to the wound, the place where she was bitten, now the venom was expressed, began to heal; she felt sufficient strength to resume her journey on horseback, and would be able to travel without too much fatigue. These good news dispersed the clouds which obscured the forehead of the *hacendero*, and he awaited, with lively impatience, the meeting with his host, which he had no doubt would not be long deferred. In fact, as soon as the Tigercat supposed that those to whom he had afforded shelter were awake, he presented himself before them to inquire how they had passed the night.

The *hacendero* thanked him warmly, assured him they were quite well, and that Doña Hermosa herself felt almost restored to health.

"So much the better," replied the Tigercat, casting a glance of fire at the girl. "It were a pity so charming a creature should perish in such a miserable manner. And now, what are your intentions? Be not offended at this question; I shall be happy to keep you at my side; and the longer you remain here, the greater my pleasure."

"Thanks for your gracious offer," said Don Pedro; "unfortunately, I dare not accept it: they will be uneasy on our account at the *hacienda*, and I must hasten in person to put an end to their alarm."

"You are right. Then you intend to depart?"

"As soon as I can; unhappily, I have no horses for the few leagues of the journey. I must put your hospitality still further to the test, although I hardly know how to thank you for what you have done already, by requesting you to sell me the animals I require to return home; at the same time, I would also crave a guide, to lead us through the forest which had nearly proved our tomb, and to put us once more on our right road. You see, *caballero*, that I make great demands on your courtesy."

"You only ask of me what is your right, señor; I will exert myself to fulfil your wishes. But how did it happen that you found yourself on foot in the virgin forest, so far from any habitations?"

The *hacendero* cast a furtive glance over the speaker; but the features of the latter continued immovable. Don Pedro then recounted all the details of the strange attack of which he had been the victim.

The Tigercat listened calmly, without interrupting him, saying, as soon as the recital was finished:

"All this seems very incomprehensible. I am annoyed at not having received this information yesterday evening. It is very late, now; but leave me to do what I can. Perhaps I may be able to cause your lost property to be restored to you; at all events I will furnish you with the means of reaching your *hacienda*. Entertain no fears on that score. I presume you would not like to leave this place before you have broken your fast; you can begin your journey as soon after breakfast as you please. I must leave you for a short time, to give the necessary orders for your departure. Excuse me. In an hour's time you shall hear from me again."

Having said this, he retired; leaving the travellers in astonishment, and perplexed as to his true character so easily did this man vary both manner and language.

An hour and a half passed over without Don Pedro receiving any news of his host. At the end of that time an Indian appeared, and without uttering a word, made a sign to the travellers to follow him. They obeyed without hesitation.

After following him for some minutes, they found themselves on the summit of the *teocali* which the evening before, under the silver rays of the moon, they had taken for a hill.

From this elevation the travellers commanded an immense extent of horizon, and enjoyed a magnificent landscape, still partially veiled by the mists of morning, but illumined here and there by the dazzling sunbeams, which produced the most striking effects amongst this chaos of trees and mountains intersecting the boundless prairies.

The morning repast was prepared on a mound of turf, covered over with the large leaves of the mahogany.

The Tigercat standing by the mound, was waiting for his guests. Some redskins, few in number, and scattered here and there about the platform, all armed, and in their war paint, were walking about with seeming indifference, and taking no apparent note of the presence of the strangers.

"I have preferred to have the meal served here," said the Tigercat, "where you can enjoy the magnificent prospect."

Don Pedro thanked him; and, at his repeated invitation, sat down by the mound with his daughter and Don Luciano. The *peones* ate by themselves.

The repast was frugal. It consisted of fritters, with red pepper, *tasajo* (sun-dried beef), a few slices of venison, and rolls made of maize flour, the whole washed down with *eau de smilax* and *pulque*,—a spirit prepared from a species of aloe. It was a true hunter's meal.

"Eat and drink," said the Tigercat; "you have a long journey before you."

"Will you not honour us by partaking of the repast you have gallantly offered us?" said Don Pedro, seeing that the old man continued standing.

"You must excuse me, *caballero*," replied the Tigercat civilly, but peremptorily. "I broke my fast long ago."

"Indeed!" said the *hacendero*, not content with the answer; "Then, at least, you will consent to empty this horn of *pulque* to my health."

"It grieves me to refuse you, señor; but it is impossible!" and he bowed.

These repeated refusals caused a sudden coolness between the guests and their host, in spite of the apparent graciousness of the old man's hospitality,—for the Americans of New Spain resemble the Arabs in this, that they only consent to eat and drink with those towards whom their intentions are friendly.

A vague suspicion crossed the mind of Don Pedro; and he looked inquiringly at his host, but could see nothing in the smiling face of the old man to justify his apprehension.

The repast was eaten silently. At its termination, Doña Hermosa, after thanking the Tigercat for his profuse hospitality, asked him if, before she left, she could not see the hunter who had rendered her such invaluable service the evening before.

"He is absent at present, señorita,—absent in your service; but I expect him to return immediately."

The doña was about to ask for an explanation of these words, when a sound, resembling distant thunder, arose in the forest, and grew louder and louder every minute.

"And here," continued the Tigercat, "comes the very man whom you desired to see; he will be with you directly. The noise you hear is caused by the galloping of the horses he brings with him."

# CHAPTER VI
# THE JOURNEY

In a very short time after the occurrences related in the preceding chapter, the travellers saw a tolerably numerous troop of riders emerge from the forest.

Stoneheart rode at their head, and Don Pedro discovered, with feelings of lively satisfaction, that the horses and mules so audaciously stolen from him were in the rear of the troop.

"Ha!" said he, "The robbers have been compelled to disgorge their prey."

"It would appear so," answered the old man, with a scarcely perceptible smile.

Meanwhile, the hunter had halted the troop at a little distance from the *teocali.* He himself had dismounted, and was now coming towards the travellers. He soon reached them.

"I perceive that you have succeeded in your enterprise," the Tigercat said to him in a tone of raillery.

"I have," answered the hunter laconically, and turning from him.

"I am rejoiced at this circumstance," resumed the old man, addressing Don Pedro; "thanks to it, you will reach your home on your own horses, and without the loss of anything belonging to you."

"How shall I ever repay all the obligations I owe you, señor?" said the *hacendero,* with great emotion.

"By not thanking me for them: my conduct towards you has been very simple, and solely dictated by the interest I took in your unlucky position."

Although nothing could be more evident than the Tigercat's intention to make a courteous answer, his words were uttered with such a hissing accent, his voice was so ironical, and his tone so sarcastic, that the effect produced was quite contrary to what he intended. Without exactly comprehending the reason, Don Pedro felt he had met with an insult instead of a compliment.

"Let us end this," said Stoneheart abruptly. "The sun is already high; and it is time to set out, if you would cross the forest before nightfall."

"In all sincerity," said the Tigercat, "notwithstanding the chagrin I feel at seeing you depart, it is my duty to warn you that, if nothing detains you here, you will do well to commence your journey."

Don Pedro and his companions rose, and, accompanied by the two hunters, descended into the plain.

During the words which had been exchanged on the *teocali*, the mounted Indians had disappeared, leaving the animals of the Mexicans at the place where they had first halted.

The *hacendero*, before he mounted, turned his head several times in the direction in which the Indian's had vanished.

"What are you looking for?" asked the old man, uneasy at this repeated movement.

"You will excuse me," answered Don Pedro; "but I am afraid to enter without a guide into that pathless forest; and I do not see the one you were good enough to promise me."

"Nevertheless he stands before you, señor," said the Tigercat, pointing to the hunter.

"Yes," said the latter, looking defiantly at the old man, "it is I who am to be your guide; and I give you my sacred word, that in despite of savages, be they beasts or men, I will conduct you in safety to your *hacienda*."

The Tigercat made no answer to these words, which were evidently spoken for his behoof; he contented himself by shrugging his shoulders, while an indefinable expression settled on his mocking lips.

"Oh!" said the *hacendero*, "We have indeed nothing to fear if you are to be our guide, señor; the generosity of your late conduct is a sure guarantee for the future."

"Let us go," said the hunter briefly, "we have already lost too much time."

The travellers mounted without replying.

"Adieu! And good luck," said the Tigercat, when he saw them ready to start.

"One word, if you please, caballero," exclaimed the *hacendero*, bowing slightly to his host.

"Speak, señor," said the latter; "is there any further service I can render you?"

"No," replied the Mexican; "I owe you too many favours already; only, before I leave you, perhaps forever, I wish to tell you, without desiring to pry too closely into the motives which prompted your actions towards me, your conduct has apparently been so cordial and noble, that I must try to express to you the extent of my gratitude. Whatever may happen, señor, and until evident proof to the contrary, I consider myself indebted to you; and if occasion offers, I shall know how to cancel the debt I owe you."

And before the Tigercat, stupefied by this adieu, which proved that the *hacendero* was not quite his dupe, had recovered, the Mexican had given both spurs to his horse, and galloped off to rejoin his companions who had already advanced some little way.

The old man remained motionless, his eyes fixed on the travellers, until they had finally disappeared within the forest; then he regained the *teocali*, muttering in a low voice:

"Has he foreseen my purpose? No, it is impossible; but his suspicion is aroused, and I must have been less prudent than my wont."

In the meantime the travellers had entered upon the forest, under the guidance of Stoneheart, who rode alone in advance, with drooping head, and apparently plunged in sombre thought.

For two hours they progressed without exchanging a word. The hunter rode on as if he were alone, without troubling himself in the least about those who followed him; without even turning his head in their direction, to see whether they were behind him.

This behaviour only moderately astonished the *hacendero*, who, recollecting the manner in which he had made acquaintance with the hunter the day before, was expecting a certain oddness of character on his part. Nevertheless, he was hurt by the coldness and indifference displayed by the man whose good will he had sought to conciliate. So he made no attempt to engage him to break the silence and become more sociable.

A little before midday the travellers reached a tolerably large clearing, in the centre of which there gushed forth, from the fissures of a rock, which rose to a grand height in the form of a pyramid, a spring of water, as clear and limpid as crystal, which ran off in a narrow stream through thick tufts of gladiolus.

This clearing, shaded by a leafy vault of gigantic trees surrounding it, offered a delicious spot for repose to the weary travellers.

"We will wait here until the greatest heat of the day is over," said the guide, breaking silence for the first time since they had left the *teocali*.

"Content," said the *hacendero*, smiling; "indeed, you could not have chosen a fitter spot."

"One of the baggage mules carries food and other refreshment, of which you may avail yourself, if you choose; they have been provided for your use."

"And you—will you not join us?" asked the *hacendero*.

"I am neither hungry nor thirsty; do not trouble yourself about me; other duties claim my attention."

Thinking it useless to insist, Don Pedro dismounted, lifted his daughter from her saddle, and placed her on the turf beside the brook. The horses were tethered, and all settled themselves to snatch a few moments of repose.

Stoneheart, after silently helping the *peones* to unload the mule which carried the provisions, and spreading them out before Don Pedro and his daughter, absented himself with hasty strides, and was soon lost in the forest.

"What a strange fellow!" said the *capataz*, while doing honour to the food before him.

"His conduct is incomprehensible," answered Don Pedro.

"But I believe him honest, in spite of his rough manner," said Doña Hermosa; "up to the present his proceedings towards us have been irreproachable."

"Very true," said her father; "yet he seems to display a coldness which, I confess, makes me uneasy."

"It is impossible to think ill of a man who, in spite of all, has shown us nothing but kindness hitherto," replied Doña Hermosa, with a certain degree of warmth of manner; "we owe him our lives, especially myself, whom he saved from a certain and horrible death."

"Very true, my daughter; yet all this is most difficult to account for."

"Not the least in the world, father: this man, accustomed to live amongst Indians, has unconsciously adopted their sententiousness, and the reserve of their manners. What you consider coldness, is probably no more than bashfulness in the presence of a class of persons he is not accustomed to; and his want of knowledge of our habits prevents his speaking."

"It is not impossible that you may be right, my child; however, I intend to ease my mind of this anxiety; and I will not leave him till I have made an effort to loosen his tongue."

"Why should you distress him, father? We cannot exact anything from him, beyond leading us in safety to the *hacienda*. Let him do as he likes, if he only fulfils the promise he made us."

"All very well, señorita," objected the *capataz*; "but you must confess that we should be seriously at a loss if he takes it into his head not to come back."

"That supposition is inadmissible, Don Luciano: his horse is feeding with ours; besides, for what purpose should he commit such an unwarrantable treason."

"This man, in spite of the whiteness of his skin, is more an Indian than an individual of our colour; and, right or wrong, señorita, I distrust the redskins amazingly."

"Moreover," added Don Pedro, "I cannot see what urgent business could induce him to leave us all alone, and to plunge into the forest."

"Who can tell, father?" said the girl shrewdly; "It may be he is gone to do us some further service."

"At all events, señorita," resumed the *capataz*, "I see one thing very clearly, which is, that if this man does not come back again, our position is still more frightful than it was yesterday, for then we had our rifles. Today we are completely without weapons, and incapable of defending ourselves if attacked by man or beast."

"It is too true," cried the *hacendero*, turning pale; "our arms were taken from us while we slept. I never thought of them before. What can be the meaning of all this? Have we again fallen into a snare, and is this man really a traitor?"

"No, my father," replied the girl, with spirit; "he is innocent; I am sure of it. You will soon acknowledge the injustice of your suspicions."

"God grant it!" said Don Pedro, with a sigh.

At this moment a sharp and prolonged whistle was heard at a distance. At the sound the hunter's horse, which had been browsing peaceably, pricked up his ears, and darting in the direction whence the whistle was heard, gave a neigh of pleasure, and galloped off into the forest.

"What did I tell you, señorita?" cried the *capataz*. "Do you believe me now?"

"No," she replied energetically; "I do not believe this man to be a traitor. Strong as appearances may be against him, you will soon see the injustice of your suspicions."

"For this once, my daughter, I concur with Don Luciano; it is evident that, for reasons of his own the miscreant has abandoned us."

His daughter shook her head, but said nothing.

The *hacendero* continued:

"What shall we do? We must decide upon something or other; we cannot stop here and wait for night."

"It is my opinion," said the *capataz*, "that we have no other alternative than to leave this place directly. Who knows whether the wretch is not preparing to swoop down upon us this very moment, at the head of a band of robbers like himself?"

"Yes; but where are we to go? None of us knows the road," interposed the *hacendero*.

"Horses have an infallible instinct which never fails to direct them to inhabited places. Let us throw the reins on their necks, and leave them to choose their road."

"It is a chance we might try; it might succeed. Let us set to work without delay."

"Father! In the name of Heaven," entreated Doña Hermosa, "Think of what you are about to do. Do not act with a precipitation you would soon regret. Wait a little while yet; it is scarcely midday, and an hour more or less is of little importance."

"I will not wait a minute, not a second!" violently exclaimed the *hacendero*, rising to his feet. "Here, *muchachos!* Saddle the horses quickly; we will be off."

The *peones* hastened to obey.

"Be careful, father," said the girl; "I hear the sound of a horse's hoofs in the thicket; our guide is returning."

The convictions of the *hacendero* were shaken by his daughter's earnest appeal. He dropped on the turf again, making a sign to his companion to do the like.

Doña Hermosa had not deceived herself. The noise she had heard was certainly the step—not perhaps of a horse, for it was slow and heavy, but at all events of an animal of great size. It was obviously approaching.

"Perhaps it is a grizzly bear," muttered the *hacendero*.

"Or a jaguar in search of prey," added the *capataz* in a low voice.

The anxiety of the travellers was intense. Abandoned in the forest, without arms to defend themselves, it was clear that they were lost if a wild beast should really attack them; for flight was impossible, as they knew not where to fly to.

"You are mistaken," said Doña Hermosa, who alone had preserved her presence of mind; "no danger threatens us. Look! The horses continue feeding without showing the least alarm."

"You are right," said Don Pedro; "they would have perceived the scent of a wild beast—have been mad with fear, and taken to flight before this."

Suddenly the bushes parted, and the hunter made his appearance, leading his horse by the bridle.

"I was sure of it," cried Doña Hermosa in triumph; while her father and the *capataz* cast down their eyes, blushing for shame.

The features of the hunter were as cold and impassive as they had been when he quitted the clearing, only their expression was more sombre. His horse carried on his back a heavy bundle, oblong in shape, carefully corded, and wrapped up in buffalo hide.

"You must excuse me for having left you," he said in a voice that sounded rather sadly; "I only perceived, when it was too late, that you had been deprived of your weapons,—at least I suppose that to be the case; for you cannot have forgotten to take them when you left the *teocali*; and as it is more than probable you will have to defend yourselves before you leave the wilderness, I have been to find arms for you."

"Is that the reason why you left us?"

"Why I left you!" he answered quietly. "I brought you to this place because a few paces off I have one of those *caches* (hiding places) which we hunters fashion, here and there in the desert, to serve us in time of need. But," he added in a bitter tone, "it has been discovered and pillaged. On that account I whistled for my horse, whose help had become indispensable; for I was obliged to go to another *cache* at some distance. If it had not been for this mishap, I should have been back at least half an hour ago."

This explanation was given by the hunter without emphasis, and in the tone of a man conscious he was merely relating a simple fact.

He unloaded his horse, and opened the bale. It contained five American rifles, knives, straight swords called *machetes*, powder, balls, and hatchets.

"Arm yourselves. The rifles are good; they will not fail you when the time to use them arrives."

The Mexicans did not wait to be asked twice; they were soon armed to the teeth.

"Now, at least," said the hunter, "you can defend yourselves like men, instead of letting yourselves be butchered like deer."

"Ah," sighed Doña Hermosa, "I was convinced he would act like this."

"Thanks, señorita," was his response; "thanks for your trust in me."

While he spoke these words, his features became animated, and his eyes flashed; but he soon resumed the impassiveness of marble.

"I promised to conduct you in safety to your home," he said, "and I will do so."

"Is there any danger to be feared?" inquired Don Pedro.

"There is always danger," he replied bitterly, "in the desert more than elsewhere."

"Are we threatened with treachery?"

"Ask me no questions; I will not reply to them. Listen to my words, and profit by them. If you wish to preserve your scalps, you must place implicit confidence in me, whatever I may do, and obey me, without fear or hesitation, in everything I may order. All I shall do will be done with but one aim—your safety. Do you consent to these conditions?"

"We do," exclaimed Doña Hermosa fervently; "we will not doubt your loyalty, and will act entirely according to your council."

"I swear it," said the *hacendero*.

"It is well; now I will be answerable for everything. Put aside all anxiety. Do not speak to me; I have need to collect my thoughts."

Bowing carelessly, he betook himself to a little distance, and seated himself at the foot of a tree.

In the meantime the curiosity of the Mexicans was strongly excited. They comprehended that serious danger was impending, and that the hunter was planning means to avert it; but now that they had excellent weapons, horns full of powder, and balls, they looked at their position in a new light, and, although their anxiety was still great, they did not despair of being able to escape from the snares laid for their feet.

The hunter, after remaining motionless as a statue for nearly half an hour, raised his head, calculated the time by the shadows of the trees, and said, rising with some impetuosity,

"To horse; it is time to go."

The horses were soon saddled, and the travellers in their seats.

"You will march in Indian file," continued the hunter; "follow exactly in my steps."

Instead of advancing in the direction he had taken hitherto, he rode his horse into the rivulet, the course of which he followed until he reached a spot where two other brooks contributed their waters. Stoneheart chose the left hand brook, and followed its windings. The Mexicans closely imitated this manoeuvre, riding in Indian file—the head of each horse at the crupper of the one in front of him.

The heat was stifling in the covert, where the circulation of the air, impeded by the foliage, was scarcely perceptible. The deepest calm prevailed through the forest; the birds, nestled under the leaves, had ceased their songs; and nothing was heard but the monotonous humming of innumerable myriads of mosquitoes hovering about the marshes.

In the meantime the brook they were following increased by degrees till it assumed the character of a river. Here and there, already, black *chicots* (trees uprooted and carried down by the rivers, often forming serious obstacles to navigation) began to make their appearance, on which rosy flamingoes and herons stood on one leg; the banks right and left became steeper, and the horses for some time past had been obliged to swim.

This unknown river, whose blue waters had never reflected anything but the azure of the skies and the green dome formed by the trees capriciously bending over its banks, presented to the eye a grand and majestic sight, impressing the mind with a kind of melancholy calm and religious awe.

The travellers, silent as phantoms, continued their journey, swimming slowly down the middle of the river, close at the heels of their guide, whose eagle glance explored its banks. Arriving at a place where an immense rock rose like a solitary watchtower, and formed an immense vault overhanging the stream, Stoneheart slipped from his horse, whose bridle he gave to Don Pedro, and swam under the arch, making a sign to the others to pursue their course. He soon reappeared in one of those Indian canoes which are built of birch bark, detached by means of boiling water, and whose lightness is unequalled. With a few strokes of the paddle he reached the travellers; the latter climbed into the canoe, and their horses, relieved from the weight of their riders, were able to swim with greater ease.

Doña Hermosa was very glad of the change. Still suffering from her wound, she began to feel much difficulty in keeping her seat on her horse, although she exerted herself to the utmost to conceal her fatigue. But the quick eye of the hunter had noticed her lassitude, and he had brought the canoe for her relief.

They still continued to advance in this manner for nearly an hour, without any occurrence to disturb their tranquillity or make them suspect the vicinity of an enemy. At last they reached a turn of the river where the banks rose, for a considerable space, to a prodigious height, and hemmed in the stream between two walls of rock terminating in peaks. In the centre of the river arose a block of grayish granite, about sixty yards in circumference, and towards it the hunter guided the canoe. The Mexicans, at first astonished at this manoeuvre, were not long before they comprehended it; for, when close in upon the rock, they discovered that one of its faces sloped down in a gentle incline, and in this face there yawned the mouth of a cavern.

The canoe touched the ground; the travellers disembarked, and hastened to bring the horses to land: the poor animals were spent with fatigue.

"Come," said the hunter, shouldering the canoe; and the Mexicans followed him.

The cavern was spacious, and seemed to extend under water to a great distance. The horses were stabled in a corner, and supplied with provender.

"Here," said the hunter, "we are as much in safety as it is possible to be in the desert. If nothing comes to trouble us, we will pass the night here, in order to give our horses the rest of which they stand so much in need. You can light a fire without hesitation; the fissures in the rock, which afford you light, will divide the smoke, and render it invisible. Although I believe I have hidden our trail from those in pursuit of us, it is still incumbent on me to make a reconnaissance outside. Be not uneasy; present or absent, I watch over you. I will return in an hour. But take heed not to show yourselves; in the virgin forest, who can tell what eyes may be upon him? Adieu for a time."

He went out, leaving his companions a prey to anxiety, which was the more lively because, although well aware that some great danger threatened, they could not foresee either whence or in what manner it would fall on them, and because they were completely at the mercy of a man whose character and ultimate intentions it was impossible to divine.

# CHAPTER VII
# THE SKIRMISH

Nature has rights she always enforces: whatever the anxiety of the Mexicans, the fatigues they had endured during the whole of that long day made them feel the imperious necessity of recruiting their strength; so, after a few gloomy reflections on their critical and almost desperate situation, Don Pedro ordered the *peones* to light a fire and prepare the evening meal.

Men whose physical faculties are more frequently called into exertion than their minds, never forget to eat and sleep, whatever situation chance may place them in; appetite and sleep never fail them. The reason is simple: constantly exposed to Titanic struggles with man or the elements, their natural forces must be maintained in an equal ratio with the efforts they have to make to surmount the obstacles which oppose, or the perils which threaten them.

The meal was sad and silent; the Mexicans were too deeply impressed by the approach of night, the time habitually chosen by the redskins for their attacks, to care for exchanging many words.

The hunter's absence was protracted; already, for more than two hours, the sun had disappeared behind the high mountaintops; thick darkness enveloped the earth as with a shroud; not a star twinkled in the sky; and great black clouds coursed through space, completely veiling the orb of the moon.

The *hacendero* would not resign to any other the duty of watching over the common safety. Lying face downwards on the platform, so that he might not be visible if an unseen enemy were lying in wait, he anxiously scanned the dark line of the water. At his side lay the *capataz*, who, equally with himself, had no wish to attempt a repose which he knew to be impossible.

The high cliffs of the banks were bare and deserted; only at one place, where the shore was accessible, they saw black shapes moving for a few seconds, with hoarse and angry growls, and then disappearing. These black forms were evidently wild animals, slaking their thirst in the river before repairing to their layers.

"Come!" suddenly exclaimed a deep and determined voice in the ear of the Mexican.

Don Pedro turned round, repressing a cry of astonishment; the hunter stood by him, leaning on his rifle.

The three men entered the cavern. The remains of the fire which had been lighted for the evening meal diffused light enough to distinguish objects.

"You are very late," said the *hacendero*.

"I have traversed six leagues since I left you," replied the hunter; "but that is no matter. A man, whose name you need not know at present, has resolved to prevent your reaching the *hacienda*. A party of Apaches is on our trail. All my precautions have not availed to conceal our tracks from these cunning demons, whose piercing eyes would detect in the air the trail of the eagle's flight. They are encamped close by; they are preparing rafts and canoes to attack you."

"Are there many of them?" inquired the *hacendero*.

"No; not above a score at most, of whom only six or seven are armed with rifles; the rest have but bows and lances. Knowing you to be without arms, or at least believing so, they count upon carrying you off without striking a blow."

"Who is the man who is so inveterate against us?"

"What is that to you? He is a strange and mysterious being, whose life is one continual round of dark conspiracies; his mind is an abyss which no one has dared to sound, the depths of which even he himself, who fears nothing in the world, would dread to fathom. But enough of him. You are to be attacked in two hours; three chances of escape from the fate prepared for you are open to you."

"And what are these chances?" said the *hacendero*.

"The first is, to remain here, await the attack, and make a vigorous resistance. The Apaches, alarmed at finding armed and on their guard the men whom they hoped to surprise weaponless and defenceless, may lose courage, and retreat."

Doña Hermosa, aroused by the sound of voices, had approached, and was listening attentively.

The *hacendero* shook his head. "The chance seems hazardous," he said; "for if our enemies succeeded in setting foot on the rock, they would overpower us by dint of numbers, and make themselves masters of our persons."

"That would most probably be the case," said the hunter, coolly.

"Let us hear the second chance; the one already proposed seems impracticable."

"This rock communicates, by a subterraneous passage under the bed of the river, with another rock, a good distance from the place where we now are. I will lead you to that rock; when we get there, we will embark in the canoe; having reached the opposite bank of the river, we will mount, and trust our safety to the speed of our horses."

"I should prefer this chance, if our horses were not so worn out that a night flight across the wilderness would be almost an impossibility."

"The redskins know as well as I do all the outlets from the rock on which we have taken refuge. Most likely they have already guarded the passage by which we might hope to escape."

"Alas!" said the *hacendero*, sorrowfully, "With all your good intention to help us, the chances you propose are against us."

"I know it; unfortunately, it does not depend upon me to make them otherwise."

"And lastly," resumed Don Pedro, with much resignation, "what is the third chance?"

"I am afraid you will find the last more desperate than the other two. It is a rash and dangerous undertaking, which might perhaps offer a hope of success if we had not with us a woman, whom we must not expose to one peril in order to save her from another."

"Then it is useless to name it," said the *hacendero*, with a mournful look at his daughter.

"You are wrong, father," said Doña Hermosa, with much animation; "let us hear, at least, what this chance is. Perhaps it is the only good one. Explain, señor," continued she, addressing the hunter. "After all you have done for us, we should be ungrateful not to listen to your counsel. I am convinced that what you hesitate to propose, for my sake, is the only means of safety open to us."

"That may be," answered the hunter; "but I repeat, señorita, that the means are impracticable—you being with us."

The girl drew herself up, a gay smile played about her rosy lips, and, commencing her speech in a voice slightly ironical, she said:

"You surely think me very weak and pusillanimous, señor, since you dare not speak out. I am but a woman, it is true, and feeble, as we all are; but I think I have proved to you, in the few hours during which we have travelled together, that my heart is above vulgar fears; and that if my physical strength is not equal to my moral energy, my will triumphs over my woman's weakness, and makes me superior to circumstances, let them be what they will."

Stoneheart listened attentively to the beautiful girl. The mask of impassiveness which covered his features melted away at the sound of that melodious voice, and a deep blush suffused his face.

"Pardon me, señorita," he said in a voice which the secret feelings agitating him caused to waver; "I was wrong; I will speak out."

"Good!" said she, with a pleasant smile; "I knew what your answer would be."

"The Apaches," began the hunter, "are encamped, as I have told you, at a short distance from the bank of the river. Certain that they will not be molested, they keep no watch; they sleep, drink the firewater, and await the time for attacking you. We are six men, well armed and determined; we know that our safety depends on the success of our expedition. Let us land on the island, surprise the redskins, and fall on them boldly. Perhaps we may succeed in opening ourselves a passage, and in that case we shall be saved, for they will not pursue us after they have been defeated. This is my proposal."

There was a long silence; it was Doña Hermosa who broke it.

"You were wrong in hesitating to acquaint us with this project," said she, fervently; "it is the only one practicable. It is better to meet danger halfway than to tremble in cowardly expectation of its advent. Let us go! Let us go! We have not a minute to lose."

"Daughter," exclaimed Don Pedro, "you are mad! Remember, we are going to expose ourselves to almost certain death."

"Be it so, my father," she replied, with feverish energy; "our fate is in the hands of God, whose protection has been so evident thus far, that I believe He will not abandon us now."

"The señorita is right," cried the *capataz*; "let us smoke these demons out of their lair. This hunter, to whom I make my most humble apologies for having suspected his loyalty for an instant, will supply us with the means of arriving, without being discovered, at the camp of the Apaches."

"I can but do my best," said the hunter modestly.

"Let us go, then, since needs must," said the *hacendero*, with a sigh.

The *peones*, who had not mingled in the conversation, seized their rifles with an air of determination which proved them resolved to do their duty.

"Follow me," said the hunter, lighting a torch of *ocote* wood, to show the way.

Without another word, the Mexicans plunged into the depth of the cavern, taking with them the horses whose strength had been thoroughly recruited by their rest of so many hours.

They continued pushing their way through the subterranean passage. Overhead they heard the dull and ceaseless noise of the waters; thousands of night birds, dazzled by the unwonted light of the torch, awoke from their slumbers, and wheeled around, uttering mournful and discordant cries.

At the end of half an hour's rapid march, the hunter halted.

"Wait for me here," he said, and passed on rapidly, after delivering the torch to the *capataz*.

Shortly after, he returned.

"Come," said he, "all goes well."

They followed him anew. Suddenly a fresh, cool breeze met their faces, and through the obscurity before them they saw two or three points of light glittering. They had reached the other rock.

"We must now redouble our caution," said the hunter; "those points of light you see shining through the mist are the campfires of the Apaches. Their ear is fine; the least noise would betray our presence."

The canoe was launched again; the Mexicans embarked, the *capataz*, at the stern of the frail bark, holding the reins of the horses, which followed swimming.

Crossing occupied only a few minutes, and the canoe soon grated against the sandy beach.

Nothing could be better than the place chosen by the hunter. A high rock threw over the water, to a considerable distance, so dark a shadow, that it was impossible to distinguish the travellers ten paces off.

The forest, scarcely twenty yards from the shore, offered, amongst its thickets, immediate protection to the fugitives.

"The señorita will remain here, with one *peon* to guard the horses," said the hunter; "we others will attempt the surprise."

"Not so," exclaimed the girl resolutely. "I want no one here. You would miss the man you wish to leave with me. Give me a pistol, to defend myself in case of attack, and go."

"Nevertheless, señorita—"

"It is my will," she peremptorily exclaimed. "Go, and God be with you!"

The *hacendero* convulsively pressed his daughter to his bosom.

"Courage, my father!" she cried, while she embraced him; "Courage; all will end well."

She took a pistol from him, and left him, waving her adieu.

The hunter for the last time warned his companions to be cautious; and the men set off, following his exact footsteps in the forest.

After marching half an hour in Indian file, they saw the fires of the Apaches glimmering close by.

At a sign from the hunter, the Mexicans threw themselves on the ground, and began to crawl forward in silence, advancing with extreme precaution inch by inch, their ears on the watch, and ready to fire at the first suspicious movement of the enemy.

But nothing stirred: most of the Apaches slept, plunged, as Stoneheart had asserted, in the brutal drunkenness caused by the abuse of the firewater.

Only three or four warriors, easily recognised as chiefs by the vulture plumes they wore in their hair, were squatting around the fire, smoking with the mechanical gravity characteristic of the Indian.

By the hunter's order, the Mexicans slowly arose, and each man sheltered himself behind the trunk of a tree.

"I leave you here," whispered Stoneheart. "I am going to enter the camp. Keep still as death; and, whatever may happen, do not fire before you see me throw my cap on the ground."

He disappeared among the underwood.

From the spot where the travellers were hidden, they could easily see all that took place in the camp of the redskins, and even hear what was said; for only a few yards separated them from the fire round which the *sachems* crouched.

With bodies ensconced behind the trees, their fingers on the triggers of their rifles, their eyes fixed in feverish impatience on the camp, the Mexicans awaited the signal to give fire.

The few minutes preceding a night attack are very solemn. A man left alone with his thoughts on such an occasion, about to risk his life in pitiless strife, however brave he may be, feels himself seized by an instinctive dread, which sends a cold shudder thrilling through his frame. In that supreme hour he sees his whole life pass, as in a dream, with giddy rapidity before him, and the most abiding and predominant sensation is the thought of that which is to happen beyond the grave,—the dread unknown.

Some ten minutes had elapsed since the departure of the hunter, when a slight noise was heard in the brushwood on the opposite side of the camp to that where the Mexicans lay in ambush.

The Apache chiefs turned their heads negligently, the bushes parted, and Stoneheart made his appearance in the circle of light caused by the watch fires.

The hunter slowly approached the chiefs. When close to them, he stopped, and bowed ceremoniously, but without speaking.

The *sachems* returned the salute with the innate good breeding of the redskins.

"My brother is welcome," said a chief. "Will he sit by the council fire?"

"No," said the hunter; "my time is short."

"My brother is prudent," resumed the chief; "he has abandoned the palefaces, because he knows that the Tigercat has delivered them over to the barbed arrows of the Apache warriors."

"I have not abandoned the palefaces: my brother deceives himself. I have sworn to defend them; I will do so."

"That is against the orders of the Tigercat."

"I take no orders from him. I hate treachery. I will not let the redskin braves accomplish what they meditate."

"Oh!" grunted the *sachem;* "My brother lifts his voice very high. I have heard the hawk mock at the eagle, but a blow of its mighty wing crushed the hawk to powder."

"A truce to sarcasm, chief. You are one of the most renowned braves of your tribe, and cannot consent to become the agent of an infamous treachery. The Tigercat has received these travellers in his *calli;* he has treated them with hospitality. Is not hospitality sacred in the desert?"

The Apache burst into a laugh.

"The Tigercat is a great chief; he would neither eat nor drink with the palefaces."

"It is an unworthy artifice."

"The palefaces are thievish dogs. The Apaches will take their scalps."

"Wretch!" cried the hunter; "I too am a paleface. Come and take my scalp."

And, rapid as thought, he cast on the ground the cap of fur which covered his head, and at the same instant precipitated himself on the Indian chief, and plunged his knife into his heart.

Five shots were heard simultaneously with this action, and the remaining chiefs sitting round the fire rolled to the ground in their death agony.

The *sachems* were the only Indians with rifles.

"Forward! Forward!" shouted the hunter; and seizing his rifle by the muzzle, he hurled himself into the midst of the panic-stricken Apaches.

The Mexicans after their first fire, rushed into the camp to reinforce the guide.

Then a terrible struggle commenced—six men against fifteen—a struggle all the more fierce and desperate because each man knew he could expect no mercy.

Happily for themselves, the whites were armed with pistols. These they discharged point-blank in the face of their opponents, attacking them afterwards with the sabre.

The Indians had been so completely surprised—they had so little expected to have to sustain such a vigorous onslaught from men who seemed to have emerged from the earth, and whose numbers they were far from suspecting—that half of them had been killed before the rest could recover from their fright, or attempt serious resistance. When at last they essayed an organised defence, it was too late. The Mexicans pressed them so hard, that a longer resistance was impossible.

"Hold!" shouted the hunter.

Whites and redskins lowered their arms at once.

The hunter continued: "Warriors of the Apaches, throw down your arms!"

They obeyed; and at a signal from the guide, the Mexicans bound their opponents without further difficulty.

As soon as the redskins acknowledged their defeat, they awaited, with complete apathy and their usual fatalism, the doom their victors might think fit to impose upon them.

Out of twenty Apache braves, only eight remained alive: the rest had fallen.

"At sunrise," said the hunter, "I will come and release you from your bonds. Till then, stir not! I pardon once; never a second time."

The Mexicans collected all the arms, freed all the horses tethered at one side of the camp, drove them into the forest, where they were soon lost to sight, and left the Apaches.

"And now," exclaimed the hunter, "let us return to the señorita."

"But," enquired Don Pedro, "is it really your intention to restore these men to liberty?"

"Assuredly. Would you have me leave them to be devoured by wild beasts?"

"It would be no great misfortune," answered the rancorous *capataz*.

"Are they not men, like ourselves?"

"They are so little like ourselves, that it is hardly worth mention," said the *capataz*.

"And will you really dare to place yourself in the power of these ferocious beings, exasperated as they are by defeat?" asked the *hacendero*. "Do you not fear they will assassinate you?"

"These men!" replied the hunter in disdain; "They would not dare."

Don Pedro could not repress his amazement.

"The redskins are the most vindictive of men," said he.

"True," was the reply; "but I am not a man in their eyes."

"What then?"

"An evil spirit," murmured the hunter in a hoarse whisper.

By this time they had reached the place where they had left their horses.

The noise of the combat had extended itself to the spot where Doña Hermosa was waiting; but that courageous girl, far from suffering herself to be overcome by the very natural fear she experienced, understood the importance of the post confided to her, and remained firmly on her guard, a pistol in each hand, attentively listening to every sound in the forest, ready to defend herself, and resolute to die sooner than fall into the hands of the Indians.

Her father having explained to her what had occurred, they began their journey at the best speed of their horses.

The whole night passed without slackening their pace. At sunrise they had cleared the forest, and there lay the bare wilderness, extending to the horizon.

They continued their route for two more hours, when they halted.

The hunter addressed them: "We must part here." He spoke in a firm, voice, yet unable completely to conceal the feeling of sorrow which pervaded him.

"So soon!" said the girl naively

"Thanks for that expression of regret, señorita; but I must go. You are but a few miles from your *hacienda:* the road is easy; my help is no longer needful."

"We must not part thus, señor," said the *hacendero*, holding out his hand; "I owe you too many obligations."

"Forget them, *caballero*," vehemently exclaimed the young hunter; "forget me too: we must never meet again. You return to civilised life, I to the desert. Our roads are far apart; for your sake and for mine, pray that we never again stand face to face. Only," he added, lifting his eyes to the señorita, "I carry with me a memory of you which can never be effaced. And now, farewell! Yonder are the *vaqueros* of your *hacienda* approaching to meet you. You are in safety."

He bent his head to his saddlebow, tuned his horse, and began to gallop away. But, looking back, he perceived Doña Hermosa riding after him.

"Stay," she exclaimed.

He obeyed mechanically.

"Look," said she, presenting to him a slender gold ring; "of all my possessions, I value this ring the most; it belonged to my mother whom I never knew. Keep it in memory of me, señor."

The señorita rode off, leaving the ring in his hand without giving him time to reply.

# CHAPTER VIII
# THE PUEBLO (THE TOWN)

After the Spanish rule had been firmly established in the New World, the government, to hold the Indians, in cheek, constructed fortified posts, at certain distances, on the extreme limits of their possessions. These posts were called *presidios*, and were peopled by criminals of every degree of whom it was deemed prudent to clear the mother country. The *presidio* of San Lucar, on the Rio Bermejo, was one of the first established.

At the epoch of the foundation of this *presidio*, the post consisted solely of a fort built on the north bank, on a steep cliff which commands the river, the plains to the south, and the surrounding country.

It is square in form, built with very thick walls of hewn stone, and flanked by three bastions,—two on the river, to east and west, the third in the plain.

The interior contains the chapel, priest's house and the powder magazine; on the other sides are the old dwelling places of the prisoners, spacious buildings for the commandant, the treasurer, and officers of the garrison, and likewise a small hospital.

All these buildings, only one story high, were finished off with flat Italian roofs. Outside, the government had also constructed vast granaries, a bakery, a mill, two workshops for saddlers and carpenters, and two *ranchos* appropriated to the horses and cattle.

In these days the fort is almost in ruins the walls, for want of repair, are crumbling in all directions; only the dwellings are kept in tolerable condition.

The *presidio* of San Lucar is divided into three sections,—two to the north, the third to the south of the river.

Its general aspect is melancholy. A few sparse trees grow here and there, in close contiguity to the river, manifesting, by their want of vitality, how ungrateful is the soil from which they draw their existence. The roads are covered with a pulverulent sand, throwing up clouds of dust at the least motion in the atmosphere.

Three days after the events recorded in our last chapter, at about two o'clock in the afternoon, five or six *vaqueros* and *leperos* were seated at a table in the drinking room of a *pulquería* (a public house) of New San Lucar, which is situated on the south bank of the river, and disputed vehemently, while they emptied, at long draughts, the *pulque* in the cups which circulated among them.

"*¡Canarios!*" exclaimed a tall and meagre fellow, with the mien and air of a brazen-faced scoundrel, "Are we not free men? If Señor Don Louis Pedrosa, our governor, persist in fleecing us in this fashion, the Tigercat is not too far off for a man to come to an understanding with him. Though he chooses to be an Indian chief today, he is a white man without alloy, and a *caballero* to the tips of his fingers."

"*¡Calla la voz!* be silent, Pablito!" said another; "You had better swallow your words with your *pulque* than utter such folly."

"I will speak!" said Pablito, who was washing the inside of his throat more than the others.

"Do you not know that invisible eyes are watching us from the shade, and that ears are open to gather up our words, and profit by them?"

"There you are again," replied the first speaker: "always in fear, Carlocho! I have no more respect for a spy than for an old *cuarta*" (hag).

"Pablito!" exclaimed the other, placing his finger on his lips.

"What! Am I not right? Why does Don Louis bear us so much malice?"

"You are wrong," interrupted a third, with a laugh. "Don Louis, on the contrary, is only too fond of you so he always keeps you under his thumb."

"This devil of a *verado* has a wit fit for such a rascal as he," roared Pablito, with shouts of laughter.

"Well, after us the end of the world."

"In the meantime let us drink," said the *verado*.

"Good! Let us drink, and drown care. Have we not Don Fernando Carril to help us when our purses run dry?"

"Another name which ought to have stuck in your throat," said Carlocho, striking the table in his irritation with his fist. "Can you never hold your tongue, cursed dog?"

Pablito frowned, and, looking angrily across the table, exclaimed: "Do you pretend to give me a lesson, *amigo? ¡Canarios!* You begin to put my blood up."

"A lesson? And why not, when you deserve it?" replied the other, without stirring. "*Caray* these two hours you have been drinking like a sponge; you are full as a vat, and talk as wildly as an old woman. Hold your tongue, or go to sleep."

"*Mil rayos*," growled Pablito, sticking his knife violently into the table; "You shall answer for this!"

"¡*Vive Dios!* A blood-letting will do you good. My hand itches to give you a *navajada* (a stroke with a knife) across your hideous snout."

"Hideous snout, did you say?" and Pablito threw himself upon Carlocho, who awaited his onset firmly.

The other *vaqueros* and *leperos* threw themselves between the pair, to prevent the meeting.

"¡Halloa, *caballeros!*" cried the *pulquero* (innkeeper), thinking it necessary to interfere. "Peace! in the name of God or the devil! No quarrels in my house: if you wish for satisfaction, the street is free."

"The *pulquero* is right!" screamed Pablito. "Come, if you are a man!"

"Gladly!" cried Carlocho; and the two *vaqueros* rushed into the street.

As to the worthy *pulquero*, he stood at his door, his hands in the pockets of his *calzoneras* (loose trousers), and whistled a *jarana* (a dance tune), while expecting the fight.

Pablito and Carlocho wrapped the left arm in the *zarapé* for a shield, took off their hats and saluted with much affectation, drew their long knives from their girdles, and, without exchanging a word, stood on their guard with remarkable coolness.

In this kind of duel—the only one, by the by, known in Mexico—satisfaction consists in slashing the adversary in the face. A blow delivered below the girdle would be considered a piece of treachery unworthy of a true *caballero*.

The two opponents, firmly planted with legs apart, bodies inclined, and heads thrown back, watched each other fixedly, in order to forestall a movement, parry a blow, or inflict a wound. The rest of the *vaqueros*, with their delicate maize cigarettes in their mouths, looked on composedly, and applauded every adroit thrust or parry.

The fight was continued for some minutes, with equal success on either side, when Pablito, whose sight was most likely obfuscated by his copious potations, came to the parry a second too late, and felt the point of Carlocho's knife rip the skin of his face from chin to forehead.

"Bravo! Bravo!" exclaimed all the *vaqueros* at once. "Well hit!"

The combatants, flattered by this approbation, stepped away from each other, bowed to the spectators, sheathed their knives, saluted one another with exquisite courtesy, and having first shaken hands, went into the *pulquería* once more.

The *vaqueros* are a peculiar race of men, whose ways and manners are quite distinct from the customs known in Europe. Those of San Lucar may serve as a type. Born on the Indian frontiers they have contracted sanguinary habits, and their disregard of life is remarkable. Inveterate gamblers, the cards are never out of their hands; and play is a fruitful source of quarrels, in which the knife is constantly called into requisition. Careless of the future, little heedful of present trouble, and enduring physical suffering hardily, they look upon death with as much contempt as on life, and recoil before no danger.

These men—who often abandon their families in order to live a life of greater license among the savage hordes of the desert; who, in shear wantonness, spill the blood of their fellow creatures; who are implacable in their hate—these men are capable of ardent friendship, and of extraordinary devotedness and self-denial. Their character presents a curious mixture of good and evil, of unbridled vice and sterling qualities. They are at one and the same time idle, gamblers, quarrelsome, drunkards, ferocious, brave to rashness and devoted heart and soul to a friend, or the patron of their choice. From infancy blood runs like water from their hands during the period of the *matanza del ganado* (slaughtering the cattle); and this familiarity with the crimson stains hardens them to the sight of human gore. Lastly, their jokes are as coarse as their habits, the threat of using the knife on quite frivolous occasions being the most delicate and the most common.

While the *vaqueros*, reseated at the table in the *pulquería*, were pouring libations to their reconciliation, and drowning the remembrance of the petty incident in floods of *pulque* and *mezcal* (a coarse kind of brandy), a man entered, muffled in the folds of a thick cloak, and with the wide brim of his hat pulled over his eyes. Approaching the table without uttering a word, he cast a look of seeming indifference around, lighted a cigarette at the brazier, and struck three blows upon it with a large piastre he held between his fingers.

The noise, which appeared to be a signal, startled the three *vaqueros*. They dropped the noisy conversation they were engaged in, as if suddenly struck by an electric shock, and became as still as death. Pablito and Carlocho began to tremble, seeking all the while to discover the features of the new arrival under the folds of his cloak; while the *verado* turned his head on one side to hide his crafty smiles.

The stranger cast his half-consumed cigar into the brazier, and retired from the filthy room in the same silence in which he came.

An instant later, Pablito, who was stanching his bleeding cheek, and Carlocho, making a pretence of important business, quitted the *pulquería*. The *verado* glided along the wall to the door, and followed at their heels.

"Holloa!" muttered the *pulquero*, "Here are three *pícaros* (villains), who seem to be concocting some devil's job, in which more broken heads than *duros* (dollars) are to be gained. ¡Caray! That is their lookout."

The remaining *vaqueros*, completely absorbed in a game at *monte*, and bending over their cards, appeared scarcely to have noticed the departure of their comrades.

At some little distance from the *pulquería* the stranger looked back. The two *vaqueros* were walking close behind him, talking carelessly, as if they were two idlers strolling along. The *verado* was not to be seen.

The stranger went on his way again, after making a scarcely perceptible sign to the two men, and pursued a road which, in a gentle curve, gradually retired from the river, and led, little by little, into the fields. At the exit from the *pueblo* this road took a sharp angle, and narrowed suddenly into a path, which lost itself in the plain among many more.

Just at the bend in the road, a cavalier, trotting hurriedly in the direction of the *presidio*, passed close to the three men; but, immersed in their thoughts, neither stranger nor *vaqueros* took notice of him. As to the cavalier, he darted a rapid and piercing look at them, and gradually slackened his horse's speed, which he stopped altogether a few yards further on.

"God forgive me!" he said to himself; that is Don Fernando Carril, or else the devil in flesh and bone. That fool, Zapote, has missed him again, then! What business can he have out here, in company with those two bandits, who look like agents of Satan? May I never be Torribio Quiroga if I don't find out, and if I do not put myself on their traces.

Señor Don Torribio Quiroga was an individual of not more than thirty-five, with a rather stout figure, under the middle height. But to make up for it, the squareness of his shoulders, and thick-set limbs, gave unmistakable evidence of great muscular power. Little grey eyes, lively, and sparkling with malice and audacity, lit up a face which was perhaps somewhat vulgar. He was dressed in the costume of all Mexicans of a certain rank.

He dismounted, and looked about for somebody to hold his horse, but could see no one; for, at San Lucar, and especially in the new *pueblo*, it was almost a miracle to meet two persons passing through the streets at the same time. He stamped in anger, threw the reins over his arm, and led his horse to the *pulquería* whence the *vaqueros* had come, confiding him to the care of the landlord.

Having carefully completed this duty—for the Mexican's dearest friend is his horse—Don Torribio retraced his steps with the most minute precaution, like a man who wishes to see without himself being seen.

The *vaqueros* had gained considerably upon him, and disappeared behind a hillock of shifting sand just at the moment when he turned the angle of the lane: however, he soon saw them again as they were toiling up a steep and rough path leading to a clump of trees, which by chance or some caprice of nature had shot up among the arid sands.

Sure of finding them now, Don Torribio began to walk more slowly, and lit a cigar, to keep himself in countenance in case of surprise, or to prevent any casual suspicion of his intentions. Luckily, the *vaqueros* never looked back once, but entered the wood close upon the heels of the man recognised by Don Torribio as Don Fernando Carril.

When, in his turn, Don Torribio arrived at the margin of the wood, he took good care not to walk straight into it. He first made a slight *détour* to the right; then, bending down to the ground, he commenced crawling on hands and knees, taking special care to avoid any noise that might excite the attention of the *vaqueros*.

The sound of voices soon reached him. Gently raising his head, he perceived, in a small clearing close at hand, the figures of the three men, who had stopped, and were engaged in a lively conversation. He rose from the ground, and hid himself behind a maple tree.

Don Fernando Carril had dropped his cloak, leaning with his shoulders against a tree, and, with his legs crossed, he was listening with visible impatience to what Pablito was saying.

The hands of Don Fernando were small, and delicately gloved; his feet, showing the nobility of his blood by their diminutive size, were encased in varnished boots,—a luxury unheard of in these distant regions. His costume, of amazing richness, was absolutely identical in shape with that of the *vaqueros*. A diamond of immense value fastened the collar of his shirt; and his *zarapé* was worth more than five hundred piastres. For the present, we will conclude the portrait here.

Two years before our narrative commences, Don Fernando Carril had arrived at San Lucar, knowing nobody; and everyone had asked, Who is he? Where does he come from? Whence does he derive his riches? And where do his estates lie? Don Fernando bought a *hacienda* a few leagues from San Lucar. Under pretence of defending it against the Indians, he fortified it, surrounded it with palisades and a moat, and furnished it with two small pieces of cannon. In this way he had kept his doings secret, and curiosity at bay. Although he never opened his *hacienda* to receive a guest, he was himself received by the first inhabitants of San Lucar, whom he visited most assiduously, till suddenly, to the great amazement of all, he disappeared for several months.

The ladies missed their practice in smiles and ogling, the men their occupation of contriving adroit questions to entrap Don Fernando. Don Louis Pedrosa, whose post as governor gave him a right to be inquisitive, could not help feeling uneasy about the stranger; but, wearied with conjecture, he was obliged to trust to time, which, sooner or later, reveals all mysteries. Nothing more was known of the man who was standing in the clearing, listening to Pablito.

"Enough!" said this personage, interrupting Pablito, in a fit of passion; "You are a dog, and a dog's son."

"Señor!" exclaimed the latter.

"I feel inclined to crush you, wretch!"

"A threat! And to me!" shouted the *vaquero* white with fury, and unsheathing his knife.

Don Fernando seized the man's fist with his gloved hand, and gave it such a sudden and violent wrench, that the *vaquero* dropped his weapon with a groan.

"Down on your knees, and ask for pardon!" the don went on, hurling the wretch to the ground.

"No! I will die first!"

"Begone! You are a brute beast!"

The *vaquero* staggered as he rose; his eyes were bloodshot, his lips blue; his whole body trembled. He picked up his knife, and approached Don Fernando, who stood there with folded arms.

"It is true; yes, I am a brute beast; but, nevertheless, I am devoted to you. Forgive me, or kill me, but do not bid me begone."

"Go! I tell you."

"And you have no more to say to me?"

"It is my last word; vex me no more."

"Your last word to me? Then I go—to the devil!" And he raised his weapon to kill himself.

Don Fernando arrested the stroke. "I forgive you," said he: "but, if you still wish to remain in my service, be mute as a corpse."

The *vaquero* fell at his feet, and covered with kisses the hand extended to him. It was like a dog licking the hand of the master who has beaten him.

Carlocho had taken no part in this scene, but remained a calm and unmoved spectator.

"What charm has this mysterious stranger," muttered Don Torribio behind his maple, "to make himself beloved like this?"

After a short silence, Don Fernando again spoke.

"I know you are devoted to me. I have great confidence in your fidelity; but you are a drunkard, and drink is an evil counsellor."

"I will drink no more," replied the *vaquero*.

Don Fernando smiled in disdain.

"Drink, but do not drown your reason. Drunkenness such as yours lets fall words for which there is no remedy,—words more murderous than the dagger. It is not the master, it is the friend who speaks to you. Can I count on you both?"

"You can."

"I leave this place for a few days; you will remain in the neighbourhood. At a short distance from the *pueblo* is the Hacienda de las Norias de San Antonio; do you know it?"

"Who does not know Don Pedro de Luna?"

"Watch that *hacienda* carefully, both without and within. If anything extraordinary befalls Don Pedro or his daughter, Doña Hermosa, one of you will come and acquaint me with it. You know where to find me?"

The men bowed their heads.

"Will you execute all my orders, however incomprehensible, with promptitude and accuracy?"

"We swear so, master."

"Good! One word more; attach to yourselves as many *vaqueros* as you can; strive to gather together a body of men to be depended on. Do this without exciting suspicion; she never sleeps with both eyes closed. Stay! I remember! Put no faith in the *verado*; he is a traitor—a spy upon me, in the service of the Tigercat."

"Shall we kill him?" coolly asked Carlocho.

"It might be, prudent; only rid yourselves of him quietly."

The two *vaqueros* looked at each other furtively.

Don Fernando seemed not to remark what happened.

"Do you want money?" he asked.

"No, master; we have still some."

"Nevertheless, take this as well: better to have too much than too little."

He placed in the hands of Carlocho a long netted purse, across the meshes of which a goodly number of gold pieces glittered.

"Now, Pablito, my horse."

The *vaquero* led from the recesses of the wood a magnificent charger. Don Fernando vaulted into the saddle.

"Remember," said he, "prudence and fidelity; one indiscretion would cost you your lives."

He waved his hand to the *vaqueros*, gave his horse the spur, and rode off in the direction of the *presidio*. The two men resumed the road to the *pueblo*.

When they were a good way off, the brushwood at one corner of the clearing began to shake, and a human head slowly emerged, the face blanched with terror.

The head was succeeded by the body of the *verado* who had risen to his feet, his knife in one hand, a pistol in the other, and now looked about him with his hair standing on end.

"*¡Canarios!*" he cried in a low tone; "rid themselves of me quietly! We shall see! we shall see, *¡Santa Virgen del Pilar!* What demons! Aha! I was right to listen."

"It is the only way to hear," said a mocking voice.

"Who goes there?" roared the *verado*, as he jumped to one side.

"A friend," replied Don Torribio, leaving his hiding place and advancing into the open.

"What! You, Señor Don Torribio Quiroga? You are welcome. Then you listened too?"

"*¡Cuerpo de Cristo!* Didn't I listen! I think I have profited by it, to get edifying news about Don Fernando."

"Since you overheard the conversation, what do you think of it?"

"This *caballero* seems to me a black villain enough; but we will thwart his infamous plans."

"God grant we may!" muttered the *verado*, with a sigh.

"And now, what are your own intentions?"

"Mine! I swear I do not know. I know nothing, except that my head swims. Did you hear? They want to rid themselves of me quietly! In my opinion, they are the greatest wretches in the prairie."

"Pooh! I have known them a long time; they give me very little uneasiness."

"And I, on the contrary, am very uneasy."

"What the devil! You are not dead yet!"

"*¡Vive Dios!* I am little better off; I am literally between death and the devil."

"How can you be afraid—you, the most daring hunter of the jaguar I know?"

"A jaguar is but a jaguar, after all; one can talk reason to him with a ball. But these two *birbones* (rascals), whom Don Fernando has maliciously set upon my trail, are veritable demons, without faith or law, who would bleed their own fathers for a small measure of *pulque*." ("To bleed" is the common Mexican expression for "to stab.")

"True; but time presses. For reasons with which I need not acquaint you, I take enormous interest in Don Pedro de Luna, and more in his lovely daughter. Don Fernando Carril, as we have just learnt, is concocting some infernal plot against this family. I mean to frustrate it. Will you assist me? Two men can do a great deal, if they work with a will."

"Do you propose a partnership with me, Don Torribio?"

"Call it what you will; but answer promptly."

"In that case, sincerity for sincerity, Don Torribio. This morning I would have refused your proposal: tonight I accept it; for I have done with soft-heartedness. My position is completely changed. Rid themselves of me quietly! ¡Vive Dios! I will have my revenge. I am yours, as my knife is to the sheath. I am yours, body and soul, on the word of a *vaquero*."

"I see we shall easily come to an understanding."

"Say, rather, we understand each other already."

"Good! But we must be cautious, if we wish to succeed: the game we are about to chase is wily. Do you know a *lepero* named Tonillo el Zapote?"

"Know Tonillo! He is my bosom friend."

"So much the better. This Tonillo is a resolute fellow, on whom one can fearlessly depend."

"That is holy truth. Moreover, he is a *caballero* of excellent principle."

"He is: find him out, and bring him one hour after sunset to the Callejou de las Minas" (the pass of the mines).

"It shall be done; I understand perfectly. We will be there."

"And then, we three will arrange our counterplot."

"Yes; and set your heart at rest. We will find a way to deliver you from this man, who wishes to rid himself of me quietly."

"That seems to lie heavily on your mind."

"¡Caray! Just put yourself in my place. After all, the longest liver will see. Don Fernando has not got quite so far with me as he fancies."

"Then you will bring Tonillo?"

"Were I to bring him by force, we would both be there."

"Now, we have nothing more to do than to go about our separate affairs."

"Which road do you take?"

"I am going direct to the *hacienda* of Don Pedro."

"Listen to me, Don Torribio: do not broach this matter to him."

"What is your reason for saying so, *verado?*"

"Because Don Pedro, excellent man and perfect *caballero* as he is, has old-fashioned ideas, and would probably attempt to dissuade you from your plan."

"Perhaps you may be right; he had better know nothing of the service I wish to render him."

"It will be better. Now Don Torribio, good-bye till evening."

"Good-bye; and good luck!"

The two men separated. Don Torribio Quiroga ran hastily down the road leading to the *pueblo*, to regain his horse from the *pulquero*; while the *verado*, whose horse had been hidden somewhere about, jumped into the saddle, and galloped off in a fury still muttering between his teeth:

"Rid themselves of me quietly! Was there ever such an idea? But we shall see. *¡Mil rayos!*" (a thousand thunders).

# CHAPTER IX
# DOÑA HERMOSA

Stoneheart was not mistaken in declaring that the dust, rising far away in the desert, was caused by the servants of the *hacienda*; in fact, the hunter had scarcely left the persons he was guiding, when the cloud of sand was blown away by the breeze, disclosing a numerous party of *vaqueros* and *peones*, well armed, who were approaching at the top of their speed.

Two horses' length in front galloped Don Estevan Diaz, chiding his companions, and urging them to increase their pace.

The two parties soon met, and mingled with each other.

Estevan Diaz, as Don Pedro had foreseen, had grown anxious at his master's lengthened absence. Fearing lest some accident might have occurred, he had assembled all the most resolute men belonging to the *hacienda*, and placing himself at their head, commenced his search at once, scouring the wilderness in all directions.

But had it not been for the lucky chance which led to the meeting with Stoneheart, in the very moment when the strength and courage of the little party were oozing away together, it is probable that the search would have been without result, and another mournful and horrible tragedy registered in the annals of the prairies.

The joy of Don Estevan and his party was great at recognising those whom they had scarcely hoped to see again, and the whole company gaily took the road to the *hacienda*, where they arrived in safety a couple of hours later.

Doña Hermosa retired to her apartment as soon as she had dismounted, excusing herself on account of the fatigue she had endured.

She reached her cool maiden chamber, which looked so calm and pleasant, cast a glance of delight at the cherished appurtenances, and then threw herself with a feeling of instinctive gratitude, at the knees of the Virgin, whose image, crowned with flowers, was placed in a corner of the chamber, and seemed to watch over her.

Her prayer addressed to the Virgin was long, very long. For more than an hour she remained on her knees, murmuring words which none save God could hear.

At last she rose, slowly, and as it were with reluctance, made a final sign of the cross, and, traversing the room, cast herself on a couch, where she nestled in a flood of drapery, like the Bengali in its bed of moss.

Then she gave herself up to thought.

What power could thus profoundly occupy the mind, hitherto so gay and cheerful, of this young creature, whose life from infancy had been one unbroken succession of gentle joys,—for whom the sky had had no cloud, the past no regrets, and the future no apprehensions Why did she frown so heavily, tracing, on her pure forehead, lines at first hardly perceptible, but deepening with her deepening thoughts?

None could tell. Hermosa herself could not, perhaps, have given an explanation.

This was the reason: without accounting to herself for the change she was undergoing, Hermosa awoke as from a long slumber; her heart beat more quickly, her blood coursed more rapidly in her veins, a flood of unknown thoughts rushed from her heart to her brain, making it whirl. In one word, the girl felt she had become a woman.

A vague uneasiness without apparent cause, a feverish irritability, agitated her by turns; sometimes a stifled sob would rend her bosom, and a burning tear show like a pearl on her eyelashes; then her purple lips would part under the influence of a charming smile, the reflection of thoughts she could not define, beseeching her to drive them away, and return to the calm and heedless joys she was losing forever.

"Yes!" she cried suddenly, bounding from her couch with the grace of a startled fawn; "Yes: I will discover who he is."

Hermosa had involuntarily allowed the key of the riddle to escape her. Possessed by the spirit whose voice was evoking her inward agitation, she loved—or at least Love was on the point of revealing himself to her.

Scarcely had she uttered the words we have reported, than she blushed deeply, and, urged by a charming impulse of maiden modesty, ran to draw before the image of the Virgin the curtain used to conceal it.

The Virgin, the habitual confidante of the girl, was not to know the secrets of the woman. Full of holy fervour, Hermosa had immediately seized upon this delicate distinction; perhaps she mistrusted herself; perhaps the feeling which had been so suddenly and violently awakened in her heart did not seem pure enough to be confided, with all its longings and desires, to her at whose feet she had hitherto deposited all her hopes and aspirations.

Feeling calmer after this action, which, in her superstitious ignorance, she fancied would shroud her from the piercing eye of her heavenly protectress, Doña Hermosa regained her couch, and touched a silver bell standing beside her. At the sound, the door softly opened half way, and the arch face of a charming *chola* (maid) appeared at the opening with a look of inquiry.

"Come in, *chica*" (girl), said her mistress, making a sign for her to approach.

The *chola*, a slim maiden, of lithe figure, and whose skin was slightly tawny, like that of all half-breeds kneeled gracefully at the feet of her mistress, fixed her great black eyes upon her, and smilingly asked what she wanted.

"Nothing," was the evasive answer, "only to see and talk to you a little."

"How glad I am!" said the girl, passionately clasping her hands together; "It is so long since I have seen you, *niña*" (a term of endearment).

"Did my absence distress you much, Clarita?"

"What a question to ask, señorita! Do I not love you like a sister? Do they not say you have been in great danger?"

"Who says that?" asked Hermosa carelessly.

"Everyone; they talk of nothing but your adventures in the prairie. All the *peones* have left their work to hear the news; the *hacienda* is in an uproar."

"Indeed!"

"For the two whole days of your absence, we did not know what saint to commend you to; I vowed a gold ring to my good patroness Santa Clara."

"Thank you," said she, with a smile.

"But you should only have seen Don Estevan! He would not be comforted; the poor fellow was like a madman, accusing himself as the cause of all that had happened: he tore his hair, asserting that he ought to have disobeyed your father, and to have remained with you in defiance of his orders."

"Poor Estevan!" said the lady, whose thoughts were elsewhere, and who began to get weary of the chattering of her maid; "Poor Estevan! He loves me like a brother."

"Yes, he does; so he has sworn by his head that such a thing shall not happen to you again, and that from henceforth he will never lose sight of you."

"Was he really in such alarm about me?"

"You cannot imagine how dreadfully frightened he was, particularly as they said you had fallen into the hands of the most ferocious robber in the prairie."

"Yet, I can assure you, *chica*, that the man who gave us shelter overwhelmed us with civility and attention."

"Exactly what your father says; but Don Estevan maintains he has known this man for a long time; that his kindness was feigned, and intended to conceal some monstrous treachery."

Doña Hermosa had suddenly become thoughtful.

"Don Estevan has gone mad," she said; "his friendship for me bewilders his brains; I am sure he is mistaken. But you remind me that I escaped from him the moment after my arrival without offering him a word of thanks. I must make reparation for this involuntary forgetfulness; is he still in the *hacienda*?"

"I think he is, señorita."

"Go and find out, and ask him to come here, if he has not gone already."

The maid rose and left her.

"As he knows him," said Hermosa, as soon as she was alone, "I will make him speak, and teach me what I want to learn."

So she awaited impatiently the return of her messenger.

The latter seemed to have divined the anxiety of her mistress, and made such haste to execute her commission that scarcely ten minutes elapsed before she announced Don Estevan.

We have already said that Don Estevan was a handsome man; he had the heart of a lion, the eye of an eagle; his carriage full of grace and suppleness, betrayed his race. He entered, saluting the lady with a winning familiarity authorised by his long and intimate connection with one whom he had known from her cradle.

"Dear Estevan," said she, stretching out her hand gaily, "how happy I am to see you! Sit down here and let us talk."

"Yes; let us have some chat," answered Don Estevan, gladly entering into the spirit of Hermosa's gaiety.

"Give Estevan a chair, *chica*, and then go; I do not want you any longer."

The maid obeyed without replying.

"What a number of things I have to tell you, my friend!" resumed the doña. "But first excuse me for running away from you. My sole thought was to be alone, and put my ideas into a little order."

"I can easily understand that, dear Hermosa."

"Then you are not angry with me, Estevan?"

"Not the least in the world, I assure you."

"Are you quite sure?" said she, pouting half seriously.

"Do not talk about it anymore, my dear child; one cannot encounter such dangers as you have been exposed to without feeling their effect upon the mind for a long time afterwards."

"But it is all over now, believe me; yet, between ourselves, my dear Estevan, these dangers have not been so great as your affection for me led you to suppose."

The other shook his head in token of his want of conviction, and replied:

"On the contrary, *niña*, these dangers have been much more serious than you choose to believe."

"No, they were not Estevan; the people we met treated us with the most cordial hospitality."

"I admit it; but will reply with one question."

"Ask it; and I will answer it, if I can."

"Do you know the name of the man who treated you with this cordial hospitality?" And he laid considerable stress on the last words.

"I confess that I not only do not know it, but that I did not even take the pains to ask him."

"You were wrong, señorita: for he would have answered that his name was 'the Tigercat.'"

"The Tigercat!" she exclaimed, turning deadly pale; "The execrable miscreant who for years has spread terror over the frontiers! You are wrong, Estevan; it could not be he."

"No, señorita, I am not wrong; I know the truth of my assertion. I can have no doubt, after what I have gathered from your father."

"But how did it happen that this man should have received us so kindly, and that he should have profited by the accident which placed us in his power?"

"No one can penetrate into the dark windings of that man's heart. Besides, who can prove he was not laying a snare for you? Were you not pursued by the redskins?"

"We were; but we escaped from them, thanks to the devotion of our guide." And she spoke with a little uncertainty of voice.

"You are right again," said Don Estevan ironically "But the guide himself—do you know who he is?"

"He constantly refused to tell us his name, in spite of the pressing entreaties of my father."

"He had good reasons for doing so, *niña;* the name would have filled you with horror."

"Then who and what is this man?"

"He is the son of the Tigercat; he is called Stoneheart."

Hermosa recoiled with instinctive terror, and hid her face in her hands.

"It is impossible," she cried: "this man cannot be a monster; this man who proved himself so faithful, so loyal—who saved my life, too."

"What!" exclaimed Don Estevan: "He saved your life?"

"Have you not heard it? Has not my father told you the story?"

"No; Don Pedro did not say anything about it."

"Then I will tell you, Estevan; for whatever this man may be, I must render him justice. I owe it to him, to him alone, that I did not die in horrible agony."

"In the name of Heaven, explain yourself, Hermosa."

"While we were wandering in the forest, a prey to despair," she replied, in extreme agitation—"while we were expecting the death that could not be long in coming,—I felt my foot bitten by a snake of the most venomous kind. At first I overcame my pain, in order not to increase the discouragement of my companions."

"How well I recognise your strength and courage there, *niña!*"

"Let me continue," said she, with a sad smile. "The pain soon became so piercing, that my strength failed me, in spite of my courage. At that moment God sent to our aid, him whom you call Stoneheart. The first thought of that man was to help me."

"It is wonderful!" said Don Estevan Diaz.

"By the use of some sort of leaf, he managed to neutralise the effect of the poison, so that, shortly after having been bitten, I felt no pain from the wound, and am quite recovered today. Can you now deny that I owe him my life?"

"No," said he frankly; "for he saved you indeed. Yet for what purpose? That is what puzzles me."

"For the sake of saving me,—for humanity's sake; his after conduct sufficiently proves it. It is to him alone we owe our subsequent escape from the Apaches, who were on our trail."

"All you say, *niña*, appears like an incomprehensible dream; I do not know whether I am asleep or awake while I listen to you."

"But has this man really been guilty of the infamous actions which excite your indignation?"

Estevan Diaz did not answer: he seemed embarrassed; and there was a short silence.

"I will be frank with you, Hermosa," said he, at last. "It is necessary that you should know who your deliverer is. I will tell you all I know of him myself; and perhaps this knowledge may be useful to you hereafter, should fate ever again bring you into the presence of this extraordinary man."

"I am listening attentively; proceed."

"Be on your guard, Hermosa; do not let the impulse of your heart carry you away too far; do not expose yourself to future heartache. Stoneheart is, as I told you, the son of the Tigercat. I need tell you nothing about his father; that monster with a human face has built up for himself an infamous notoriety, too well known for me to enter into its details. The infamy of the father has reflected on the son, and enveloped him in a halo of murder and rapine which makes him almost as much dreaded as his father. However, in justice to the man, I must confess that, although he is accused of a thousand evil deeds and odious crimes, it has been impossible hitherto to obtain positive proof of any accusation preferred against him. All they say of him is wrapped up in impenetrable mystery; yet everyone relates the most horrible tales of him, although nobody can speak with certainty as to the truth of one of them."

"They are not true," said Hermosa.

"Do not be too eager to pronounce him innocent, *niña*; recollect that a modicum of truth is to be found at the bottom of every suspicion; and, strictly speaking, this man's trade would of itself suffice as proof against him, and bear testimony to his natural ferocity."

"I cannot understand you, Estevan. What dreadful trade is it?"

"Stoneheart is a bee-hunter."

"A bee-hunter!" she exclaimed, with a burst of laughter. "Truly there is nothing offensive in that?"

"The word is pleasant to the ear; the trade itself one of the most inoffensive; but the bees, those advanced sentinels of civilisation, who, in proportion as the whites push forward in America, bury themselves deeper in the prairies, and take refuge in more inaccessible wildernesses, require a special organism in the men who hunt them,—a heart of bronze in a body of steel, a fortitude beyond proof, indomitable courage, and unswerving will."

"Excuse me for the interruption, Estevan; but in all you have told me, there seems nothing that is not highly honourable to the men who devote themselves to this perilous trade."

"Your observation would be just, if these men—half savages from the life they lead, ceaselessly exposed to most serious danger, constantly obliged to strive, in defence of their lives, against the wild beast and the redskin, by whom they are perpetually threatened—had not contracted, perhaps in spite of themselves, the habit of shedding blood; a habit of such cold-blooded cruelty, in a word, that they set no value on human life,—kill a man with the same indifference as they smoke the bees from the tree, and often, for mere pastime, fire on the approaching stranger, white or redskin. For this reason, the Indians dread them more than the fiercest animals, and, unless they happen to be in force, fly before a bee-hunter with more terror and precipitation than from the grizzly bear, that redoubtable inhabitant of our American forests. Believe me, niña, I am not exaggerating. It results from what I have related, that when these men reappear upon the frontiers, their arrival creates a general panic; for their road is a bloody one, marked by the corpses of those whom they have slain under the most frivolous pretexts. In one word, niña, the bee-hunters are completely beyond the pale of humanity,—beings with all the vices of whites and redskins, and without the virtues of either: both races abjure and repudiate them with horror."

"Estevan," gravely replied Doña Hermosa, "I have listened seriously to what you have said. I thank you; but, in my opinion, it proves nothing either for or against the person about whom I questioned you. I grant you that the bee-hunters maybe semi-savages, of profound cruelty; yet, are there no noble and loyal hearts, no generous spirits, among them? You have spoken of the rule; who will tell me that Stoneheart is not the exception? His conduct compels me to think so. I am only a young, ignorant, and inexperienced girl; but were I bidden to open my heart, and speak frankly, I should answer: 'My friend, this man, condemned from infancy to a life of shame and trial, has striven valiantly against the current which was dragging him away, and the force of bad example assailing him on every side. Son of a criminal father, associated, against his will, with bandits to whom every restraint is an abomination, and by whom every sentiment of honour has been trodden under foot, this man, far from imitating their actions,—far from burning, pillaging and assassinating as they do,—has preferred to adopt a career of perpetual peril. His heart has remained pure; and when chance offered him an opportunity of doing a good deed, he seized it eagerly and gladly.' This is what I should say to you, Estevan,—and if, like me, you had studied this strange man for two whole days, you would be of my opinion,—which is, that he is more to be pitied than blamed; for, placed among ferocious brutes, he has retained his humanity."

Don Estevan remained for a time lost in thought; then he turned towards the girl, took her hand, pressed it in his own, and looked at her with tender compassion.

"I pity and admire you, Hermosa. You are just what I thought you—I, who have watched the development of your character from your infancy. The woman fulfils all the promise held out by the child and the girl. Your heart is noble, your sentiments are exalted; you are indeed perfect—a chosen soul. I do not blame you for following the impulse of your heart— you are only obeying the instinct for good or evil which sways you in spite of yourself; but, alas! Dear child, I am your elder brother, and my experience is larger than your own. To me, the horizon seems to be clouding over. Without prejudging what the future may be preparing for us, let me prefer one entreaty."

"An entreaty! You, Estevan! Oh, speak; I shall be so happy to do anything to please you."

"Thanks, Hermosa; but the entreaty has no connection with myself—it concerns you alone."

"So much the greater reason for my granting it," she said with a gracious smile.

"Listen, child: the events of the last two days have completely changed your life, and feelings have germinated in your mind of which you ignored the existence until now. You have always placed entire confidence in me: I demand the continuance of that confidence. My only desire is to see you happy; all my thoughts, all my actions, tend to that goal. Never believe that I dream of betraying you or thwarting your projects. If I am tenacious on this point, it is to aid you with my counsel and experience; it is to save you even from yourself; to insure your escape from the snares which the future may lay for your innocent frankness. Do you promise what I entreat?"

"Yes," she replied, without hesitation, and looking firmly in his face; "I promise, Estevan, my brother—for you are in truth a brother to me—whatever may happen, I will have no secrets from you."

"I thank you, Hermosa," said the young man, rising, "I hope soon to prove myself worthy of the name of brother. Come tomorrow, in the afternoon, to my mother's *rancho* (farmhouse); I shall be there, and most likely able to clear up certain matters which are so obscure today."

"What do you mean?" cried she, in great agitation.

"Nothing at present, dear child; leave me to take my own measures."

"What are your projects? What do you intend to do? Oh, do not attach more importance to my words than I attach to them myself. Involuntarily I have been constrained to utter words from which you would be wrong to draw conclusions—"

"Be calm, Hermosa," said he, interrupting her, with a smile. "I have drawn no conclusion derogatory to you from our conversation. I understand that you have avowed an immense amount of gratitude to the man who saved your life. I see it would make you happy to know that this man is not unworthy of the feelings he has inspired. I draw no other conclusion."

"It is exactly what I feel, Estevan; and I think the wish natural, and one to which no blame can be attached."

"Certainly, my dear child. I do not blame the feeling in the least; only, as I am a man, and can do many things interdicted to a woman, I will try if I can lift the mysterious, veil which conceals the life of your liberator, so as to tell you positively whether he is or is not worthy of the interest you take in him."

"Do that, Estevan, and I will thank you from the bottom of my heart."

The young man only replied by a smile to this passionate outbreak: he saluted Hermosa, and retired.

As soon as he was gone, she hid her face in her hands and burst into tears. Did she regret the confidence into which she had been led, or was she afraid of herself? Only women can decide the question, and only Spanish-American women, who are so impressionable, and through whose veins rushes the lava of their native volcanoes.

Don Fernando Carril, as we have already related, after his conversation with the *vaqueros*, had taken, at a gallop the route to the *pueblo*; but when he was within a hundred yards of the first houses, he slackened his pace to a walk, and cast glances right and left, as if in the expectation of meeting some person he wished to see. But if such were his thoughts, it seemed as if he were doomed to disappointment; for the road was completely deserted in all directions as far as his eye could reach.

# CHAPTER X
# EL AS DE COPAS (THE ACE OF HEARTS)

Don Fernando checked his steed, and remained motionless as an equestrian statue on a marble pedestal.

"He will not come," he muttered, after a while.

"Can he have deceived me? — It is impossible."

Casting, as a last hope, one more look around him, he dropped the reins, but seized them again an instant later with a suddenness which made his horse perform a curvette and wince with pain. Don Fernando had just seen two cavaliers advancing towards him — one approaching from the *pueblo*, the other riding down the road he had himself taken.

"Come, come, it is all right," he said to himself; "This one is Don Torribio Quiroga. But who is this other cavalier?" he added, turning to the man who had just left the *pueblo*.

He frowned, seemed to hesitate for an instant, but soon formed his decision, smiled ironically, and saying half-aloud, "It is better as it is," made his horse execute a traverse, and placed himself exactly across the middle of the road, so as to bar the passage completely.

The two arrivals, who greedily watched all his motions, took good note of the hostile appearance of Don Fernando's position: neither seemed to feel alarm, and both advanced at the same speed as before. The cavalier coming from the *pueblo* was much nearer Don Fernando than Don Torribio was, and was soon close to him.

Mexicans, of all ranks and however little education, have an instinctive knowledge of social decorum, which never deceives them, and a refined politeness which would astonish the inhabitants of the Old World.

As soon as Don Fernando found the stranger within reach of his voice, he slightly altered the position of his horse, doffed his hat, and said, with a low bow:

"Señor *caballero*, permit me to ask you a question."

"*Caballero*," replied the stranger, with no less politeness, "it will be an honour to me."

"My name is Don Fernando Carril."

"And mine, Don Estevan Diaz."

"Señor Don Estevan, I am happy to make your acquaintance. Would you throw away ten minutes in my company?"

"Señor Don Fernando, however pressed for time I might be, I would stop to enjoy your society."

"You are excessively kind; accept my thanks. I will explain in half a dozen words. The *caballero* who is approaching is Señor—"

"Don Torribio Quiroga," interposed Don Estevan; "I know him."

"So much the better; the matter is simplified. That honourable personage, as I found out by a strange chance is my bitter enemy."

"That is a pity."

"It is; but what shall I say? He is so thoroughly my enemy, that he has tried four times to have me assassinated; has made me serve as a target to banditti."

"It is grievous. He plays an evil game with you, Don Fernando."

"The very reflection I made myself; so, as I wish to have done with him, I have resolved to offer him the means of getting out of the scrape."

"It is the act of a true *caballero*."

"*¡Caray!* I can fancy how furious he will be. I am charmed at your consenting to be witness of the transaction."

"With pleasure, *caballero*."

"A thousand thanks; I will gladly return the compliment. But here is our man."

Don Torribio had continued to advance during this short conversation, and was now only a short distance from the speakers.

"*¡Válgame Dios!*" he cried gaily; "If I do not mistake, it is my admirable friend, Don Fernando Carril, whom I have the good fortune to meet."

"Himself, my dear friend; and as happy as you can be at the chance which has thrown us together."

"*¡Vive Dios!* Since I have got you, I will not let you go; we will ride together as far as the *pueblo*."

"I should like it, Don Torribio; but first of all, with your permission, I have a few words to say which may upset that plan."

"Speak then, señor; you can only utter words I shall be happy to hear in Don Estevan's presence."

"In fact, Don Fernando has requested me to be present at the conversation," said the latter.

"Nothing could be better! Let us hear, señor."

"Suppose we dismount," said Don Estevan; "the conversation may be a long one."

"Well observed, *caballero*," replied Don Fernando; "I know a grotto where we shall be quite at our ease. It is close at hand."

"Let us go there at once," said Don Torribio.

The three cavaliers left the beaten track, took a turn to the right, and directed their steps towards a little wood of plane trees and mahoganies, which stood at a short distance.

Anyone who had seen them thus, riding side by side, chatting and smiling to each other, would have incontestably believed them to be intimate friends, delighted at having met. However it was, nothing of the kind, as our readers will soon see.

Exactly as Don Fernando had predicted, they soon gained the wood, and found the natural grotto of which he had spoken.

The grotto was in the side of a hill of no great elevation, and its proportions were scanty enough. Carpeted with verdure inside and out, it was a charming place of repose for passing away the stifling heat of the sun at midday.

The cavaliers dismounted, took the bridle from their horses, leaving them to graze at will. They entered the grotto, and inhaled with ineffable delight the freshness caused by a slender stream of water which ran between its banks with a melancholy murmur, forming a pleasant contrast with the burning atmosphere to which they were recently exposed. They threw their *zarapés* on the ground, stretched themselves out comfortably, and lit their maize *pajillos* (cigarettes).

"I am greatly obliged to you, Don Fernando, for thinking of this delicious retreat," said Don Torribio; "now, if it is your pleasure to speak, it will be an honour to me to listen."

"Señor Don Torribio, you really overwhelm me by so much courtesy. Heaven bear witness, that if I were not your most implacable enemy, I could be your dearest friend."

"Alas!" said Don Torribio, "Heaven has disposed otherwise."

"I know it, my good señor, and regret it with all my soul."

"Not more than I do, I swear."

"Well, as that is the case, we must act accordingly,"

"Alas! That is just what I mean to do."

"I thought so. Then, in your interest and mine, I have resolved to make an end of it."

"I do not exactly see how we can get at that result, unless one of us consents to kill the other."

"I presume this hatred of yours has cost you a round sum of money?"

"Four hundred piastres, which the rascals have stolen from me, as you are still alive; to say nothing of two hundred others I propose to present to a *pícaro* who has sworn to kill you tonight."

"It is perfectly distressing! If this goes on, you will ruin yourself."

Don Torribio sighed, but made no reply.

Don Fernando resumed, while he threw away his cigarette and occupied himself in rolling another:

"For my part, señor, I confess that, in spite of the lamentable clumsiness of the people you employ, I begin to be tired of serving as a target at moments when I least expect it."

"I can understand that; it must be very disagreeable."

"It is. Well, then, wishing to reconcile our mutual interests, and to put an end to it, once for all, I have racked my brains until I think I have hit on a method of arranging these matters to our mutual satisfaction."

"Well, let us hear this method; I know you to be a man of imagination, Don Fernando. It is doubtless ingenious."

"Oh, no; on the contrary, it is quite simple. Do you ever play?"

"So seldom, that it is hardly worth mentioning."

"Precisely the case with me. This is the proposal I have to make: it is evident you will not succeed in assassinating me."

"Do you think so, señor?" said Don Torribio, still smiling.

"I am sure of it, else you would have succeeded already."

"I will admit it: what, then, do you propose?"

"This: we will have a game at cards—the first to whom *el as de copas* (the ace of hearts) falls shall win, and be master over the life of his opponent, who shall be bound to blow out his brains as he sits there."

"Not so bad; the idea is ingenious."

"And why not señor?—It is just like a common game, only the loser cannot have his revenge. Now, where are the cards?"

It was then discovered that these three gallant *caballeros*, who never played, had each a pack of cards in his pocket. They produced them with such spontaneousness, that all three could not help bursting into Homeric laughter.

We have already said, somewhere, that in Mexico the passion for gambling is carried beyond the verge of madness; so that the facility with which Don Torribio accepted the game proposed by his foe has nothing in it to astonish those who know the character of those strange Mexicans, who carry everything to extremes, and for whom anything unexpected and extraordinary has always an irresistible attraction.

"One moment, señores," said Don Estevan, who had hitherto listened without joining in the conversation; "perhaps there might still be another way."

"What other?" exclaimed Don Fernando and Don Torribio, turning briskly to him.

"Is your mutual hatred so great, that in reality it can only be satisfied by the death of one or the other?"

"It is," said Don Torribio hoarsely.

Don Fernando merely replied by a nod.

"In that case," continued Don Estevan, "instead of having recourse to blind chance, why cannot you fight it out with each other?"

Both men made a gesture of disdain.

"What!" exclaimed Don Torribio, "Fight like wretched *leperos*, at the risk of disfiguring or crippling ourselves, which would be worse than death! No! I will never consent to that."

"Nor I; it is better that chance shall decide."

"As you please, *caballeros*; do as you like."

"But," said Don Torribio, "who is to deal?"

The Bee Hunters | 109

"The devil!" said Don Fernando; "that is a good remark: I never thought of that."

"I will, if you have no objection," said Don Estevan; "and so much the more readily, as my friendship for both of you señores, makes me perfectly disinterested."

"It will do," said Don Torribio; "only, to avoid all cause for dispute, you must choose at hap-hazard the pack you are to use."

"Very well: place the three packs under a hat; I will take the first I touch."

"That will do. What a pity you did not think of this game sooner, Don Fernando!"

"What could I do, señor?—I have only just hit upon the idea."

Don Estevan rose and left the grotto, to afford the two foes every facility for arranging the three packs under the hat. He was very soon recalled.

"So," said he, "you are determined to play out this game?"

"We are, they replied."

"You swear, by all the world holds most holy, and whichever of you it may be whom fortune favours, to submit yourselves to the fiat of fate in all its entirety?"

"We swear, Don Estevan, by the word of *caballeros*."

"Enough, señores," he replied, passing his Hand under the hat and drawing out a pack of cards. "And now recommend your souls to God; for a few minutes hence, one of you will be in his presence."

The two men crossed themselves devoutly, and fixed their eyes anxiously on the pack of cards.

Don Estevan shuffled the cards with the greatest care, and then made each of the adversaries cut them in turn.

"Attention, señores," said he; "I am going to begin."

The two, negligently leaning on their elbows, smoked their *pajillos* with a perfect assumption of indifference, which was only belied by the flashing of their eyes.

Meanwhile the cards continued to fall on the *zarapé*: Don Estevan held only about a dozen more in his hand, when he paused.

"*Caballeros*," said he, "for the last time—reflect."

"Go on, go on!" cried Don Torribio excitedly; "the first card belongs to me."

"Look at it," said Don Estevan, turning it up.

"Oh," said Don Fernando, throwing away his cigarette, "*el as de copas*. Look, Don Torribio; it is curious. ¡*Vive Dios!* you can reproach no one; you are the author of your own death."

Don Torribio made a violent gesture, which he repressed immediately, and resumed the tone of affected civility which had characterised the conversation.

"Upon my honour, it is true," said he. "I must confess, Don Fernando, I have no chance with you in anything."

"I am quite in despair, dear Don Torribio."

"Never mind; it was a capital game; I never felt so interested."

"Nor I either. Unfortunately, I cannot give you your revenge."

"Right! And now I must pay my debt."

Don Fernando bowed without answering.

"Be quite easy, dear señor; I will only keep you waiting such time as is absolutely necessary. If I could have foreseen this, I would have brought my pistols."

"I have brought mine; they are perfectly at your service."

"Then pray be kind enough to lend me one."

Don Fernando rose, took a pistol from his holsters, and offered them to Don Torribio.

"It is primed and loaded; the trigger is a little stiff."

"What a capital man of business you are, Don Fernando! You provide for everything; no detail escapes you."

"My traveller's habits, Don Torribio,—nothing more."

Don Torribio took the pistol and cocked it.

"Señores," said he, "I beg you not to leave my body to the mercy of the wild beasts; it would distress me dreadfully to become their food when I am dead."

"Set your mind at rest, dear señor; we will carry you home across your own horse. We should be in despair if the body of so accomplished a *caballero* were thus profaned."

"That is all I have to request of you, señores; now accept my thanks, and farewell."

After this he cast one last look around him, and coolly placed the muzzle of the pistol against his right temple.

Don Fernando suddenly arrested his hand.

"I have one remark to make," he said.

"Upon my honour, you are only just in time," said Don Torribio, without exhibiting emotion: "two seconds more, and it would have been too late. But let us hear this remark. Is it of much interest?"

"You yourself shall judge. You have lost your life fairly to me."

"As fairly as possible."

"Well, then, it belongs to me. You are dead; I have the right of disposing of you as I think fit."

"I cannot deny it. You will observe that I am ready to pay my losses like a *caballero*."

"I render you full justice, dear señor; therefore if I allow you to live for the present, you are bound to kill yourself at my first requisition, and to employ the life I leave you (which I could deprive you of at this very moment) solely in my interest, and at my good pleasure."

"Then you offer me a bargain?" said Don Torribio.

"Yes, you have hit the word; it is a bargain."

"H'm!" said Don Torribio; "That requires consideration. What would you do, if you were in my place, Don Estevan?"

"I?" replied he; "I would accept without hesitation. Life is so beautiful, take it all in all, it is best to enjoy it as long as possible."

"There is something true about what you say; but recollect I should become Don Fernando's slave as I could only employ my life in his service, and should be bound to kill myself whenever he gives the word."

"True; but Don Fernando is a *caballero* who will only exact this sacrifice in so far as to protect his own life."

"I will even go further," broke in Don Fernando; "I will limit the duration of our bargain to ten years. If by that time Don Torribio is not dead, he will again enter upon his rights in all their plenitude, and can dispose of his life after his own fashion."

"That really touches me to the heart! You are a perfect *caballero*, señor; and I accept the life you offer me so gracefully. A thousand thanks!" added he, uncocking the pistol. "I have no further use for this weapon."

"One thing more, Don Torribio. As no one can read the future, you will not object to have this bond drawn up in writing?"

"Certainly not; but where shall we get the paper?"

"I think I can find the writing materials in my *alforjas*."

"How right I was in pronouncing you a perfect man of business, whom nothing escapes, dear señor!"

Don Fernando, without answering, went to fetch his *alforjas*, a kind of double pocket, which is fastened behind the saddle, to hold the necessary articles for travelling, and used throughout the whole of Spanish America instead of the common European valise.

Don Fernando took out pens, ink, and paper, and laid them in order before Don Torribio.

"Now," said he, "write as I shall dictate."

"Proceed, my dear señor; I will write."

Don Fernando began:

"I, the undersigned, Don Torribio Quiroga y Carvajal y Flores del Cerro, acknowledge that I have fairly lost my life to Don Fernando Carril, in a game played with the aforesaid señor; I acknowledge that the life belongs henceforth to Don Fernando, who shall have the right to dispose of it as he thinks fit, without my having power to raise objection in any case, or to refuse obedience to the orders he may give me, whether they be to kill myself before his eyes, or to risk in any perilous adventure the life I have lost, and which I acknowledge to hold only at his pleasure. I farther acknowledge that all sentiments of hatred to the aforesaid Don Fernando Carril are extinguished in my heart, and that I will never seek to injure him directly or indirectly. I enter into this bond for the space of ten years, beginning from the day on which this deed is signed; it being formally stipulated by me, that at the end of the aforesaid ten years I shall resume all my rights in full, with the entire possession of my life, and that from thenceforth I shall not be responsible to Don Fernando Carril for any account of it."

"Written and signed by me, this 17th March 18—, and subscribed, as witness, by Señor Don Estevan Diaz y Morelos."

"Now," said Don Fernando, "sign: pass the paper to Don Estevan, for his signature; then give it to me." Don Torribio signed with the greatest good humour, added a tremendous flourish to his signature, and gave the pen to Don Estevan, who affixed his name without making the slightest objection to this strange arrangement.

When all this was over, Don Torribio scattered a little sand over the paper, to dry the ink, folded it neatly in four, and placed it in the hands of Don Fernando, who read it attentively, and put it in his bosom.

"There, that is finished," said Don Torribio. "Now señor, if you have no commands for me, I ask your permission to retire."

"I should be distressed to detain you longer, *caballero*; go where your engagements call you; may they be pleasant ones!"

"Thanks for the wish, though I fear it will scarcely be fulfilled; I have had bad luck for some time past."

He saluted the others once more, put the bridle on his horse, and departed at a gallop.

"Do you really intend to demand the execution of this bond?" asked Don Estevan, as soon as he found himself alone with Don Fernando.

"Most certainly," replied the other; "you forget that this man is my mortal foe. But I must leave you, Don Estevan; I must be today at Las Norias de San Antonio, and it is growing late."

"Are you going to the *hacienda* of Don Pedro de Luna?"

"Not exactly to the *hacienda*, but to the neighbourhood."

"Then we can ride together; for I, too, am going in that direction."

"You," said he, looking at him inquisitively.

"I am the *major-domo* of the *hacienda*," replied Don Estevan.

The two men left the grotto, and mounted their horses. Don Fernando rode pensively by the side of his companion, only replying in monosyllables.

# CHAPTER XI
# THE RANCHO

The road the two men had to travel together was tolerably long. Don Estevan would not have been sorry to shorten it by talking to Don Fernando, particularly as the manner in which he had made acquaintance with the latter, and the light in which he had shown himself, excited the curiosity of the former in the highest degree. Unfortunately, Don Fernando did not seem in the least inclined to keep up the conversation; and, in spite of all his efforts, the *major-domo* found himself obliged to conform to his companion's state of mind, and imitate his taciturnity.

They had already left the village a long way behind them, and were cantering along the undulating banks of the Rio Bermejo, when they heard, at a short distance in front of them, the sound of a horse at full gallop. We say, they heard; for, shortly after leaving the grotto, the sun had finally disappeared below the horizon, and there had been a sudden transition from the glorious light of day to thick darkness.

In Mexico, where there is no police, or, at all events, only a nominal one, every man is obliged to take care of himself. Two men, meeting on a road after nightfall, cannot accost each other without the greatest precaution, nor approach each other until fully assured they have nothing to fear.

"Keep your distance!" shouted Don Fernando, as soon as he thought the person approaching was within reach of his voice.

"And why so? You know you have nothing to fear from me," answered somebody; the sound caused by the horse's hoofs ceasing at the same time, denoting that the rider had halted.

"I know that voice," said the Mexican.

"And the man, too, Señor Don Fernando, for it is not very long since we met; I am El Zapote."

"Aha!" laughed Don Fernando; "Is it you, Tonillo? Come on, *muchacho*."

The latter rode up directly.

"What the devil are you doing on this road, at this hour of the night?"

"I am coming from a rendezvous, and returning to the pueblo."

"I fancy that rendezvous has been a slippery affair."

"You insult me, Don Fernando. I am an honourable man."

"I have no doubt of it. Moreover, your affairs are not mine; and I do not choose to be mixed up with them. Come, adieu, Tonillo."

"A moment if you please. Since I have been lucky enough to meet you, grant me five minutes: I was going to look for you."

"You! Is it a case like the last? I thought you had had enough of that speculation, which hardly succeeds with me."

"Here is the matter in two words, Don Fernando. After what happened the other day, I considered that I owed you my life, and, consequently, had not full liberty of action where you are concerned. But you know, señor, I am a *caballero*; and as an honest man can but stick to his word, I resolved to see the person who had paid me to kill you, and return him the money. It was hard to disburse so large a sum; but I did not hesitate. One may well say, a good action always brings its own recompense."

"You ought to know that better than anyone else," laughed Don Fernando.

"You laugh! Very well; judge for yourself. I sought this person, whose name it is needless to mention."

"So much the more so, as I know it already."

"You do? Very well, then. This morning a *caballero*, one of my friends, gave me notice that the person in question also wished to speak to me. All was working wonderfully. But guess my amazement when, just as I was going to refund the money and throw up my engagement, this personage announced to me that he had been reconciled to you, that you were the best friends, and begged me to keep the hundred piastres as an indemnification for the damage he had caused me."

"Was it this person, then, whom you went to meet tonight?"

"The same. I have only just left him."

"Very well: go on, *compadre*" (comrade).

"Well, *caballero*, since this affair has ended in a manner honourable to me, as I flatter myself, I am at liberty to follow my own inclinations, and am quite at your service, if you will do me the honour to employ me."

"I will not say no; perhaps in a day or two I may find a use for your services."

"You will not repent having employed me, señor. You will be always sure to find me at—"

"Not a word on that subject," said Don Fernando, interrupting him suddenly; "when the time comes, I shall find you."

"As you please, señor. Now permit me to take leave of you and this honourable *caballero*, your friend."

"Adieu, Zapote. A happy journey."

The *lepero* joyfully took to his road again.

"Señor," said Don Estevan, as soon as the latter had gone, "in a short time we shall reach the *rancho* (farmhouse) I inhabit with my mother; it would glad me to offer you shelter for the night."

"Thanks for your courtesy, which I gratefully accept. Is the *rancho* far from Las Norias?"

"Hardly a league. Were it daylight, you would be able to see from hence the tall walls of the *hacienda*. Permit me to be your guide on the road to my poor dwelling."

The cavaliers then bent to the left, entering a broad path lined with aloes. Very soon the barking of several watchdogs, and two or three specks of light which twinkled through the darkness, apprised them that it would not be long before they reached the end of their tedious journey. In fact, after riding some ten minutes longer, they found themselves in front of a house, small, but apparently comfortable, under the *zaguán* (veranda) of which several persons, provided with torches, seemed to be expecting their arrival.

They stopped before the porch, dismounted, gave their horses to a *peon*, who led them away, and entered the dwelling, Don Estevan preceding his guest in order to do the honours of his house.

They found themselves in a chamber of good dimensions, furnished with sundry chairs, a few armchairs, and a massive table, on which the cloth was laid for several persons. The whitewashed walls of the room were adorned with prints, frightfully coloured, representing the four seasons, the five quarters of the globe, &c.

A woman, no longer young, dressed with a certain degree of refinement, and whose features, although marked by age, still preserved traces of great beauty, stood in the middle of the room.

"Mother," said Don Estevan, bowing respectfully before her, "permit me to present to you Don Fernando Carril, an honourable *caballero*, who consents to be our guest tonight."

"He is welcome," answered Doña Manuela, with a gracious smile; "this house and all that is in it is at his disposal."

"Many thanks, señora, for this kind reception."

At first sight of the stranger Doña Manuela had begun to tremble, and had scarcely repressed an exclamation of surprise. The sound of his voice struck her no less, and she cast a profoundly scrutinising look over him; but after a moment she shook her head gently, as if mistrusting the thought which had arisen.

"Be seated, señor," she said, pointing to the table with great cordiality; "the supper shall be served directly. Your long ride will have sharpened your appetite, and will make the frugality of the viands less distasteful."

In fact, the meal was frugal, consisting of beans with red pepper, beef dried in the sun, a fowl boiled in rice, rolls of maize, with *pulque* and *mezcal* to drink With great pleasure Doña Manuela watched the viands disappear with which she loaded their plates. She encouraged them by all the means in her power to satisfy their hunger.

When supper was over, they passed into an inner chamber, more comfortably furnished, which appeared to be the reception room.

The conversation, which had naturally been rather languid at dinner, now, little by little, grew more animated, and soon reached, thanks to the efforts of Doña Manuela, that tone of pleasant familiarity which banishes every constraint, and doubles the charms of familiar chat.

Don Fernando seemed to enter with all his heart into the desultory conversation, which leaped without ceasing from one subject to another; listening with complacency to the long stories of Doña Manuela, and answering with apparent rankness the questions she asked him.

"Are you a *costeño*" (an inhabitant of the sea border), "or a *tierras a dentro*" (one of those who dwell inland), "*caballero?*" the good dame suddenly asked her guest.

"By my faith, señora," replied he, laughing, "I confess I feel some difficulty in replying."

"Why so, señor?"

"For the simple reason that I have no idea where I was born."

"But you are *hijo del país*" (literally, a son of the country), —"a Mexican, at all events?"

"Everything leads me to think so, señora; but I would not swear it."

"That is very singular. Does not your family reside in the province?"

A shadow crossed the face of Don Fernando. "No, señora," he replied dryly.

The mistress of the house perceived she had touched a tender chord, and hastened to turn the conversation.

"Of course you know Don Pedro de Luna?"

"Very little, señora; accident threw us together once. It is true the circumstances were too singular for him to forget them easily; but it remains to be seen whether I ever set foot in his *hacienda*."

"You are wrong, *caballero*; Don Pedro is a *cristiano Viejo*" (an old Christian, i.e. a descendant of the early conquerors), "who exercises hospitality after the fashion of old times: nothing makes him happier than to practise it."

"Most unfortunately, important affairs call me to some distance, and I fear I shall have no time to stop at his *hacienda*."

"Forgive the question," said Don Estevan; "but have you really the intention of entering the prairie?"

"Why do you ask, *caballero?*"

"Because we are here on the extreme Indian frontier; and unless you retrace your steps, it is only towards the wilderness you can bend them."

"Well, then, it is my intention to go into the desert."

Don Estevan made a gesture of surprise.

"Forgive my pertinacity," said he; "but without doubt you must be acquainted with the desert you intend to enter?"

"By your leave, señor, I am thoroughly acquainted with it."

"And knowing its dangers, dare you enter it alone?"

"I thought I had given you a proof today," said he, with an indefinable smile, "that I dare many things."

"Yes, yes; I know your courage carries you on to rashness: but what you would undertake is worse than temerity—it is madness!"

"Madness, señor! The word is too strong. Can a resolute man, well armed and mounted, have anything to fear from the Indians?"

"If you had nothing to do but defend yourself against Indians and wild beasts. I should be somewhat in your way of thinking, señor: a determined white can make head against twenty redskins. But how will you escape from the Tigercat?"

"From the Tigercat? Excuse me, *caballero*, but I do not understand you at all."

"I will soon explain, señor. The Tigercat is a white. This man, from reasons unknown to all, has joined the Apaches, has become one of their chiefs, and sworn implacable hatred to all men of his own colour."

"I have heard vaguely of the man you mention; but, after all, he is the only one of his race among the Indians. Redoubtable as he may be, he is not invulnerable, I suppose; and a brave man might kill him."

"Unfortunately you are mistaken, *caballero*; this man is not the only one of his race among the Indians; other bandits of his class are with him."

"Yes," cried Doña Manuela; "his son among the rest, who, they say, is as fierce a bandit as his father."

"Mother, that is only a surmise. If you come to proof, nothing can be affirmed against Stoneheart."

"Who is the man of whom you speak?"

"His son, as people say; but one cannot be sure of it."

"And you call this man Stoneheart?"

"Yes, señor. For my own part, I know several instances of his generosity, which indicate, on the contrary, a heart in its right place, and an ardent spirit capable of noble deeds."

A slight blush overspread the face of Don Fernando.

"Let us return to the Tigercat," said he. "What have I to dread from this man?"

"Everything. Concealed in the prairie, like a hideous *zopilote* (vulture) on its point of rock, this wretch pounces upon the caravans, whatever their strength, and pillages them; he murders in cold blood the solitary travellers whom their evil destiny delivers into his hands: his nets are stretched with such cruel skill, that none may escape him. Listen to me, *caballero*: give up this journey, or you are a lost man."

"I thank you for your advice, which, I know, is prompted by the interest you take in me; nevertheless, I cannot follow it. But it is too late; allow me to retire. I observed a hammock under the *zaguán*, in which I could pass the night admirably."

"I will give orders to have my son's chamber prepared for you."

"I could not allow anyone to be disturbed on my account, señora; I am an old traveller. Moreover, the night is already far gone. I swear you would disoblige me by forcing me to accept the chamber of Don Estevan."

"Do as you think proper, *caballero*. A guest is one sent from God; he ought to be master in the house he inhabits, as long as he chooses to honour it with his presence. May the Lord watch over your repose and bless your slumbers! My son shall show you the *corral* (outhouse) where your horse has been stabled, in case you should wish to depart before the household is awake."

"Many thanks, once more, señorita. I hope to pay my respects to you before I go."

Having exchanged a few more compliments with his hostess, Don Fernando rose and left the room, accompanied by Don Estevan. The wish he expressed, to sleep in a hammock under the *zaguán*, was not at all extraordinary, and perfectly in accordance with the customs of a country where the nights, by their beauty and freshness, compensate the inhabitants for the overpowering heat of the day.

The American *ranchos* all have a porch, formed by four, and often six columns, outside the house, and which support an *azotea* (flat roof). In the large space between these columns, which are placed on either side of the main entrance, hammocks are slung, in which the owners of the dwellings themselves often pass the night, preferring to sleep in the open air rather than endure the torrid heat which literally converts into a stove the interior of the houses.

Don Estevan led his guest to the *corral*, explained to him the mechanism of the lock, asked if he could be of any further service, wished him good night, and retired into the house, leaving the door open, so that Don Fernando might enter if he thought fit.

Doña Manuela awaited her son's return in the apartment where he had left her. The old lady seemed restless.

"Well," she asked, immediately her son made his appearance, "what do you think of this man, Estevan?"

"I, mother!" he answered, looking astonished; "What can I think of him? I saw him today for the first time."

The old señora shook her head impatiently.

"You have been side by side for many hours; such a long *tête-à-tête* should have given you an opportunity of studying and forming an opinion of him."

"That man, my dear mother, during the short time I have been with him, has appeared under so many different aspects, that it has been altogether an impossibility, I will not say to form an opinion, but even to gain a ray of light by means of which I could direct my study of him. I believe his to be a strong nature, full of nerve, capable of good or evil, accordingly as he follows the impulse of his heart or the calculations of his egotism. At San Lucar everyone seems to dread him instinctively,—for nothing ostensible in his conduct justifies the repulsion he inspires; no one can say positively who he is: his life is an impenetrable mystery."

"Estevan," said his mother, placing her hand heavily on his arm, as if to lend force to the words she was about to utter, "a secret presentiment warns me that the presence of this man in these parts presages great misfortune. I cannot explain why. The moment he entered, his features recalled a confused recollection of events that happened long ago. I saw in his face points of resemblance with that of a person dead, alas! How long?" She sighed. "When he spoke, the tone of his voice sounded mournfully on my ear; for the voice completed the likeness I had found in his face. Whoever this man may be, I am convinced there is trouble, perhaps danger, in store for us. I am old, my son; I have much experience; and, you know, one is seldom mistaken at my age. Presentiments come from God; we must have faith in them. Watch that man's doings as long as he remains here. I could wish you had never brought him under our roof."

"What could I do, mother? Hospitality is a duty from which no one should shrink."

"I do not reproach you, Estevan; you have acted according to your conscience."

"God grant that you delude yourself, mother! After all, whatever the man's intentions may be, if he seeks to injure us, as you suppose, we can but countermine his machinations."

"No, Estevan; it is not exactly for ourselves I fear."

"For whom, then, mother?"

"Cannot you understand me?" said she, with, a mournful smile.

"¡*Vive Dios*, mother! Let him beware. But no, it is impossible. Nevertheless, I will go to the *hacienda* at daybreak, and put Don Pedro on his guard."

"Do not say a word to them, Estevan; but watch over them like a faithful friend."

"Yes, mother, you are right," said Estevan, who had suddenly become thoughtful. "I will surround Hermosa with a vigilant protection, so secret that no one shall suspect it. I swear it, ¡*vive Dios!* I would a thousand times rather die under the most atrocious torture, than see her exposed anew to dangers like those of the last few days. And now, mother, give me your blessing, and let me go."

"Go, my son; and God protect you!"

Don Estevan bent respectfully before his mother, and retired; but before seeking repose, he made a minute examination of the house, and did not extinguish his lamp till after he had convinced himself that all was in perfect order.

As soon as Don Estevan had left him, Don Fernando threw himself into the hammock, and closed his eyes. The night was calm and beautiful; the stars studded the heavens with an infinite number of diamonds; the moon spread her silver rays over the landscape; at intervals, the prolonged baying of the watchdogs mingled with the abrupter bark of the *coyotes* (prairie-wolves), whose sinister forms were often perceptible in the distance, the transparency of the atmosphere permitting remote objects to be easily distinguished.

All slept, or seemed to sleep.

Suddenly Don Fernando raised his head, and peered cautiously over the edge of his hammock. Thoroughly convinced that silence reigned throughout the house, he slipped to the ground; after carefully listening, and prying into the darkness in all directions, he placed on his head the accoutrements of his horse, and turned his steps towards the *corral*.

Opening the door noiselessly, he whistled gently. At the signal, the horse raised his head, and walked up to his master, who was holding the door half open.

The latter caught him by the mane, caressed him playfully, and then saddled and bridled him with the dexterity and speed only acquired by constant habit. The task over, his master wrapped his hoofs in four pieces of sheepskin, to deaden the sound of his steps, vaulted into the saddle, and bending over the neck of the noble brute: "Santiago!" cried he, "now is the time to prove your mettle."

The horse, as if he understood his master, dashed off into the darkness, and took the direction of the river at the top of his speed.

Meanwhile the greatest silence pervaded the *rancho*, none of the inhabitants of which seemed to be aware of this sudden flight.

# CHAPTER XII
# THE REDSKINS

We must now return to the Far West.

On the banks of the Rio Grande del Norte, about ten leagues' distance from the *presidio* of San Lucar stood the *atepelt*, or temporary village, of Des Venados.

The *atepelt*, a simple camp, like most of the Indian villages, consisted of about a hundred *callis*, or huts, irregularly grouped near each other.

Each *calli* was built of about a dozen stakes driven into the ground, four or five feet high at the sides, and six or seven in the centre, with an aperture towards the east, for the master of the *calli* to throw water in the direction of the rising sun—a ceremony by which the Indians conjure the Wacondah to befriend their families during the course of the day just breaking.

These *callis* were covered with bison hides sewn together, with a hole in the centre to admit the exit of the smoke of the fires kindled in the interior,— fires which equal in number the wives of the owner, each wife having a right to a fire of her own.

The hides which formed the outer walls were carefully dressed, and painted of divers colours; the painting, by its extravagance, enlivening the aspect of the *atepelt*.

The lances of the fighting men were planted upright in the ground in front of the entrance to the *calli*. These light lances, made of flexible reed, sixteen or eighteen feet long, and armed at one end with a long grooved iron, forged by the Indians themselves, are the most redoubtable weapons of the Apaches.

The liveliest joy seemed to animate the *atepelt*. In some *callis* the women were spinning the wool of their flocks with their spindles; in others they wove those *zarapés*, so renowned for their fineness and the perfection of the work, at looms of primitive simplicity.

The young people of the tribe, assembled in the centre of the *atepelt*,—a large open space,—were playing at *milt* (an Indian word signifying "arrow") a singular game, to which the Indians are greatly addicted.

The players trace a large circle on the ground, into which they step, arranging themselves in two opposite rows. The leader of one row, holding a ball filled with air in the right hand, the leader of the other in the left, they throw their balls backwards with a motion which brings them in front again. The left leg is then lifted, the ball caught and hurled at the opposite player, whose body it must touch, under penalty of losing a point. A thousand extravagant contortions ensue on the part of the latter, in order to avoid the ball: he stoops, he rises, bends himself backwards or forwards, jumps up where he stands, or bounds to one side. If the ball quits the ring, the first player loses two points and runs after it; if, on the contrary, the second is struck, he must seize the ball and throw it back at his opponent, whom it must hit, or he loses a point. The next in order, at the opposite side of the ring, begins the game again; and so on, till the close of the sport.

One can understand what shouts of laughter arise from the grotesque attitudes into which the players fall as the game goes on.

Other Indians of riper age, were gravely playing with curious packs of cards, made of squares of hide, coarsely painted with figures of different animals.

In a *calli* larger and better painted than the other huts of the *atepelt*—the dwelling of the *sachem*, or principal chief, whose lances, ornamented at the foot with pieces of skin-dyed red, were the distinguishing badge of power— three men, crouched round the embers of a fire, were, talking, heedless of the uproar without. They were the Tigercat, the Zopilote, and the *amantzin*, or the sorcerer of the tribe.

The Zopilote was a half-breed, who had taken refuge with the Apaches long ago, and been adopted by them. This man, every way worthy of the name he bore, was a wretch whose cold and malignant cruelty revolted the very Indians, who are themselves not delicate in matters of this kind. The Tigercat had made this ferocious miscreant, who was devoted to him, prime-minister of his vengeance, and the docile instrument of his will. His latest wife, to whom he had been married a year, had given birth to a boy that morning—hence the rejoicings of the Indians; and he had come to take the orders of the Tigercat—the great chief of the tribe—with respect to the ceremonies usual on the like occasions.

The Zopilote left the *calli*, to which he speedily returned, followed by his wives and all his friends, one of whom held the infant in his arms. The Tigercat, placing himself between the Zopilote and the *amantzin* at the head of the party, led them towards the Rio Grande del Norte.

The procession halted on the bank of the river; the *amantzin* took a little water in the hollow of his hand, and threw it into the air, muttering a prayer to *the Master of the life of men*. He next proceeded to *the great medicine*; that is, the newborn child, wrapped in his woollen swaddling bands, was five times plunged into the waters of the river, while the *amantzin* repeated, in a loud voice:

"Master of life, look upon this young warrior with favourable eye; remove from him all evil influences; protect him, Wacondah!"

At the termination of this part of the ceremony, the procession returned to the *atepelt*, and arranged itself in a circle in front of the Zopilote's *calli*, at the entrance of which lay a young mare on her back, with her four feet tied together. A new *zarapé* was stretched under the belly of the animal, on which relations and friends deposited, one after the other, the gifts intended for the child—spurs, arms, and clothing. The Tigercat, out of friendship for the Zopilote, had consented to act as godfather to the infant. He placed it in the midst of the various gifts which filled the *zarapé*.

Then the Zopilote seized his scalping knife, opened at one slash the flanks of the mare, tore out the heart, and gave it, bleeding as it was, to the Tigercat, who made a cross with it on the forehead of the child, addressing him thus:

"Young warrior of the tribe of Apache-Bisons, be brave and cunning. I name thee *Mixcoatzin*—Cloud-Serpent."

The father took the child, and the chief, raising the bleeding heart above his head, shouted thrice:

"Long live the Cloud-Serpent!"

The cry was enthusiastically repeated by the bystanders. The *amantzin* then commended the child to the Spirit of Evil, praying him to make the young warrior brave, eloquent, and cunning; terminating his prayer in these words, which found an ardent response in the hearts of all those fierce beings:

"Above all, may he never be a slave!"

Thus terminated the ceremony: every religious rite had been performed. The poor mare, the victim of this stupid superstition, was cut into pieces; a great fire was kindled; friends and relations took their seats at a feast, which was intended to last until nothing was left of the mare.

The Zopilote was about to seat himself, and feast with the others; but, at a sign from the Tigercat, he followed the great chief to his *calli*, where they once more took their seats by the fire. The *amantzin* was also with them.

The Tigercat waved his band to his wives, who left the *calli*, and after a short meditation, spoke as follows:

"I trust my brothers, and my heart opens before them like a *chirimoya*" (a kind of American pear), "to show them my secret thoughts: I have sorrowed for many days."

"My father sorrows for his son Stoneheart," said the *amantzin*.

"No; I care not where he is now; I can find him again when I want him. But I have a secret mission to confide to a safe man. Till this morning, I hesitated to open my heart to you."

"Let my father speak; his sons listen."

"To hesitate longer would be to compromise things sacred. You will to horse, Zopilote; I have no words for you: you know where I send you. Induce these men to aid our enterprise; it will be a notable service."

"I will do it. Do I go at once?"

"Without delay."

"In ten minutes I shall be far hence;" and, saluting the chiefs, he went out.

A few minutes later, the sound of a horse's hoofs fading away in the distance announced his departure.

Tigercat gave a sigh of satisfaction.

"Let my brother, the *amantzin* open his ears," said he. "I am about to leave the *atepelt*, I hope to be back tonight; but my absence may be for two or three days. I leave my brother in my stead and place; he will command the warriors, and will forbid them to go far from the village, or approach the frontiers of the palefaces. It is important that the Gachupinos (Mexicans) should not learn that we are so near them; to do so would mar our plan. Does my brother understand?"

"The Tigercat has no forked tongue; the words breathed from his mouth are clear. His son understands."

"Good. I can go in peace: my brother will watch over the tribe."

"I will obey the orders of my father. If he is absent many suns, he will not have to reproach his son."

"Ugh! My son's words lift the skin that covered my heart and filled it with sorrow. The Master of Life watch over him! I go."

"Ugh! My brother is a sage warrior. The Wacondah will protect him on his road; he will succeed."

The two men gravely saluted each other. The *amantzin* remained by the fire; the chief departed.

It is probable that, if the old *sachem* had remarked the expression of knavish hate on the face of the sorcerer at the moment they parted, he would not have quitted the village.

As the Tigercat threw himself into the saddle with a lightness hardly to be expected at his years, the sun disappeared behind the mountains, and night enveloped the prairie.

The old man, without seeming to care for the darkness, pressed his horse with his knees, gave him his head, and galloped off.

The sorcerer, with bent person and head stretched forward, listened anxiously to the lessening sound of the chief's rapid course. When all was still again, he raised himself erect, a smile of triumph played across his thin and livid lips, and he uttered triumphantly the words, "At last!"—a summary of the thoughts secreted in his heart.

Then he arose, left the *calli*, seated himself a few paces from it, crossed his arms over his chest, and chanted, in a deep bass and a mournful and monotonous rhythm, the Apache lament, beginning with the following verse, which we reproduce as a specimen of the language of this barbarous people:

> "El mebin ni tlacaelantey
> Tuz apan Pilco payentzin
> Ancu maguida coaltzin
> Ay guinchey ni polio menchey."

[I have lost my *tlacaelantey* in the country of Pilco. Oh, murderous knives, which have changed him into shades and flies!]

As the sorcerer went on with his song, his voice became by degrees louder and more confident. In a short time, warriors, wrapped in their bison robes, issued from several of the huts, and, with furtive steps, approached the sorcerer, and entered the *calli*. At the close of the lament, the sorcerer rose, ascertained that no other person was coming towards him, that no laggard was loitering at his call, and in his turn entered the *calli*, to join those whom he had convoked thus singularly.

There were twenty men in all; they stood silent and motionless, like bronze statues, round the fire, whose flames, revived by the draught caused by their entrance, threw sinister shadows over their stern and determined features. The *amantzin* placed himself in the midst, and said:

"Let my brothers sit at the council fire."

The warriors squatted down in a circle.

The sorcerer then took from the hands of the *hachesto*, or public crier, the great calumet, the bowl of which was of red clay, and the tube six feet long, of aloes wood, garnished with feathers and hawks' bells. He filled it with a washed tobacco, called *morriche*, which is never used except upon great occasions, lighted it with a medicine stick, and having drawn a long breath of more than a minute, and discharged the smoke through mouth and nose, presented the calumet to the warrior on his right. The latter followed his example; and the calumet passed thus from hand to hand, till it returned to the *amantzin*.

The latter shook the ashes into the fire, muttering, in a low voice, a few unintelligible words; after which, be restored the calumet to the *hachesto*, who went out to watch, in order to ensure secrecy to the deliberations of the council.

There was a long silence; the profoundest calm brooded over the village; no sound disturbed the tranquillity of the *atepelt*; and one might have thought oneself a hundred leagues from a human dwelling.

At length the *amantzin* rose, cast a searching look over the assembly, and spoke.

"Let my brothers open their ears," he said in measured tones. "The spirit of the Master of Life has entered into my body; it is he who dictates the words which spring from my lips. Chiefs of the Bison-Apaches! The spirit of your ancestors has ceased to animate your souls. You are no longer the terrible warriors, who declared war, without truce or mercy, against the palefaces—those cowards, and hateful despoilers of your hunting grounds; you are only antelopes, who fly with faltering feet from the distant sound of an *erupha* (gun) of the palefaces; you are old women, to whom the *Yorris* (Spanish) give their petticoats; your blood no longer runs bright in your veins, and a skin stretches over your heart and covers it completely. You, formerly so brave and terrible, have made yourselves the coward slaves of a dog of a paleface, who chases you like frightened rabbits, and holds you trembling under his eye. Thus speaks the Master of Life. What do you answer, warriors of the Apaches?"

He ceased, and waited for one of the chiefs to take up the word. During this insulting speech, a tremor of indignation agitated the Indians; it was only by great efforts they obtained the mastery over their passion. But when the *amantzin* ceased, a chief rose.

"Is the sorcerer of the Apaches-Bisons mad," said he in a voice of thunder, "that he should speak thus to the chiefs of his nation? He who counts the foxes' tails attached to our heels will see if we are women, and if the courage of our ancestors is dead in our hearts. What if the Tigercat is a paleface?—His heart is Apache. The Tigercat is wise; he has seen many things; the counsels he gives are good."

The *amantzin* smiled with disdain.

"My brother the White-Eagle speaks well; it is not for me to answer him."

He struck his hands thrice. A warrior appeared.

"Let my brother," said the *amantzin* to him, "tell the council the mission with which he was charged by the Tigercat."

The redskin advanced to the circle, and bowed low before the chiefs, who were all gazing at him.

"The Tigercat," spoke a deep and mournful voice, "had ordered the Black-Falcon to form an ambush with twenty warriors on the path of the palefaces, whom Stoneheart pretended to guide to their big stone huts. The Black-Falcon followed the palefaces a long time in the prairie. Their trail was clear; they had no arms; nothing seemed more easy than to seize them. An hour before the time fixed for the attack, Stoneheart appeared alone in the camp of the warriors. The Black-Falcon received him with the signs of friendship and praise, because he had abandoned the *Yorris*. But Stoneheart replied, that Tigercat forbade the attack on the palefaces, and, throwing himself on the Black-Falcon, thrust the knife into his heart; while the *Yorris*, who had stolen upon the camp, surprised the warriors, and massacred them with *eruphas* given by Tigercat himself. This treachery was done to put Black-Falcon out of his path, whose fame he envied. Twenty warriors followed the war path; six returned with me to the *atepelt*: the others have been slain by the Tigercat. I have said."

This astonishing revelation created a stern silence of amazement and rage. It was the calm that harbours the tempest. The chiefs looked from one to the other with eyes of wrath.

Of all races, the redskins are the most remarkable for the rapidity with which their moods change, and are most easily led away by feelings of rage. The *amantzin* was aware of this; therefore he was sure of his triumph, after the terrible impression made by the recital of the warrior.

"Ugh!" said he, "What do my brothers think now of the counsels of the Tigercat? Does the White-Eagle still think he has the heart of an Apache? Who will avenge the death of the Black-Falcon?"

Most of the chiefs rose at once, brandishing their scalping knives.

"The Tigercat is a thieving dog, and a coward!" they shouted. "The Apache warriors will tie his scalp to their girdles."

Only two or three of the *sachems* attempted to protest; they knew the *amantzin's* inveterate and long-standing hatred of Tigercat; they knew the knavish character of the sorcerer; and suspected that, in this affair, the truth had been disguised and garbled in order to serve the vengeance of the man who had vowed the death of a foe whom he would never dare to face openly.

But the voices of these chiefs were soon stifled by the clamorous ire of the other Indians. Renouncing, for the present, a useless discussion, they withdrew from the circle, and grouped themselves in a corner of the *calli*, resolved to remain the impassive, if not indifferent, witnesses of the resolutions to be taken by the council.

The Indians are grown-up children, who lash themselves into fury with the sound of their own words and, when excited by their passions, forget all prudence and moderation.

However, in the present case, although they felt the fiercest desire to avenge themselves on the Tigercat,—whom at this moment they hated so much the more because they had loved and respected him so highly,—although the most violent measures were proposed against him, still it was not without some degree of hesitation that they proceeded to act against their aged chief. The reason was simple enough: these primitive beings recognised only one kind of superiority,—that of brute strength; and the Tigercat, in spite of his great age, enjoyed among them a reputation for strength and courage, too well established for them not to look forward with a certain degree of fear to the consequences of the action they meditated.

The *amantzin* tried in vain, by all the means in his power, to convince them how easy it would be to seize Tigercat on his return to the village. The sorcerer's project was excellent; if the chiefs chose to avail themselves of it, it would be impossible to fail. The plan was this: the Apaches were to feign ignorance of the death of the Black-Falcon; they were to receive him on his return with the greatest protestations of joy, in order to lull the suspicions he might entertain, and seize him while he slept; they were to bind him securely, and tie him to the torture stake. One sees that the plan was extremely simple; but the Apaches would not listen to it, so great was the dread they felt for their foe.

Finally, after a discussion which lasted the greater part of the night, it was definitely settled that the tribe should strike their camp, and bury themselves in the desert, without troubling themselves with any further thought of their old leader.

But just at that moment the dissentient chiefs who, up to that time, had taken no part in what was going on, left the corner of the *calli* to which they had retired, and one of them, called Fire-Eye, taking up the word in the name of his companions, observed that those of the *sachems* who wished to depart might do so, but could not impose their will on others; that the tribe had no great chief legally chosen; that each was at liberty to act as he pleased; and that, as for themselves, they were resolved not to repay with black ingratitude the eminent services the Tigercat had rendered the tribe for many years past; and they would not quit the village before his return.

This determination gave great anxiety to the *amantzin*, who vainly sought to overcome it: the chiefs would listen to nothing, and adhered firmly to their determination.

At sunrise, by order of the sorcerer, who already acted from that time forward as if he was the recognised grand chief of the tribe, the *hachesto* summoned the warriors to the open space of the village, by the ark of the first man, and orders were given to the women to pull down the *callis*, and harness and load the dogs, that they might depart as soon as possible. The order was promptly executed; the pickets were drawn, the bison hides folded, household utensils carefully packed, and placed on sledges, to be drawn by the dogs.

But the dissentient chiefs had not been idle on their side: they had managed to win over to their opinion several renowned warriors of the people, so that only about three-quarters of the tribe prepared to emigrate, while the other quarter remained stoical spectators of the arrangements for travel which were going on before them.

At last the *hachesto*, at the order of the *amantzin*, gave the signal to march.

Then a long line of sledges drawn by dogs, and of women laden with children, quitted the village, escorted by a numerous band of warriors, and was soon winding its way, like a great serpent, through the prairie.

When their brothers had disappeared in the depths of the wilderness, the warriors who had remained faithful to the Tigercat assembled to deliberate on the measures to be taken until his return.

# CHAPTER XIII
# THE MIDNIGHT MEETING

In the meantime Don Fernando Carril, bending over his horse's mane, was gliding through the night like a phantom.

Thanks to the precaution he had taken of wrapping pieces of sheepskin round the hoofs of the horse, he passed on silently and rapidly as the spectre-horseman of the German ballad, making the frightened packs of *coyotes* fly before his career.

Gradually he neared the banks of the river, which he forded without slackening his speed; inciting his steed by voice and gesture, and throwing sharp glances to right and left, before and behind him.

His flight lasted full three hours, during which the Mexican never allowed his favourite a moment's respite to fetch his breath and rest his tired limbs.

But when at last he arrived at a spot on the narrow river, where it rolled its muddy waters between low banks lined with tufted cotton trees, he alighted in a thick coppice, and, having convinced himself he was alone, plucked a handful of grass, and rubbed his horse down with that care, and solicitude of which those alone are capable whose lives may at any moment depend on the speed of their faithful and devoted companion. Then taking off the bridle, and leaving him to graze on the tall and abundant grasses, the Mexican spread his *zarapé* on the ground, and closed his eyes.

Nothing troubled the silence of the night; no sound arose in the desert. Don Fernando lay motionless as a corpse, his eyes still closed, and his head supported by his left arm; and thus he lay for two hours.

Did he sleep? Did he wake? None could say. Suddenly the hooting of an owl arose on the air. In an instant Don Fernando half-raised himself, bent his head forward, and listened, with his eyes fixed on the heavens.

It was deep in the night; the stars were shedding on the earth their obscure and doubtful light; nothing foretold the approach of day.

It was scarcely two o'clock in the morning; the owl is the first bird to announce the approach of the sun, but owls do not proclaim the day three hours before it breaks. Notwithstanding the perfection of the imitation, the Mexican hesitated. Soon a second hoot, followed by a third, dispersed the doubts of Don Fernando; he rose, and thrice repeated the cry of the water hawk.

A similar cry issued immediately from the opposite bank of the river.

Don Fernando bridled his horse, cast his *zarapé* over his shoulders, examined his weapons to ensure their efficacy, flung himself into the saddle without touching stirrup, and crossed the river.

A short distance in front of him lay an islet, covered with poplars and cotton trees, towards which he bent his steps. The approach to the islet was easy; the horse, recruited by his two hours' rest, swam strongly, and touched the ground nearly in a straight line from the spot where he had plunged in.

Scarcely had the Mexican reached the land, when a rider emerged from the thicket, and halting some twenty paces off, exclaimed, in a loud voice, and an accent of great discontent:

"You were late in replying to my signal. I was on the point of leaving."

"Perhaps it would have been better had you done so," sharply replied Don Fernando.

"Aha!" said the other mockingly, "Does the wind blow from that quarter?"

"Never mind whence it blows, if I do not sail before it. I am here; what do you want with me? Be short; for I have no time to give you."

"*¡Vive Dios!* Something very interesting must entice you to the place whence you came, if you are so anxious to be there again."

"Listen, Tigercat," roundly and sharply replied the Mexican; "if you have summoned me here so urgently merely to chafe and laugh at me, it is useless to stay longer; so, adieu!"

As he said this, Don Fernando turned as if to retire and quit the island.

The Tigercat—for his interlocutor was no other than that extraordinary personage—quickly seized a pistol, and cocked it.

"*¡Rayo de Dios!*" said he; "if you stir a foot, I will blow your brains out!"

"Pooh!" replied the other, with a sneer; "What should I be doing in the meanwhile? A truce to threats, or I kill you like a dog."

With action as prompt as the Tigercat's, he too had drawn a pistol, cocked, and presented it at his opponent.

"You would not dare to do it."

"You know I dare all," said the Mexican.

"We have lost time enough; let us proceed to business," said the old man, alighting from his horse.

"Well, let us proceed to business. What is it you want with me?" replied Don Fernando, also dismounting.

"Why have you deceived and turned against me, instead of serving me, as you are bound?"

"I was bound to nothing with you; on the contrary, I roundly refused the mission which you persisted in forcing upon me."

"Could you not have remained neuter, and allowed these people to fall into my hands again?"

"No; my honour compelled me to defend them."

"Your honour!" burst out the Tigercat, with a cynical laugh.

The Mexican was confused: he frowned, but recovered himself, and continued:

"Hospitality is sacred in the prairie; its rights are indefeasible. The people I guided had placed themselves, of their own accord, under my protection: to abandon, or refuse to defend them, would have been to betray them. You yourself would have done as I did."

"It is useless to recur any more to this, or to discuss a deed that is done. Why did you not return to me?"

"Because I preferred to stay at San Lucar."

"Yes; civilized life is sure to attract you; I can understand that this double part you are playing, at your own risk and peril, has charms for you. Don Fernando Carril is received with open arms in the circles of the highest Mexican society. But believe me, boy, you had better take heed lest your adventurous spirit lead you into some false steps, from which not all the courage of Stoneheart could save you."

"I did not come here to listen to sermons."

"True; but it is my duty to read you the sermons you did not come to hear. As long as I remain in the desert, I will not lose sight of you for a moment. I know all your doings; I am ignorant of nothing regarding you."

"And why have you surrounded me with spies?" said Don Fernando haughtily.

"In order to know if I could still repose the same confidence in you."

"And what have you learned from your spies?"

"Nothing but what is satisfactory; only I insist on knowing how we stand towards each other."

"Do not your spies make you aware of my slightest doings?"

"Yes, of all that concerns you personally: thus I know you have not yet ventured to present yourself to Don Pedro de Luna;" and he sneered.

"True; but I intend to see him tomorrow."

The Tigercat shrugged his shoulders in disdain.

"Let us speak of more serious matters," said he. "How do we stand?"

"I have followed your instructions in everything. For two years, since the time I first made my appearance in San Lucar, I have lost no single opportunity of forming connections, which will, I hope be of service to you later on. Although my appearance at the *pueblo* is rare, and my visits are short, I still think I have attained the object you proposed to yourself when you gave me my orders. The mystery with which I surround myself has been of more use to me than I dared to hope. I have attached to myself the greater number of the *vaqueros* and *leperos* in the *presidio*—gallows birds, but I can count upon them; they are devoted to me. These fellows only know me as Don Fernando Carril."

"Ah, I know all that," said the Tigercat.

"You do?" said the Mexican, looking at the old man with a glance of anger.

"Have I not told you I never left you out of my sight?"

"Yes—as far as my personal affairs are concerned."

"Well, the hour is come to gather the harvest we have sown among these villains. They will serve me better against their countrymen than the redskins in whom I dare not place perfect confidence. They are acquainted with Spanish tactics, and accustomed to firearms. Now that your part with the *picaros* is over, I shall begin to play mine. I must enter into direct relation with them."

"As you please; I thank you for releasing me from the responsibility of an affair the object of which you have never thought fit to confide to me. I shall be glad to procure you the means of treating personally with the rascals I have engaged in your service."

"I understand your longings to be free, and approve them the more, since it was I who first inspired you with the wish to become better acquainted with the charming daughter of Don Pedro de Luna."

"Not a word of her," said Don Fernando fiercely. "If, up to the present time, I have consented to be guided by you, and to obey your orders without discussing them, the time has now come to place the question clearly and categorically before us, so that no misunderstanding may arise between us in the future. It is this reason alone which had weight enough to bring me tonight in answer to your summons."

The Tigercat looked at the Mexican long and fixedly; then he replied:

"Speak, then, madman, who do not see the gulf which yawns at your feet: speak; I listen."

Don Fernando remained some time lost in thought, leaning against the knotted trunk of a poplar, and with his eyes cast on the ground.

"Tigercat," said he at length, "I know not who you are, nor the motives which have induced you to renounce civilisation, to take refuge in the desert, and adopt the life of the Indian; I do not wish to know them. Every man is responsible for his own actions, and must render an account of them to his own conscience. As to myself, never has a word from your mouth taught me in what place I was born, or to what family I belong. Although you brought me up—although, as far back as my memory carries me, I have seen no one belonging to me but yourself—yet I cannot think you are my father. Had I been your son, or even only a distant relative, it is evident my training would have been widely different to that which I received at your express commands."

"What are those words your bold lips utter?—How dare you venture to fling reproaches at me?" said the old man, bursting into a fit of passion.

"Interrupt me not, Tigercat; let me open my thoughts to you entirely," sadly replied the Mexican. "I do not reproach you; but from the time when, under the name of Don Fernando Carril, you forced me into the whirl of civilised life, in spite of myself, and no doubt in spite of you, I have learned two things, and my eyes have been opened. I have comprehended the meaning of two words, the significance of which was unknown to me till then. These two words have changed not only my character, but the light in which I used to look at things; for, with a purpose I cannot divine, you applied yourself from my infancy to foster every evil sentiment germinating within me, while you carefully stifled the few good qualities which my heart might haply have possessed, had it not been for the system you adopted. In a word, I have now arrived at the knowledge of good and evil. I know all your efforts have been exerted to make me a human wild beast. Have you succeeded? The future shall show. To judge by the feelings that are surging in my heart while I speak to you, you have not reached the result you aimed at; be that as it may, I am no longer your slave. I have served too long as the instrument in your hands of deeds whose aim I cannot see. You have yourself taught me that family bonds do not exist in nature; that they are absurd prejudices, trammels invented by civilisation; that no man has a right to impose his will as law on others; that the real man is he who walks free through life, unincumbered by relation or friend, recognising no master but his own desires. Well, then, I will now put in practice these precepts you have so long and steadily inculcated. What matters to me whether I be Don Fernando Carril, or Stoneheart the Bee-hunter? Following the law laid down by yourself, and elevating ingratitude into a virtue, I take back my own free liberty and independence of you, recognising no claim of yours to influence my life for good or for evil, and assuming from henceforth the right to walk after my own impulses, whatever may happen in consequence of my resolve."

"Go, my child," said the Tigercat, with his mocking sneer; "go, act as you think fit; but, in spite of all your efforts, you will soon come back to me; for say what you will, you belong to me, and will soon know it. But it does not rouse my ire to hear you speak thus; it is not you who speak—it is love. I am very old, Fernando, but not so old as to have lost all recollections of my youth. Love has mastered your heart; when he has utterly burnt it up, you will return to the desert; for then you will have learnt what that life is into which you, poor, ignorant child, are just plunging. You will have learnt that life in this world is but a feather blown hither and thither by every varying breeze; and that at the breath of love, the man who thinks himself the strongest becomes more feeble than the weakest and most wretched of created beings. But let us break off: it is your will to be free; be so. First of all, however, you have to render me an account of the mission with which I charged you."

"I will do so. Present yourself to the *vaqueros* in my name; this diamond"—and he drew one from his finger—"will be your passport. They have been warned: show it to them, and they will obey you as they would myself."

"Where do these men meet?"

"You will find most of them at a low *pulquería* in the new Pueblo de San Lucar. But do you really intend to venture within the *presidio*?"

"Assuredly. Now, one word more: can I count upon you when the hour for action arrives?"

"You can, if what you purpose is right."

"Aha! You are already beginning to impose conditions."

"Have I not told you so?—Or shall I remain neuter?"

"No; I have need of you. You will, I suppose, inhabit the house you bought? Every day a trusty person shall inform you of the course of events; and when the proper moment comes, I know you will be with me."

"Perhaps I may; but happen what will, do not depend too much upon it."

"I do depend upon it, nevertheless, and I will tell you why. At present you are under the impulse of love, and naturally your reasoning succumbs to the influence of the passion that masters you. But before a month is over, see what will inevitably happen. Either you will succeed,—and satiety, following on the heels of sated passion, will make you glad to return to the wilderness,—or you will fail, and jealousy and wounded pride will inspire the lust for vengeance, and you will seize with joy the opportunity I shall offer you to glut it."

"I see clearly that very shortly we shall not understand each other at all," said the Mexican with a melancholy smile. "You always reason from your evil passions, so great is your hatred of men, and the contempt you feel for the human race; while I only listen to my good feelings, and suffer myself to be guided by them."

"Well, well, child; I give you a month to finish your caterwauling. That time passed, we will resume our conversation. Adieu."

"Adieu. Are you bound for the *presidio?*"

"No; I return to my village, where, too, I have a little matter of business; for, unless I am mistaken, curious things have happened since I left it."

"Do you dread a revolt there against your power?"

"I do not dread, I wish it," was the enigmatical answer.

The old man then bid the Mexican farewell, mounted his horse, and rode into the thicket.

Don Fernando stood there some time, plunged in serious thought, listening mechanically to the sound of the horse's hoofs as they died away in the distance. When he could no longer hear them, he turned his head in the direction Tigercat had taken.

"Go," said he hoarsely; "go, savage, in the belief that I have not discovered your project. I will dig a mine under your feet to explode and crush you. I will foil your attempt. I would dare more than man dares to baffle your machinations. It is three o'clock," he continued, after looking at the sky, from which the stars were fading out; "I shall have time."

He called his horse and mounted, took the direction of Don Estevan's *rancho*, and recommenced his headlong course across the wilderness.

The horse, fresh from his long rest, stretched himself out freely; and daylight was just beginning to appear when they reached the *rancho*.

Don Fernando gave a sigh of satisfaction. All was quiet about the dwelling; all the inhabitants seemed wrapped in repose. The secret of his nocturnal excursion was safe.

He unsaddled his horse, groomed him carefully,—so as to leave no signs of his ride,—and led him to the *corral*, where he carefully divested his hoofs of the pieces of sheepskin, turned him in, closed the door, and softly returned to the zaguán.

Just as he was about to climb into his hammock, he observed a man, who, leaning against the doorpost with his legs crossed, was calmly smoking his *pajillo*.

Don Fernando recoiled on recognising his host; it was, in fact, Estevan Diaz.

The latter, without the slightest semblance of surprise, took the cigarette from his mouth, blew out an enormous mouthful of smoke, and addressed his guest in a tone of the most polished courtesy.

"You must be greatly fatigued with your long ride tonight, *caballero*. Will you have anything to restore you?"

Don Fernando, horrified at the coolness with which this was uttered, hesitated for a moment.

"How am I to understand you, *caballero?*" said he.

"How?" said the other. "Pooh! What is the use of dissembling? I assure you, it is useless to attempt to blind me: I know all."

"You know all! What do you know?" replied the Mexican, anxious to ascertain how far Don Estevan was acquainted with what had occurred.

"I know," replied the *major-domo*, "that you rose, that you saddled your horse, and that you went to meet one of your friends who was waiting for you at the Isle de los Pavos."

"What!" cried Don Fernando, scarcely repressing his rage; "You dared to follow me?"

"¡*Vive Dios!* I should think so; it is my way of thinking to fancy that a man who has been all day long on horseback does not take another ride through the whole of the following night for mere pleasure, particularly in a country like this, which, dangerous enough by daylight, is doubly so when night has fallen. Moreover, I am inquisitive by nature—"

"You are a spy!" broke in Don Fernando, in a fury.

"Fie, *caballero!* What a strange expression you use! I a spy! No, no; only as the simplest way of learning what I wanted to know was to listen, I listened."

"Then you were present at the conversation on the Isle de los Pavos?"

"I will not deny it, caballero; indeed, I was very close to you."

"And heard everything that was said there?"

"To be sure; yes, very nearly all," replied Don Estevan, still smiling.

Don Fernando threw himself upon the *major-domo*, but was stopped by him with a strength the former hardly expected to meet with.

Don Estevan continued, in the same placid tone in which he had hitherto spoken:

"*¡Cuerpo de Cristo!* you are my guest. Wait a little; we shall have time to finish this matter here, after, if it must be."

The Mexican, overwhelmed by these words, stepped back from him, crossed his arms, and, looking him full in the face, replied, "I will wait."

# CHAPTER XIV
# DON ESTEVAN DIAZ

For some little time the two men stood thus face to face, looking at each other with the dogged resolution of two duellists who are watching an opportunity to close.

The eyes of Don Estevan, whose face was in other respects impassive, betrayed a sorrow which he could not dissemble.

Don Fernando, with folded arms, his head erect, his forehead frowning, and his lips livid with the fury that boiled within him, waited for the words that were to fall from Don Estevan's mouth, in order to decide whether he should attack him at once, or pretend to be satisfied with the excuses the latter would probably utter.

By degrees the darkness had become less palpable: the sky decked itself in iris colours, the horizon grew red, the sun, although not yet visible, gave tokens that it would not be long ere he rose, to replace with floods of dazzling light the pale rays of the few stars still visible in the profound blue of heaven.

A thousand pungent odours rose from the earth; and the morning breeze, passing over the foliage of the trees, made it tremble and murmur, while it twisted the mists hanging over the river into the most fantastic folds.

At length Don Estevan, to whom the pause was becoming as embarrassing as it was to the other, determined to break the silence.

"I will be frank with you, *caballero*," said he. "I heard everything that passed in your conversation with the Tigercat; not a word escaped me. This will show you that I know all, and am aware that Don Fernando Carril and Stoneheart are one and the same person."

"Yes," said the Mexican, bitterly, "I see you are an excellent spy. You have chosen a sorry trade, *caballero*."

"Who can tell? Perhaps, before we have finished our conversation, you may be of a different opinion, señor."

"I doubt it. But allow me to remark, that you have a singular mode of showing hospitality towards the guests God sends you."

"Let me explain first; then, after you have heard what I have to tell you, I shall be ready, *caballero*, to give you the satisfaction you demand—if you still insist on it."

"Speak, then; and let us finish this somehow or other," replied Don Fernando impatiently. "The sun has already risen; I hear them moving and talking in the *rancho;* the people will soon make their appearance, and hinder, by their presence, any explanation between us."

"You are right; we must settle this; and as I have as little inclination to be interrupted as you, follow me. What I have to say is too long to be spoken here."

Don Fernando complied. They entered the corral, and saddled their horses.

"Now mount and be off," said Don Estevan, as he vaulted into the saddle; "there is plenty of room for talk in the desert."

The plan proposed was very acceptable to the Mexican, as it gave him freedom of action, and the means of hurling consummate vengeance at the head of the *major-domo,* if the latter wished, as he fancied, to betray him.

It was a splendid morning: a dazzling sun showered down his hot rays in profusion over the country, making the stones glitter like diamonds; the birds warbled gaily among the leaves; *vaqueros* and *peones* began to disperse themselves in all directions, urging on to the pasturage the horses and cattle of the *hacienda;* the landscape increased in beauty every moment, and bore a smiling aspect, very different to the one it wore under the terrors of darkness.

The two men rode on for an hour, when they came to a half-ruined and uninhabited *rancho,* which, covered with climbing plants, and almost hidden under their leaves and flowers, offered an excellent refuge from the heat; for, though the day was still young, the sultriness of the air was overpowering.

"Let us stop here," said Don Estevan, breaking silence for the first time since they left his home; "we shall scarcely find a fitter place."

"Stop, if it suits you," said Don Fernando, carelessly; "to me all places are alike, provided you give me the explanation I demand; only, let it be short and frank."

"Frank it shall be, I give you my honour; short I cannot say, for I have a long and sad tale to relate."

"To me? And for what purpose, pray? Must I hear it? Tell me only—"

"Most surely," said Don Estevan, as he dismounted, "what I have to say will touch you very nearly. You will shortly see the proof."

Don Fernando shrugged his shoulders, and alighted in his turn.

"You are mad, *Dios me libre*," (God forgive me), said he. "Since you overheard our conversation so clearly, you must know that I am a foreigner, and anything that occurs in this country can be but of slight importance to me."

"*¿Quién sabe?*" (Who can tell?) replied Don Estevan, sententiously, throwing himself on the floor of the *rancho* with great content.

Don Fernando followed his example, his curiosity beginning to get the better of him.

When the two men were comfortably stretched opposite each other, Don Estevan turned his face to the Mexican:

"I am going to talk of Doña Hermosa," said he of a sudden.

Surprised by these words, the Mexican blushed deeply. He tried in vain to conceal his emotion.

"Ah!" said he in a stifled voice, "Doña Hermosa! You mean the daughter of Don Luna?"

"The same. In a word, the very girl you saved a few days ago."

"Why recur to that event? Everyone else in my place would have done the same."

"It may be so. I do not wish to appear sceptical, but I think you are mistaken there. However, that is not our question. I say, you saved Doña Hermosa from a frightful death. At the first impulse, yielding to your feelings of pride, you left her abruptly, determined to return to the desert, never again to see the face of her who would have overwhelmed you with gratitude."

Don Fernando, astonished and galled at finding his feelings so well understood, briskly interrupted the speaker.

"To our business, if it so please you, *caballero*," he said sharply; "it is better to begin your explanation at once than launch out into suppositions which may be very ingenious, but have the one fault of being erroneous."

"Look, Don Fernando," replied the other, "you will try in vain to lead me on a false trail; so all denial is useless. You are young and handsome. Passing your life among savages, you are utterly ignorant of the great key to human passions. You could not see Doña Hermosa with impunity. As soon as you saw her, your heart trembled; new ideas developed themselves; and, forgetting all else, despising every other consideration, you have retained only one object, one desire,—that of seeing this girl, who appeared to you as a dream, and brought trouble into a heart so calm before. You have longed to see her, if only for a minute—for a second."

"You are right," cried Don Fernando, carried away by the force of truth; "I feel all you describe. I would joyfully give my life to see but a corner of her *rebozo* (veil). But why is it so? I seek in vain to understand it."

"It is what you would never understand if I did not come to your aid. A man brought up like you, beyond the pale of social considerations,—whose life as yet has only been one long strife with the imperious necessity of each day; who has never employed his physical powers except in the cares of the chase or the struggles of war,—your moral faculties lay dormant within you; you were ignorant of their power. Love brought about the transformation, the effects of which are now confounding you. You love Doña Hermosa."

"Do you think so?" said he simply. "Is this what is called love? In that case," he added, speaking more to himself than to Don Estevan, "its pains are cruel."

The latter looked at him with a mingling of pity and sorrow, and continued:

"I followed you last night because your actions seemed suspicious, and a vague fear led me to distrust you. Concealed in a bush only a yard or two from the spot where you were talking to the Tigercat, I overheard all you said. I changed my opinion of you; I recognised—forgive me if I speak frankly—that you were better than report would make you, and that it would be wrong to take you for such a man as the one you spoke to. The peremptory manner with which you repulsed his insinuations proved that you have a heart. Upon that I determined to support you in the strife for which you are preparing against this man, who has ever been your evil genius, and whose pernicious influence has so malignly brooded over your youth. These are the reasons why I have spoken thus; these the reasons why I brought you here for an explanation. Now, here is my hand; will you take it? It is that of a friend and brother."

Don Fernando rose, and eagerly seizing the hand so frankly held out to him, pressed it again and again.

"Thanks," said he; "thanks, and forgive me. Truly I am, as you say, a savage, taking offence at every trifle. I did not recognise your noble character."

"Do not say a word on that subject. Listen to me: I do not know whence my idea springs, but I suspect that the Tigercat is the implacable enemy of Don Pedro de Luna; his purpose is to make you the instrument of some devilish attempt upon the family at the *hacienda*."

"It is just what I thought myself," said Don Fernando. "The Tigercat's strange conduct during the time they were his guests, and the deception practised upon them, which would have been successful but for my intervention, roused my suspicions. You yourself heard last night the obloquy he heaped on me. Let him beware."

"Let us not be too precipitate," said Don Estevan; "we cannot be too prudent. On the contrary, let us leave the Tigercat to develop his schemes, that we may check them the more readily."

"That, perhaps, would be the better plan. He is going to San Lucar shortly: it will be easy to watch all his steps and counteract his projects. Although this man is subtle, and his cunning and knavery astute, I swear to God I will be no less wily than he."

"More so, as I shall be in the background to support you, and be at your side in the hour of need."

"It is Doña Hermosa who must be specially guarded."

"Alas, Don Estevan, how happy you will be in having it in your power to watch over her hourly."

"Nonsense, my friend; I hope to take you to her in the course of an hour or two."

"Can such a thing be possible?" cried Don Fernando, rapturously.

"Of course it can; particularly as you ought to be placed on a certain footing of intimacy with those at the *hacienda*, that we may the better mislead the Tigercat. Have you forgotten his sarcasms and insinuations apropos of the love he fancies you feel for the charming girl,—the love he boasts of having instigated himself, by throwing her into your way without your suspecting it?"

"True; the man has certainly some hideous project concerning her."

"Be not alarmed; with God's help, we will checkmate him. Now, two words more. Do you really believe this wretch to be your father? The question is one of more importance than you imagine."

Don Fernando became restless; his forehead clouded over with thought; he remained some time in profound meditation. At last he raised his hat and replied:

"I have often asked myself the question you have propounded without ever coming to a satisfactory conclusion. Nevertheless, I am almost certain he is not my father; I cannot be his son. His conduct towards me, the cruel care with which he inspired me with thoughts of evil, and developed in me all the bad instincts of nature,—prove to me that, if any relationship exists between us, it can only be a distant one. It is not to be imagined that a father could take absolute pleasure in thus perverting his own son. Nature revolts so utterly against such a proposition, that the mind cannot accept it. On the other hand, I have always felt for this man a secret repulsion and invincible dislike approaching to hatred. This repulsion increased instead of diminishing with time, a rapture became daily more imminent, and only a pretext was wanting to bring it about. This pretext has been unconsciously found by the Tigercat; and now I am hugging myself with joy at finding my freedom restored, and myself eased of the heavy burden of subjection which weighed me down so long."

"I am quite of your opinion; the man cannot be your father. We shall shortly find that we are right in our conviction; and this moral certainty will allow us to take any measures we please to counteract and foil his machinations."

"In what way do you intend to introduce me to Doña Hermosa, my friend?"

"I will tell you directly. But first I must relate a long and mournful tale, requisite for you to know in all its details, lest, in your intercourse with Don Pedro, you should unwittingly touch upon a wound still secretly bleeding in his heart. This dark and mysterious affair happened long ago. I was hardly born at the time of its occurrence; yet my mother has so often told me the details, that they present themselves to my memory as if I had been an actor in the terrible drama. Listen attentively, my good friend. Who knows whether God, who has inspired me with the wish to tell you the tale, may not have reserved for you the elucidation of its mysteries."

"Does this tale relate to Doña Hermosa?"

"Indirectly it does. Doña Hermosa was not born at the time, and her father did not inhabit the *hacienda*, which he purchased subsequently. At that time the family lived in retirement at a town in the Banda Oriental; for you must know that Don Pedro de Luna is not a Mexican, and the name by which you know him is not his; at least he has only adopted it, the name belonging to the original branch of his family in Mexico. He did not assume it till after the occurrence of the events I am about to relate, when he came to settle here, having bought Las Norias de San Antonio from his relations, who, established for many years in Mexico, only occasionally, and at long intervals, paid a visit of a few days to this distant *hacienda*. The people at San Lucar, and the other inhabitants of the province, knowing Don Pedro de Luna under no other name, imagined it was really that person who had chosen to retire to his estate. My master, when he came here, cared the less to disabuse them, as, when he bought the *hacienda*, he had stipulated with his relations for the right to bear their name. The latter naturally found nothing extraordinary in this; and now that, after a lapse of twenty years, Don Pedro, by the death of his relations, has become the head of the family, this borrowed name has become effectually his own, and none can dispute his right to bear it."

"You excite my curiosity to the utmost; and I wait with impatience for the beginning of your tale."

The two men seated themselves as comfortably as they could in the *rancho*; and Don Estevan Diaz, without farther digression, commenced his long-deferred story. He spoke the whole day long, and when night fell was still speaking.

Don Fernando, his eyes eagerly fixed on the narrator, his heart palpitating, and his eyebrows compressed, listened with liveliest interest to the tale, the strange events of which, as they were unrolled before him, made him shudder with emotions of mingled rage and horror.

Taking Don Estevan's place, we will ourselves recount to the reader this mournful history.

# CHAPTER XV
## DON GUZMAN DE RIBERA

In the year 1515 Juan Diaz de Solis discovered the Rio de la Plata,—a discovery which cost him his life.

According to Herrera, this river to which Solis had first given his own name, took the one it now bears from the fact that the first silver brought from America was shipped at this point for Spain.

In 1535 Don Pedro de Mendoza, appointed *adelantado*, or governor general, of the country between the Rio de la Plata and the Straits of Magellan, founded on the right bank of the river, opposite the mouth of the Uruguay, a town called at first Nuestra Señora de Buenos Aires; later, La Trinidad de Buenos Aires; and finally, Buenos Aires,—a name it has since retained.

The history of this town would be a curious study, full of interesting particulars, as from its earliest days it seems stamped with the seal of fatality.

One should read, in the narrative of Ulrich Schmidel, a German adventurer, and one of the original founders of Buenos Aires, to what depths of misery the wretched conquerors of the country were reduced: how they were constrained by famine to devour the dead bodies of their companions, who had been killed by the Corendian Indians, whom their exactions and cruelties had driven to exasperation; and who, believing the white men who had landed amongst them in such an extraordinary way to be evil genii, had sworn their extermination.

The destiny of this town is a singular one, condemned, as it has been, to an unceasing strife, sometimes with enemies from without, at others, with more formidable foes from within; and which, in spite of these ceaseless struggles, is still one of the richest and most flourishing cities of Spanish America.

Like all the towns founded by the Castilian adventurers in the New World, Buenos Aires is placed in a lovely situation. Its streets are broad, laid out by rule and line; the houses are well built, with a garden to each, thus affording a pleasant prospect. It contains many public buildings, among which we may name the Bazaar de la Recoba. At intervals vast squares occur, well furnished with magnificent shops, which give it an appearance of life and prosperity unhappily too rare in this unfortunate country, so long distracted by civil wars.

Taking an immense leap backwards, we will now introduce our readers to Buenos Aires at a time about twenty years previous to the period to which our story belongs. It is ten o'clock in the night of one of the last; days of September 1839, *i.e.* at the time the tyranny of that extraordinary man who, for twenty years, subjected the Argentine provinces to a yoke of iron, had reached its climax.

Nobody in these days could imagine the hideous tyranny which the Government of Rosas inflicted on this beautiful country, nor the frightful system of terrorism organized by the Dictator from one extremity to the other of the Banda Oriental.

Although it was only ten o'clock, as we said above, a deathlike silence hovered over the town. All the shops were shut, all the streets dark and deserted, save when, at long intervals, they were traversed by strong patrols, whose heavy footsteps resounded on the pavement; or by a few solitary *serenos* (watchmen), who, in fear and trembling, shambled through their duty as guardians of the night.

The inhabitants, shut up in their dwellings, had timidly extinguished their lights, for fear of exciting the suspicions of a police ever ready to take offence, and had sought a temporary refuge in slumber from the evils of the day.

On this particular night Buenos Aires was more desolate-looking than usual. The wind had blown, in a storm from the Pampas during the whole of the day, and filled the atmosphere with an icy chill. Large vivid clouds, laden with electricity, were moving heavily through the sky; and the hoarse rumbling of distant thunder, and the nearer and nearer approaching flashes of lightning, gave warning that a fearful storm was on the point of breaking over the city.

Nearly in the centre of the Calle Santa Trinidad, one of the finest streets in the city, which it traverses almost from end to end, a feeble light, placed behind the muslin curtain of a window on the ground floor, twinkled, like a star in a dark sky, through the tufted branches of some trees planted in front of a noble mansion.

This light seemed to be a blot upon the universal obscurity; for every patrol that passed, every *sereno* whom chance brought to the spot, could not refrain from pausing, and observing it with an expression of anger and ill-dissembled fear: after which they would resume their march, the soldiers growling, in a tone of ill humour boding no good:

"There is that traitor, Don Guzman de Ribera, hatching some new conspiracy against his Excellency the Dictator."

The others saying, in a tone of subdued pity:

"Don Guzman will go on till he gets himself arrested some day."

It is into this house, and into the room itself where the light is shining, which gave rise to so many surmises, that we will introduce our readers.

After having crossed the garden and cleared the *zaguán*, we find on our right hand a massive door of walnut, fastened simply by a latch, on lifting which we enter a large room, well lighted by three windows opening on the street.

The furniture of this apartment was of the greatest simplicity. The whitewashed walls were decorated with a few of those abominable coloured prints which the trade of Paris has exported into all regions of the globe, and which are supposed to represent the death of Poniatowski, the seasons, &c. The inevitable Soufleto's piano—which in all Spanish-American houses one sees thrust forward into the most conspicuous place, but which is happily beginning to be replaced by the Alexandre harmonium—a dozen chairs, a round table covered with a green cloth, two armchairs, and a clock with alabaster columns, on a pier table, completed the inventory.

In this room a man, dressed in a travelling costume, with *poncho* (cloak) and *polenas* (boots), was striding up and down, casting impatient and restless looks at the clock every time he passed the table.

Sometimes he paused, lifted the curtain of a window, and tried to pierce the obscurity of night and see into the street; but in vain; the darkness was too great for him to distinguish objects. Sometimes he listened attentively, as if amongst the noises of the town the breeze had brought him the distant echo of a sound significant to him; then he resumed, with a gesture of ill humour and increasing agitation, the walk he had so often interrupted.

This man was Don Guzman de Ribera.

Belonging to one of the best families in the country, and descending in a direct line from the first conquerors, Don Guzman, when still very young, had served a rude apprenticeship in arms under his father. During the war of independence, as aide-de-camp to San Martin, he had followed that general when he crossed the Cordilleras at the head of his army, and revolutionised Chili and Peru.

Since that period he had served continually, sometimes under one chief, sometimes under another; always striving, to the best of his ability, to avoid ranging himself under a flag hostile to the true interests of his country — a difficult task amidst those perpetual convulsions caused by the petty ambition of men without real importance, who were contending for power amongst themselves. Nevertheless, thanks to his dexterity, and still more to the uprightness of his character, Don Guzman had managed to keep himself stainless: yet two years previously, suspected by Rosas, to whom his ideas of true liberality were odious, he had retired from the service, and settled himself at home.

Don Guzman, a true soldier in the most honourable acceptation of the word, although never ostensibly meddling with politics, was greatly dreaded by the Dictator, on account of the influence his loyal and resolute character gave him over his countrymen, who felt for him a sympathy so profound, and a devotedness so complete, that more than once General Rosas, a man of few scruples, had been forced to relinquish the idea of ridding himself, by exile or worse means, of a man whose seclusion and noble pride seemed to cast a shadow over the actions of the Dictator.

At the moment we bring him before our readers, Don Guzman had just reached his fortieth year; but notwithstanding the countless fatigues he had undergone, and which had only hardened him, age seemed to have taken no hold of his vigorous organism.

His tall and muscular figure was as upright, the expression of his face as full of calm intelligence, his eye as brilliant as ever. A few silver threads among his hair, and one or two wrinkles, written on his forehead more by thought than by time, were the only signs that he had already attained middle age.

The clock had struck half past ten some minutes ago, when several rude blows were struck on the door, making Don Guzman tremble.

He stopped and listened.

A lively altercation appeared to be taking place under the *zaguán* of the house. Unfortunately, the room being too far from the porch, Don Guzman could only hear a confused uproar, without being able to distinguish the sounds. But in a short time the noise ceased, the door of the room was opened, and a domestic entered. We must suppose him to be a confidential servant, judging by the manner in which his master spoke to him.

"Well, Diego, what is it? What is the meaning of all this noise at such an hour?"

The servant approached his master before he answered, and bowing, whispered in his ear: "Don Diego Pedrosa."

"He!" said the master, frowning. "Is he alone?"

"I do not think he has more than two or three soldiers with him."

"Which means," said Don Guzman, looking more and more gloomy —

"That he has another score or two concealed close at hand."

"What does the man want with me? It is hardly the hour for a visit. Don Bernardo is scarcely so intimate with me," he added, with a bitter smile, "that he would act with so little ceremony towards me without an urgent reason."

"Exactly what I did myself the honour to remark to him, your Excellency."

"And he persists?"

"Yes, Excellency. He tells me he has business of the utmost importance to communicate."

Don Guzman strode up and down with a pensive air.

"Listen, Diego," said he, at last; "see that the servants arm themselves quietly, and be ready at the first signal; but act prudently, so as to avoid suspicion."

"Trust me, Excellency," said the old servitor, with a smile of intelligence.

For thirty years Diego had been in the service of the Ribera family; many a time had he given his master proof of his boundless attachment.

"Ah, well," replied Don Guzman good humouredly; "I know pretty well what you can do."

"And the horses?" continued the servant.

"Let them stay where they are."

"Even if we are to be off directly?" said Diego, in amazement.

"We shall be off so much the sooner, *muchacho*," said the don, whispering to his servant, "if they do not think we have seen their trap and are about to throw dust in their eyes."

Diego nodded.

"And Don Bernardo?" he asked.

"Admit him. I had rather know the worst at once."

"Is it quite prudent for your Excellency to see this man alone?"

"No fear, Diego; he is not so terrible as you think. Are my pistols in my *poncho?*"

The old servant, probably tranquillised by these words, left the room without replying; but returned almost immediately, showing in a man of about thirty, dressed in the uniform of a staff officer of the Argentine army.

At sight of the stranger, Don Guzman smiled pleasantly, and advancing a few steps towards him, said:

"You are welcome, Colonel Pedrosa"—he made a sign to Diego to retire—"although the hour is rather late for a visit. I am delighted to see you. Pray be seated."

"Your Excellency will excuse me, on account of the business which brings me here," replied the colonel, with a polished bow.

Here Diego, obeying the reiterated signs of his master, left the room, although much against his will.

The two men, seated face to face, looked at each other much like two duellists about to cross their blades.

Don Diego was a handsome man, of slender and upright figure, all whose movements betrayed his noble birth, and were marked by the most consummate elegance.

His face, a perfect oval, was embellished by two large black and sparkling eyes, from which, when he grew excited, fire seemed to flash, possessing an electric power so potent, that few could support their dazzling effulgence. His straight nose, with its open and flexible nostrils; his well-formed mouth, with its astute and sarcastic outline, and its set of brilliant teeth, surmounted by an ebon and well-trimmed moustache; his open forehead, and his complexion slightly tanned by exposure to the sun,—gave to his face, which was encircled by long silky curls of magnificent black hair,—a haughty and commanding expression, inspiring an instinctive repulsion by its frigid energy.

His bands, ensconced in admirably fitting gloves, and his varnished boots, were of wonderfully small size,—in fact, his whole person was a type of his race.

Such was the personage who, at eleven o'clock at night, knocked at Don Guzman's door, and insisted on admittance, under the pretext of important business. As for his moral qualities, the progress of our story will exhibit them so perfectly, that it would be useless to enter into the details at present.

However, as the silence between these two personages threatened to prolong itself indefinitely, Don Guzman, in his quality of host, thought it incumbent on him to put an end to a situation which began to be embarrassing to both; so he broke it.

Bowing with courtesy, he said:

"*Caballero*, I am waiting for what you may please to communicate to me. It grows late."

"Aha! You wish to get rid of me," said the colonel, with a sardonic smile. "Is that what you wish me to understand?"

"It is always my aim to make my speech so clear and open, colonel, that there may be no possibility of my words bearing a double interpretation."

Don Bernardo's cheeks, which had flushed up when Don Guzman spoke, resumed their natural colour, and assuming a tone of pleasantry, he said:

"Look you, Don Guzman; we will put away all idea of sparring with each other. I have a great desire to serve you."

"Me!" said Don Guzman, with a look of ironical amazement; "Are you quite sure of that?"

"If we continue in this strain, *caballero*, we shall only envenom our discussion, without coming to an understanding."

"Alas, colonel, we live in an era (and you know it better than most men) in which the most innocent actions are so often made to look like guilt, that no one dares to take a step or hazard a word without dreading to excite the suspicions of a power that broods darkly over us all. How can I put faith in the words you have just spoken, when your whole conduct towards me has hitherto been that of an inveterate enemy?"

"Allow me to waive for the present the discussion of the question whether I have acted for or in opposition to your interests. The day will come, *caballero*—at least I hope so—when you will judge me according to my deserts. My present hope is, that you will lay aside all prejudice as regards the step I am now taking."

"If that be the case, have the goodness to explain your intentions, that I may act accordingly."

"Certainly, *caballero*. I have just left Palermo."

"Palermo, indeed!" said Don Guzman, shuddering imperceptibly.

"I have; and do you know what they are doing at Palermo tonight?"

"By my faith, I confess I trouble myself very little about the Dictator, especially when he is busy at his *quinta* (country house). They are dancing, or otherwise amusing themselves there, I suppose?"

"Quite right: they are dancing and amusing themselves."

"By heavens!" said the other, "I did not think I was so good a diviner."

"Well, you have guessed a part of their occupation, but not the whole."

"The devil! You puzzle one," replied Don Guzman laughing sardonically. "I do not see too clearly what his Excellency can have to do beyond dancing, unless he amuses himself with signing warrants against the suspected. His Excellency is endowed with great capabilities for business."

"This time you have divined the whole, *caballero*," said the colonel, without appearing to notice the ironical tone of the speaker.

"And amongst these warrants there is, I dare say, one which concerns me more particularly."

"Precisely so," replied the colonel, with a bland smile.

"Very good. What follows is quite simple: you are charged to put it in execution."

"Just so," said the colonel coolly.

"I would have laid a hundred to one on it! And this warrants enjoins you —"

"To put you under arrest, *caballero*."

No sooner had the colonel uttered these words with the most charming indifference, than Don Guzman was standing before him, a pistol in each hand.

"By heavens!" said he resolutely, "Such an order is easier given than executed when the person to be arrested is Don Guzman de Ribera!"

The colonel had not stirred; he had remained lounging in his armchair, in the attitude of a man quite at home with his host. He made a sign to the *caballero* to be seated again.

"You are quite mistaken," said he coolly. "Nothing would have been easier for me than to execute the warrant, if I had any intention to carry it out, especially as you yourself have furnished me with the means."

"I!" said Don Guzman.

"Yourself: you are a resolute man; you would have resisted it, as you have just proved. Now, what would have happened? I should have killed you. General Rosas, in spite of the interest he feels for you, has not absolutely ordered me to take you alive."

The reasoning was brutal, but perfectly logical. Don Guzman bowed his head: he felt he was in this man's power.

"Nevertheless, you are my foe," he said.

"¿Quién sabe?" (who can tell?) "Señor, in times such as we live in, no one can say who is friend or who is foe."

"But finally, what are your intentions?" exclaimed Don Guzman, in a state of nervous excitement, increased by the necessity of dissembling the fury that was raging in his mind.

"I will tell you; but I beg you will not interrupt me. We have already lost much time—which is valuable just now, more especially to yourself, as you ought to know. At the very moment when I came to disturb you, you were giving orders to your confidential servant Diego to get ready your horses."

"Indeed!" said Don Guzman.

"It is the fact. You were only deferring your flight till the arrival of a certain *guacho*" (Mexican inhabitant of the prairies) "to guide you through the Pampas."

"Do you know that too?"

"We know everything. As for the rest, judge for yourself. Your brother, Don Leoncio de Ribera, a refugee with his family for many years in Chili, is to arrive this very night within a few leagues of Buenos Aires. You have been advised of his coming for some days. It was your intention to repair to the Hacienda del Pico, where he was to expect you; then to introduce him surreptitiously into the city, where you have prepared what you fancied would be a safe hiding place for him. Is this the whole, or have I forgotten any minor particulars?"

Don Guzman covered his face with his hands, discouraged, thunderstricken by what he had just heard.

A horrible gulf yawned before his eyes. If Rosas was master of his secret—and that he was, the revelations of the colonel left no room to doubt—his death and that of his brother had been sworn by the ruthless Dictator. Hope would have been a folly.

"Good God!" cried he; "My brother—my poor brother!"

The colonel seemed to enjoy for a moment the effect produced by his words; then he resumed, in a quiet and insinuating manner:

"Calm yourself, Don Guzman; all is not yet lost. The details I have mentioned, and which you thought such a profound secret, are known to me alone. The order for your arrest does not come into execution before sunrise tomorrow. The stop I have taken should prove to you that I have no wish to make an unfair use of the advantage chance has placed in my hands."

"But again I say, What is your intention? In the name of the devil, what are you?"

"What am I?—Your enemy. My intention?—To save you."

Don Guzman did not reply. A prey to the most violent emotion, his whole body trembled with agitation. The colonel shrugged his shoulders impatiently.

"Let us understand each other," said he. "You wait in vain for the *guacho* on whom you reckoned: he is dead."

"Dead!" cried Don Guzman, struck with astonishment.

"The man," continued Don Bernardo, "was a traitor. He had hardly entered Buenos Aires, before he attempted to make money by the sale of the secret confided to him by your brother. Chance would have it that he should apply to me, in preference to anyone else, on account of the hatred I seemed to entertain for your family."

"That you seemed to entertain!" bitterly repeated Don Guzman.

"Yes, that I seemed to entertain," Don Bernardo went on, laying great stress upon the words. "In short, this man revealed everything. I paid him well, and let him go."

"What an imprudence!" exclaimed Don Guzman, highly interested.

"Was it not?" said the colonel quickly. "But what could I do? For the first moment I was so thunderstruck by the news, that I did not think of detaining the fellow. I was on the point of sending in search of him, when I heard an uproar in the street. I inquired the cause; I confess I was not quite satisfied with what was told me. It appears that the fool had hardly put foot in the street before he began to quarrel with another *pícaro* of his own kind; that the latter, in a fit of impatience, had given him a *navaja*" (a cut with the knife) "across his belly, and, luckily for you, killed him outright. It is miraculous, is it not?"

The colonel had related this strange tale with the same negligent indifference he had exhibited during the whole meeting, and which he had not dropped for an instant. Don Guzman cast a penetrating glance at him, which he bore with the greatest unconcern. Then all irresolution seemed to vanish. He raised himself to his full height, and made a courteous inclination to Don Bernardo.

"Excuse me, colonel," said he fervently, "for having mistaken your character; but up to this day everything seemed to justify my conduct; only, in the name of Heaven, if you are my foe—if you have a hate to satisfy—take your revenge on me—on me alone—and spare my brother, against whom you can have no cause for animosity."

Don Bernardo frowned, but replied quickly:

"*Caballero*, order your servants to bring round your horses; I myself will escort you out of the city. You could not possibly quit it without me; you are so thoroughly surrounded by spies. You have nothing to fear from the men who are with me; they are trusty and faithful, and I chose them on purpose. Besides, they shall leave us a few paces hence."

Don Guzman hesitated for a while. He watched Don Bernardo with anxious eyes. At last he seemed to have formed his resolve; for he rose, and said, looking the colonel full in the face:

"No; whatever may happen, I will not take your advice."

The colonel suppressed his feeling of dissatisfaction.

"Are you mad?" said he; "Remember—"

Don Guzman interrupted him:

"My decision is made," said he dryly. "I will not leave this room without a perfect knowledge of the reason of this strange conduct on your part. I have tried to overcome it, but a secret presentiment assures me that you are still my foe; and if you now utter a feigned wish to serve me, colonel, it is only with the purpose of carrying out some diabolical plan against me and mine."

"Beware, *caballero*! When I came here, my purpose was friendly. Your obstinacy will compel me to break off a colloquy which we can never resume. I have but one thing to add: whatever the reason for my actions may be, I have only one wish—to save you. This is the sole explanation I have the right to give."

"But that will not suffice, *caballero*."

"And why, if it please you?" said the colonel haughtily.

"Because matters have occurred between you and a certain member of my family which give me a right to look upon any intentions of yours as hostile."

The colonel trembled; a livid pallor stole over his countenance.

"Indeed!" said he hoarsely. "So you know that, Señor Don Guzman?"

"I will answer you in the exact words in which you replied to me a few minutes ago; I know all!"

Don Bernardo cast down his eyes, and clenched his hands in concentrated rage.

There was silence for a time.

Just at this moment a *sereno* passed through the street, paused close to the walls of the house, and cried, in a cracked and drunken voice, the hour of the night:

"*¡Ave, María purísima! Las doce han dado y sereno!*" ("Hail, purest Mary! Twelve o'clock, and a fine night!")

Then his heavy step was heard as he went on his rounds, until it gradually died away in the distance.

The two men shuddered, thus suddenly aroused from their preoccupation.

"Midnight already!" muttered Ribera in a tone of mingled regret and anxiety.

"Let us end this," resolutely exclaimed Don Bernardo. "Since nothing will convince you of the honesty of my intentions; since you exact from me revelations which concern myself alone—"

"And one other person," supplied Don Guzman.

"I will admit it," continued the colonel impatiently.

"Well, are you satisfied now? It is solely because I know I shall meet this person at the Hacienda del Pico, that I wish to accompany you. I must have an interview. Do you understand me now?"

"Yes; I understand you perfectly."

"Then what are your objections?"

"You are deceiving yourself, *caballero*," answered Don Guzman coolly.

"Oh! This time I swear you are mistaken."

"Then I shall go alone!—That is all."

"Beware, once more!" said the colonel; "My patience is exhausted."

"And mine, colonel! Yes, I repeat, I scorn your threats! Do what you think fit, *caballero*. God will aid me."

At these words a disdainful smile passed over the lips of the colonel; he rose, and planted himself before Don Guzman, who was standing in the middle of the room.

"Are those your last words, señor?" said he.

"The last."

"Your blood be upon your own head! It is you who have willed it so," shouted the colonel, casting on him a glance of fury.

And without taking any further notice of his foe, who remained apparently cold and impassive, he turned to leave the chamber, a prey to the most violent emotion.

Don Guzman, profiting by this movement of the colonel, dexterously threw off his *poncho*, cast it over the head of Don Bernardo, muffling him up in it in such a manner that he was bound and gagged before he could attempt to defend himself.

"For one trump a higher!" laughed Don Ribera.

"As you are determined to go with me, you shall, but in a different fashion to what you expected."

For answer, the colonel made a vain but desperate effort to free himself from his bonds.

"And now for the others!" exclaimed Don Guzman, with a triumphant look at his enemy, who was rolling on the floor in a paroxysm of impotent rage.

Five minutes later, the few soldiers who had been left in the *zaguán* were disarmed by the servants, bound with cords they had themselves brought for a far different purpose, and deposited on the steps of the neighbouring cathedral, where they were left to their fate.

As to the colonel, the old soldier, who had just shown so much presence of mind, had no idea as he had said himself, of leaving him behind. On the contrary, he had weighty reasons for taking him with him in the hazardous adventure he was about to undertake. So, as soon as he was on horseback, he threw his prisoner across the pummel of his saddle, and left the house attended by several trusty servants, well mounted, and armed to the teeth.

"Speed! Speed!" he cried, as soon as the door was closed. "Who knows but that this traitor may have sold us beforehand?"

The little party started at a gallop, and traversed the city—deserted at that time of night—with the speed of a storm wind.

But as soon as the riders reached the commencement of the suburbs, they gradually slackened their pace, and finally halted, at a sign from Don Guzman.

That gentleman had totally forgotten one thing, and a very important one. It was, that during the time the city was suffering under the rule of Rosas, it was under martial law; and consequently, after a certain hour, it was impossible to pass out without the watchword, which was changed every night, and given by the Dictator himself. It was an embarrassing situation. Don Guzman's looks fell upon the prisoner in front of him; for a single moment he thought of liberating his head, and demanding the watchword, which he would certainly know. But another moment's reflection made him relinquish the idea of trusting to a man to whom he had just offered a mortal insult, and who would certainly embrace the first opportunity that offered for revenge. He determined, therefore, to trust to audacity, and act according to circumstances. Consequently, having warned his servants to look to their arms, and be in readiness to use them at his first signal, he gave the order to advance.

They had ridden a few hundred paces farther, when they heard the sound of a musket being cocked, followed immediately by the words, "Who goes there?" lustily halloaed.

Luckily, the night was intensely dark. The moment for audacity had come.

Don Guzman responded, in a sharp and firm voice:

"Colonel Pedrosa! ¡Ronde mashorca!" [1]

"Where are you going?" said the sentry.

"To Palermo," replied Ribera, "by orders of the well-beloved General Rosas."

"Pass!" said the sentry.

The little party was swallowed up in the jaws of the ponderous gate; it galloped through, and was soon lost in the darkness.

Thanks to his audacity, Don Guzman had escaped from utmost peril.

The serenos were chanting the half-hour after midnight when the travellers left the last houses of Buenos Aires behind them.

[1] The "mashorca rounds," —a nickname given to the bodyguards of the Dictator; literally, "more gallows."

# CHAPTER XVI
# THE POST HOUSE IN THE PAMPAS

The Pampas are the *Steppes* of South America, with this difference, that these immense plains, which extend from Buenos Aires, as far as San Luis de Mendoza, to the foot of the Cordilleras, are clothed with a thick carpet of long grass, undulating with the softest breath of the wind, and are intersected by numerous water courses, some of great magnitude, which cut it up in every direction.

The aspect of the Pampas is desperately monotonous and mournful. There is neither wood nor mountain; not a single break of ground to form an oasis of sand or granite, on which to rest the eye in the midst of this ocean of green.

Only two roads traverse the Pampas, and connect the Atlantic with the Pacific.

The first leads to Chili, passing by Mendoza; the second to Peru, by Tucumen and Salta.

These vast solitudes are infested by two races of men, perpetually at war with each other: the Indian Bravos, or Pampas, and the Guachos.

The Guachos, a caste peculiar to the Argentine provinces, are not to be met elsewhere.

These men, charged with the supervision of the wild cattle and horses which range at large through the whole extent of these wide plains, are, for the most part, whites by race; but, crossed in blood with the aborigines for many years, they have in time become almost as barbarous as the Indians themselves, from whom they have learnt their cunning and cruelty.

They live on horseback, lie in the bare sun, support themselves on the flesh of their beasts when unlucky in the chase, and only approach the towns and *haciendas* for the purpose of exchanging their skins, their *ñandú* (the ostrich of the Pampas) plumes, and furs, for spirits, silver spurs, powder, knifes, and the cloths of gaudy colours with which they delight to adorn their persons.

The true Centaurs of the New World, as rapid as the Tartar riders of the *Steppes* of Siberia, they transport themselves with prodigious speed from one extremity of the Banda Oriental to the other. They recognise no law beyond the whim of the moment; no master but their will. For the most part, they do not know the proprietor who employs them, and whom they only see at rare intervals.

The Guachos are almost as much to be dreaded as the Indians by travellers, who dare not venture upon the Pampas except in considerable numbers, so as to afford mutual protection against the aggressions to which they are constantly exposed, either from Indians or from the wild beasts.

The caravans are usually composed of fifteen, or even twenty, wagons, or *galeras*, drawn by six or eight oxen apiece. Their drivers, crouching under the hide covering of the *galeras*, urge them on with long goads, slung over their heads, with which they can easily reach the leading oxen of the team.

A *capataz*, or *major-domo*,—a resolute man, thoroughly acquainted with the Pampas,—commands the caravan, having under his orders some thirty *peones*, who, like himself, are mounted, and gallop around the convoy, watch the relief cattle, and, in case of attack, defend the travellers of every age whom they escort.

Nothing can be seen at once so picturesque and sad as the aspect the caravans present as they extend themselves in a long serpentine line over the Pampas, advancing at a slow and regular pace along roads full of quagmires, over which the immense *galeras* roll, groaning on their croaking and massive wheels, tottering with indescribable swayings and joltings along ruts, out of which the oxen, lowing and stretching their smoking nostrils to the ground, can hardly drag them.

Ofttimes these heavy caravans are passed by *arrieros* (muleteers), whose *recua* (string of mules) trots gaily on, to the tinkling of a silver bell attached to the neck of the *yegua madrina* (the leading mule), and to the sound of "*Arrea, mulos*" (Get on mules), incessantly repeated, in all notes of the gamut, by the *arriero* chief and his *peones* who gallop about the mules to prevent their straying to right or left.

When night comes, the muleteers and ox drivers find precarious shelter in the post houses—a kind of *tambas* or *caravanseries*, built, at considerable distances apart, in the Pampas. The *galeras*, detached from the oxen, are ranged in single file; the burdens of the mules are piled up in a circle; then, if the *corral* (stables) be full, if there be many travellers at the post house, beasts and men encamp together, and spend the night under the open sky,—a mode of sleeping which is no hardship in a country where cold is almost unknown. Then commence, by the fantastic light of the bivouac fires, the long tales of the Pampas, interspersed with joyous bursts of laughter, with songs, and words of love uttered in whispers.

Yet it is rare for the night to pass over without a quarrel of some sort arising between the muleteers and the drivers, who are by nature jealous of each other, and enemies by profession. Then blood flows, the consequence of a *navajada* or two; for the knife always plays a too active part among these men, whom no fear of consequences restrains in their unbridled frenzy.

Now, on the night of the day on which our story begins, the last post house on the Portillo road, when you leave the Pampas, going to Buenos Aires, was overfilled with travellers. Two numerous *recuas de mulas* (strings of mules), which a month before had crossed the Alto de Cumbre, and encamped on the Rio de la Cucoa, close to the Inca's Bridge, one of the most singular natural curiosities in the country, had lighted their fires before the post house, close to two or three convoys of *galeras*, whose oxen were quietly lying in the interior of the circle formed by the wagons.

The post house was a building of considerable extent, constructed of *adobas* (sundried bricks.) The entrance was furnished with a portico—a species of peristyle formed of the trunks of four large trees, planted in the ground in lieu of pillars, and supporting a veranda broad enough to afford shelter from the piercing rays of the sun.

In the interior of the *toldo*, as they call these miserable hovels, resounded the songs and laughter of the drivers and muleteers, mingling with the notes of a *vihuela* (Spanish guitar), scraped with the knuckles of the hand in a manner sufficient to drive one to despair, and with the sharp and clamorous outcry of the postmaster, whose squeaking voice strove in vain to quell the uproar, and regulate the disorder.

Just at this moment the rapid gallop of many horses was heard; and two parties of riders, coming from points diametrically opposite, stopped, as with one accord, before the porch of the *toldo*, after passing with great dexterity through the encampments before the post house, the approaches to which were vastly obstructed by the *galeras*.

The first of these parties, consisting of only six riders, came from the direction of Mendoza; the second from the opposite side, from the heart of the Pampas: the latter comprised some thirty individuals at least.

The unexpected arrival of the newcomers stopped, as by enchantment, the clamour which the *ranchero*, or owner of the house, had been unable to still, and a sudden silence seized on the company, which had been so joyously uproarious a few minutes before.

The muleteers and drivers glided like shadows out of the house, and, with furtive steps, regained their respective encampments, exchanging uneasy looks amongst themselves; so that the room was empty in a twinkling, and the *ranchero* was able to come forward and receive the guests who had arrived so unexpectedly. But he had scarcely reached the threshold, and cast a glance outside, when a mortal pallor overspread his visage, a convulsive shudder shook his frame, and his tones were almost unintelligible, as he managed to stutter forth the essential phrase of welcome in South America; "¡*Ave, María purísima!*" (Hail, purest Mary!)

"¡*Sin pecado concebida!*" (immaculately conceived) answered the rough voice of a tall cavalier, with harsh features and a ferocious eye, who seemed to be the leader of the more numerous party.

We must observe that the second party appeared in some degree to share the terror felt by the inhabitants of the post house; and having perceived the others before their own presence was remarked, the six cavaliers had prudently reined in their horses, and thrown themselves into the shade as far as possible, being little desirous, in all probability, of being inadvertently seen by the dangerous fellow travellers amongst whom chance or ill luck had unfortunately thrown them.

Now, who were these persons, the sight of whom sufficed of itself to inspire a general panic and womanly consternation in the breasts of the hardy explorers of the wilderness—of men whose life was a perpetual struggle against the wild beasts, and who had so often confronted death without blenching, that they almost fancied they were beyond his grasp?

At the time in which this story happens, the hateful and bloody tyranny of that half-breed—that Nero who had nothing belonging to humanity but its semblance, that ignorant and brutal *guacho*, that man-faced tiger, in a word, Don Juan Manuel de Rosas—which had so long crushed the Argentine provinces, was still all-powerful; and these men were *federales*, hired assassins of that butcher in cold blood, whose name is now damned by the execration of the world; in short, they were members of that horrible *restauradora* (regeneratory) society, better known under the name of *mashorca* (*mashorca* signifies literally "more gallows"), which for several years filled all Buenos Aires with mourning. Constrained by public indignation, the Dictator, later on, had made a pretence of dissolving this society; but he did nothing of the sort, in reality; and up to the final fall of the unclean tyrant, it existed *de facto,* and at the slightest sign of its master scattered murder, violation, and fire through the length and breadth of the confederation.

The reader can now understand the terror which seized upon the careless and peaceable travellers assembled in the *toldo*, at the appearance of the ominous uniforms of these hired ruffians, to whom pity was unknown.

Compelled by one of these instinctive presentiments which are seldom fallacious, they felt that some misfortune threatened them. They crept out with slouching heads, and hiding themselves behind their bales, began to shudder in the darkness, without attempting to prepare for resistance, which they knew would be futile.

In the meantime, the *colorados*, or *federales*, had dismounted, and entered the *rancho*, marching on their toes, on account of their enormous spur rowels, and allowing their heavy iron scabbards to trail beside them: The clang made by these in their contact with the flooring seemed a sound of evil augury to the terrified listeners.

"Halloa!" cried the leader, in a harsh voice; "*¡rayo de Dios!* What does this mean, *Caballeros?* Does our arrival banish all pleasure from this dwelling?"

The *ranchero* multiplied his obeisances till he addled his brains with bowing, and twisted his shapeless hat in both hands without finding a word to say. At the bottom of his heart, this worthy man, who was acquainted with the expeditious habits of his unwelcome guests, had the greatest dread of being hanged forthwith; a thought which by no means helped him to recover his presence of mind, and the coolness required by circumstances.

The large room was barely lighted by a single smoky candle, shedding a yellow and doubtful light. The *colorado*, coming from the open, his eyes still clouded with the thick darkness on the Pampas, had not been able to distinguish objects at first; but as soon as he had got accustomed to the semi-obscurity which reigned around him, and perceived that, with the exception of the *ranchero*, the place was empty, he frowned, and stamped on the ground in ire.

"*¡Válgame Dios!*" he exclaimed, looking furiously at the poor devil perspiring with fear before him, "Have I fallen unawares into a nest of serpents? Is this miserable hut the meeting place of *salvajes unitarios?* Answer, wretch, or I will have your tongue torn out and thrown to the dogs!"

The post master grew green with fear when he heard this menace,—a threat he well knew these men capable of executing. He was still more frightened at the expression *salvajes unitarios*, an epithet used to designate the enemies of Rosas, and generally the prelude to a massacre.

"Señor General," cried he, with an heroic effort to utter a few words.

"I am not a general," broke in the *colorado* in a somewhat smoother tone, for his pride was secretly flattered by the sonorous title; "I am not a general yet, though I hope to be one someday. I am only *teniente* (lieutenant), which is already a pretty step; so call me nothing else for the present. Now, go on."

"Señor *Teniente*," replied the *ranchero*, a little comforted, "there is nobody here except good friends of the well beloved General Rosas; we are all federals."

"Ha! I doubt that," said the terrible lieutenant. "You are too close to Monte Video to be thorough Rosistas."

We must state here that throughout the Argentine provinces there was only one town which had the noble courage to oppose itself to the savage tyranny of the ruthless Dictator. This town, whose devotion to the sacred cause of liberty has made it celebrated throughout both the Old and New Worlds, is Monte Video. Resolute to perish, if it must be, in the holy cause it bad embraced, it heroically sustained a siege of nine years against the troops of Rosas, whose impotent efforts were repeatedly shattered against its walls.

"Señor *Teniente*," replied the *ranchero* obsequiously, "the people who meet here are solely *arrieros* and wagoners, who are only passers-by, and never meddle with politics."

This explanation, which the postmaster thought most adroit, had no influence on the *colorado*.

"¡*Vive Dios*!" he cried, with haughty voice, "We will see; and woe to the traitor I discover! Luco," he continued addressing his *cabo*, or corporal, "just step and rouse up those brute beasts, and bring them hither. If any sleep too soundly, stir them up with the point of the sabre; it will exhilarate them and induce them to move more quickly."

The *cabo* gave a malicious grin, and went out immediately to execute his orders.

The lieutenant, after addressing a few more questions of minor importance to the *ranchero*, at last thought fit to seat himself on the bench which ran round the room, and, to enliven the time of the corporal's absence, set himself to consume the liquor and food assiduously placed before him by the host, who was swearing to himself all the while at being obliged to find drink gratis for so many. He knew well that, though the consumption of liquors by the soldiers would be enormous, he would never see the colour of their money, and might think himself happy if he escaped without other damage.

The soldiers, except five or six who remained without in charge of the horses, seated themselves by their officer, and followed his example in drinking like sponges.

The corporal's task was easier than he expected, for the poor devils of muleteers and drivers had overheard the peremptory order of the leader. Comprehending that resistance would not only be useless, but make their situation worse, they obeyed their officer's orders with resignation, and came back again into the room, attempting to hide their fright with ill-counterfeited smiles.

"Aha!" cried the lieutenant; "I knew we should find some malcontents here,—ay, good people?"

The peasants multiplied their excuses and protestations, to which the lieutenant listened with the greatest indifference, taking all the while short sips from an enormous goblet, filled to the brim with *refino de Catalonia*, the strongest spirit known.

"There, that will do," said he at last, making the steel scabbard of his sword rattle against the bench; "let us reconnoitre a little; and first of all, for whom are you, in the devil's name?"

The travellers, terrified by this demonstration, answered the question by hastening to shout at the top of their voices, and with an enthusiasm the more demonstrative the less it was real:

"*Viva el benemérito General Rosas, Viva el libertador, Vivan los federales, Mueren los salvajes unitarios. A degüello, a degüello con ellos.*" [1]

These well-known federal cries, which served as rallying calls in their bloody expeditions, dispelled the doubts of the officer. He deigned to smile; but it was a tiger's smile, exposing the white fangs ready to bite.

"*Bravos, Bravos,*" he cried: "that is right at all events. These are true Rosistas. Come, *ranchero, trago de aguardiente*" (a draught of brandy) "for these worthy people. I intend to treat them."

The *ranchero* could have easily dispensed with this factitious generosity of the officer, the cost of which he well knew he should have to pay out of his own pocket. However, he executed the order, hiding the chagrin he felt under the most gracious air he could assume. The cries and protestations of federalism were renewed with redoubled ardour: the brandy circulated, and joy seemed to have reached a climax.

The lieutenant next took a guitar, which happened to lie beside him.

"Come, *muchachos,*" said he; "a *zambacueca*" (a Mexican dance). "*Voto a Dios*, Room for the dance."

There was no refusing. Whatever the secret fears of those present, the gracious invitation of the *colorado* was so neatly put, that they were obliged to take heart of grace, as the saying is, and play their parts to the end. It was the best plan to resign themselves to their lot. They were in the claws of the tiger, who might devour them at any moment if the fancy seized him.

The middle of the room was cleared; the dancers, male and female, took their places, their eyes fixed on the officer, in expectation of his signal.

They had not long to wait; as soon as the lieutenant saw his victims prepared, he swallowed an enormous bumper of *refino*, and set himself to rattle on the guitar with his knuckles; while he sang, or rather screeched, in a shaky voice, the gay *zambacueca* so well known in the Argentine provinces, and which begins with the following charming verse:

"Para que vas y vienes,
Vienes y vas.
Si otros andar menos,
Consiguen más?" [2]

It has been truly said that the Spaniards are excessively fond of dancing; but in this, as in many other matters, the South Americans have left them far behind They have carried this passion to such a pitch, that it reaches the limits of folly. The scene we are about to describe will prove the truth of our assertion.

These very men, who had only consented to dance because, as one may say, the knife was at their throats, and were still under the influence of extreme terror, had scarcely heard for a few minutes the groaning chords of the guitar, and the words which marked the time, than they immediately forgot their precarious position, and gave themselves up heart and soul, in a sort of savage frenzy, to their favourite pastime.

Those who at first had prudently kept themselves within bounds, in consequence of their anxiety, were soon fascinated by the bounds of the dancers, and leaped and stamped, howling, like the others, with all the strength of their lungs.

Thus at the close of a few minutes all constraint had vanished, and the noise had again grown as deafening, and the uproar as stunning, as it had been when the federals arrived.

Meanwhile the corporal had diligently carried out the orders he had received from his superior; but, as we said above, the muleteers and wagoners, having accidentally stopped in front of the *rancho*, and then entered the room of their own accord, had materially lightened his task. But that worthy officer, zealous in the performance of his duty, had taken half a dozen soldiers with him, and scoured the several encampments, passing the blades of their swords between the bales, looking into the insides of the *galeras*,—in a word, ferreting about everywhere, with the sagacity of an old bloodhound which it is impossible to baffle.

Persuaded at last, after the most minute search, that all those whom he thus looked after had entered the *rancho*, he determined to follow them. But the uproar he heard inside convincing him that all was going right, for the time at least, he changed his mind, and dismissing the soldiers who were with him, and who desired nothing better than to join the merriment, remained outside.

As soon as he found himself alone, the corporal's whole demeanour changed. He first satisfied himself that no indiscreet eye observed his motions; he then rolled a cigarette between his fingers, lit it, and, walking backwards and forwards with the air of an idler enjoying his leisure, gradually increased his distance from the porch.

After some ten minutes of this manoeuvring, which bore no bad resemblance to a ship tacking against a contrary breeze in her endeavours to get away from her port, he found he had passed beyond the wagoners' camps, and was so far from the *rancho*, that, thanks to the obscurity of the night, it was impossible to see him from thence. He immediately stopped, looked once more round him, and threw the lighted cigar in the air.

The light *pajillo* described a brilliant parabola against the sky, and then fell to the ground, when the corporal extinguished it with his foot.

At the same moment a slender line of fire sparkled in the obscurity a little way off.

"Good," growled the corporal; "see what it is to be prudent."

A second time he scanned the neighbourhood narrowly; then, reassured by the obscurity which reigned around, he resolutely turned aside into the darkness, humming under his breath these three verses of a song well known in the Pampas:

"O Libertad preciosa No comparado al oro Ni al bien mayor de la espaciosa tierra." [3]

Directly, a voice, low as a whisper, took up the subsequent verses:

"Más rica y más gozosa Que el más precioso tesoro." [4]

At this response, which he doubtless expected, the corporal stopped short. He struck the end of his scabbard on the ground, rested himself on the hilt, and said aloud, as if talking to himself:

The Bee Hunters | 173

"I should like to know why the *ñandús* (ostriches) have so suddenly taken themselves off into the Pampas?"

"Because," answered the voice which had continued the song, "they smelt the odour of dead bodies."

"That may be true," said the corporal, without seeming astonished at the answer which came so oddly; "but then the *condors* would come down from the Cordilleras."

"It is already twenty-one days since they passed the Alto de Cumbre."

"The sunset yesterday was red."

"His rays reflected the light of the conflagrations caused by the *mashorca*," said the voice again.

The corporal hesitated no longer.

"Approach, Don Leoncio," cried he; "you and your companions."

"We are here, Luco;" and the corporal was immediately surrounded by six persons, armed to the teeth.

It is useless to say that these men were the six persons who an hour before had arrived at the post house simultaneously with the *colorados*, and whom prudence had induced to remain concealed.

The dancing and shouting in the *rancho* still went on. The merriment was gradually growing into a gigantic orgy.

Consequently the strangers were sure they should not be disturbed. Moreover, although the moon had now risen, and gave a certain amount of light, the little group, sheltered by the wagons behind which they stood, was in no danger of discovery; while, thanks to its position, nobody could leave the *rancho*, without being seen directly by those composing it.

We will profit by the moonbeams to depict in a few words these fresh personages; a task made more easy by the fact that they had dismounted, and were holding their horses by the bridles.

We said they were six in number: the first three were evidently *peones*; but their heavy silver spurs, their *tirador*, or girdle of embroidered velvet, their beautifully chased weapons, their rich *ponchos* of fine Bolivian vicuña wool, and, above all, the respectful familiarity which they used towards their masters, indicated that they had earned for themselves a certain degree of consideration.

These *peones* were, in fact, not only servants, but friends; humble ones, it is true, but devoted ones, tried many a time in scenes of frightful danger.

Of the masters, two were men of about thirty-five, in all the vigour of their age and strength. Their dress, similar in cut to that of their servants, was only distinguished from it by the superior richness and fineness of its texture.

The foremost was a tall and well-built person, with graceful manners and elegant gestures. The outline of his face was proud and decided, and his hardy features expressed a kindness and frankness which, at first sight, won the sympathy and regard of all.

His name was Don Leoncio de Ribera.

His companion, of the same size and figure, and endowed with the same manners, formed, nevertheless, a perfect contrast to Don Leoncio.

His soft blue eyes; the thick curls of blonde hair, which escaped in large masses from under his Panama hat, and flowed in disorder on his shoulders; the cream-coloured skin, which contrasted with the olive and slightly bronzed complexion of Don Leoncio,—seemed to indicate that he was not born under the burning sun of South America. Yet this cavalier could proudly claim, even more than the latter, the quality of a veritable *hijo del país* [5] since he descended in a direct line from the brave and unhappy Tupac Amaru, the last Inca, so basely assassinated by the Spaniards.

He was called Manco Amaru, Diego de Solis y Villas Reales; and we beg our reader's pardon for this litany of names.

Don Diego de Solis concealed the courage of the lion under the effeminacy of a woman, and nerves of steel under the skin of his soft white hands.

As to the third cavalier, who kept himself modestly retired behind the others, he had wrapped himself up so carefully in the voluminous folds of his *poncho*, and the rim of his hat was so well pulled down over his countenance, that is was impossible to distinguish any part of him except two large black eyes, which flashed forth flames of fire. His small size, delicate limbs, and a certain soft smoothness about his movements, would lead one to suppose that he was still a youth, if this masculine attire did not conceal a woman, which seemed more probable.

However that may be, no sooner did the corporal find himself in the presence of the persons we have described, than there was a complete metamorphosis in his whole appearance. His rough and fierce demeanour was exchanged for a flattering obsequiousness, denoting complete devotedness; and his countenance lost its mocking expression, to take that of decided pleasure.

Don Leoncio had difficulty in moderating the outbursts of foolish joy to which the soldier gave vent, with the unconstraint of a man who at length enjoys a happiness he has long been vainly expecting.

"There, there, Luco," said he; "be calm. You see it is I. There, there; be moderate, *muchacho* this is not the time for outpourings of affection."

"It is true, *mi amo*" (my master); "but I am so happy to see you again after such a length of time," and he brushed away the tears which rolled down his bronzed cheeks.

Don Leoncio felt deeply moved by the affection of his old servant, and replied:

"Thanks, Luco; you are indeed a good and trusty fellow."

"And yet, in spite of the happiness I feel in seeing you once more, I wish you had not returned at such an unlucky moment. *Mi amo*, the times are bad; the tyrant is more powerful than ever in Buenos Aires."

"I know. Unfortunately, I could not postpone my journey, in spite of the perils to which I should be exposed."

"¡*Válgame Dios*, señor! This is a terrible life we are now leading."

"What is to be done? We must all take our share of the unavoidable. Are my orders fulfilled?"

"Yes, all, *mi amo*: your brother is forewarned. Unluckily, I could not go myself to inform him: I was forced to send a *guacho*, of whom I knew little. But do not be uneasy, señor; your brother will not fail to be here in a few hours."

"Good; but you seem to have come here in considerable numbers."

"Alas, it could not be helped; I am so spied after, *mi amo*. I was obliged to use the most extraordinary efforts to induce the lieutenant to bring so few."

"We had very nearly run into his arms."

"Yes; and I was in a dreadful fright at the moment, for I had recognised you already, señor: God knows what would have happened had you met."

"And now, is this lieutenant to be trusted?"

Luco shook his head sorrowfully.

"He! *Mi amo*, take heed. He is one of the most ferocious *mashorqueras* of that evil dog Rosas."

"The devil he is!" said Don Leoncio, with a troubled look. "I fear, my poor Luco, your too great confidence has led us into a hornet's nest, out of which we shall have some trouble to escape safe and sound."

"It is a difficult case—I will not attempt to deny it. You must be very cautious, and let no one strike your trail. The principal thing is to gain time."

"True," said Don Leoncio, plunging into a reverie.

"How many are there of you?" said Don Diego, mixing in the conversation for the first time.

"Thirty-five, counting the lieutenant, señor; but he is a devil incarnate, and counts for four at least."

"Pooh!" replied Don Diego carelessly, while he stroked his blonde moustache; "we are seven when we count you, my good fellow."

"Who is this lieutenant?"

"Don Torribio, formerly a *guacho*."

"Oh," said Don Leoncio, disgusted, "Torribio *Degüello!*" (literally, Torribio the Butcher).

"¡*Voto a brios!*" replied Don Diego; "How I should like to plant my knee on the breast of that wretch! Well, what are we to do?"

"You forget who is with us," said Don Leoncio, quickly, casting a glance at the motionless figure behind.

"It is true," said the young man; "I am mad. Forgive me, friend; we cannot be too cautious."

"It is lucky," observed Luco, "that you have not brought Doña Antonia with you. Poor dear niña! she would die here, were she exposed to the devils in whose midst we are."

All of a sudden before Don Leoncio had time to reply, a horrible clamour arose in the *rancho*, several shots were heard, and a score of men and women, frantic with fear, rushed into the open with shouts of terror, and dispersed in all directions.

"Hide yourselves!" cried Luco. "Good God! What can this mean? I will be back directly; but, for God's sake, do not let them see you. Farewell for a time! I must go and see what is the matter."

Leaving Don Leoncio and his companions in dreadful anxiety, the corporal ran towards the house, where the tumult was increasing every minute.

[1] "Long live the well-beloved General Rosas! Long live the liberator! Long live the federals! Death to the unitarian savages! Slay them! Slay them!"

[2] These words will hardly bear translation Their general meaning is this: Why do you go and return, return and go; if others go less far, they gain more by it.

[3] "O precious Liberty! One cannot compare you to gold nor to the greatest riches in the spacious world."

[4] "More rich and more cherished than the most precious treasure."

[5] Child of the country; a very common expression in South America.

# CHAPTER XVII
# A DELICATE FEDERAL ATTENTION

We will run before the corporal, in order to explain to the reader what had happened in the *rancho*.

At first everything went off well. After the first moment of distrust and fear, the muleteers and wagoners, involuntarily submitting to the influence of their favourite pastime, had utterly forgotten their apprehensions, and fraternised with the soldiers. The *aguardiente* went round uninterruptedly from one end of the room to the other; the merriment increased in proportion to the draughts, which, by frequent repetition, began to heat the brains of the drinkers, among whom the first symptoms of drunkenness were showing themselves here and here.

Nevertheless the lieutenant, Don Torribio, his eyes sparkling and his countenance excited, continued to sing, to torture the guitar, and specially to drink, without any signs of meditated evil; and perhaps all might have ended well, but for an incident which suddenly changed the aspect of things, and turned a scene of joy into a spectacle of terror.

One of the best and most brilliant dancers of the *zambacueca* was a young muleteer of from twenty to twenty-five, with fine and intelligent features, well-knit figure, and easy manner, who distinguished himself greatly by the lightness and grace of his dancing. The women crowded round him, cast the most killing looks at him, and applauded extravagantly the eccentric steps it was his pleasure to execute.

Among these females were two, both girls of sixteen, radiant with the beauty peculiar to South America, and which finds no equivalent in Europe. The black eyes, shaded by long silken lashes; the mouth, with lips red as the fruit of the *chirimoya* (Mexican pear); the face, slightly bronzed by the heat of a tropical sun, over which fell the long tresses of bluish-black hair; the rounded figure, supple and slender; the wavy movements, full of inimitable grace; all these charms united constituted that intoxicating and voluptuous kind of beauty, which it is impossible to analyse, but of which the most frigid mortal cannot resist the magnetic influence and fascinating spell.

These two females made themselves conspicuous by the exuberant praises they showered on the object of their predilection. The latter, we must do him the justice to say, seemed to take very little notice of the enthusiasm he excited. He was a good fellow, whose heart, if not his head, was perfectly free; who danced for dancing's sake, because it pleased him, and because the rough life he led rarely afforded an opportunity for enjoying his favourite amusement; moreover, he was totally indifferent about inspiring either one or the other of his admirers with any kind of passion whatever. The two latter, although with a woman's innate instinct they understood his indifference, and were secretly hurt at it, nevertheless continued to lavish on him the most passionate expressions of admiration of which the Spanish language is capable, as a means of evincing the interest they took in his proceedings.

These demonstrations grew at last so lively and pointed, that the greater number of the men present—who would each, in his secret heart, have given a good deal for the preference of either of these beautiful creatures—began, as is generally the case, to hate the muleteer for the indifference he displayed, and to upbraid him for serious want of politeness and unpardonable ignorance of good manners, in showing no gratitude for such enthusiastic praise.

The muleteer, embarrassed by the position in which he had involuntarily been placed while he was only laudably endeavouring to amuse himself, and compelled, as we may say, by his companions' murmurs of disapprobation, to re-establish his impugned reputation for courtesy, decided on finding some means or other of withdrawing honourably from his disagreeable situation, and with that purpose determined to ask the two girls to dance with him one after the other.

Full of these good intentions, as soon as the lieutenant—who had temporarily interrupted his inharmonious strumming to help himself to an immense goblet of *aguardiente*—began to rattle a fresh *zambacueca* on his guitar, the *arriero* advanced with a smile on his lips, and graciously saluted the two girls.

"Señorita," said he, to the one who chance to bed nearest, "will you make me happy by dancing this *zambacueca* with your humble servant?"

The girl, all rosy with delight at what she imagined the preference of the handsome dancer, was coming forward with outstretched hand, and beginning to reply, when suddenly her companion, who had turned pale on hearing the *arriero's* invitation, bounded between them like a tigress, and, with trembling lips and flaming eyes, confronted the young couple.

"You shall not dance together!" she cried in menacing tones.

The spectators of this extraordinary and unexpected scene recoiled in amazement: they were unable to comprehend this sudden burst of anger. The two would-be dancers exchanged looks of astonishment.

The situation grew intolerable, and the *arriero* determined to put an end to it.

The second girl was still standing right in front of him, her figure slightly thrown back, and firmly planted on her feet, her head erect, her cheeks inflamed, her nostrils quivering like those of a wild beast, and her arm extended in an attitude of menace and defiance.

The *arriero* took a step forward, and made a very respectful bow to the damsel.

"Señorita," said he, "allow me to remark—"

"*Calle Vd. la boca*" (hold your tongue), "Don Pablo!" she angrily exclaimed, interrupting him in the middle of his speech; "I have nothing to say against you; but look at this *chola sin vergüenza*" (shameless hussy), "who, knowing you to be the best dancer in the *rancho*, wants to monopolise you for her own benefit."

On hearing the insult her companion had thus boldly cast in her teeth, the other damsel hastily shook off Don Pablo, and placed herself face to face before her assailant.

"You lie, Manonga!" cried she: "It is jealousy that made you utter these words; you are furious at the preference with which this *caballero* honours me."

"I!" said the other disdainfully; "You are a fool, Clarita; I care no more for the *caballero* than for a sour orange."

"Indeed!" sneered Clarita; "Then, pray what may be the reason of this sudden fury?"

"Because," sharply retorted Manonga, "I have known you for a long time; you want a lesson, and I am going to give you one."

"You, indeed!" said the other, shrugging her shoulders; "Take care lest you get one yourself!"

"*Ojalá*; add another word, and, by my soul, I will knife you!"

"Pooh! you don't even know how to handle a navaja" (knife).

"*A ver;*" (we will see), shouted Manonga, beside herself with rage; and, bounding back, she drew a knife from her bosom, wrapped her *rebozo* (veil) round her left arm, and threw herself on guard.

"*A ver;*" screamed Clarita, echoing the words, and taking up her position with the same celerity as her adversary.

A duel between the two girls was imminent.

Don Pablo, the innocent cause of this combat, had several times vainly tried to mediate between the two females. Neither one nor the other would listen to his speech, nor attend to his remonstrances. When matters had reached this point, he wanted to make a fresh effort: but this time he was more sharply repulsed than before; for the bystanders, interested in the dispute, and infinitely attracted by the longing to see a duel with knives between two women, turned against him, and peremptorily bade him be quiet, and leave the *niñas* (darlings) to amuse themselves as they thought fit.

The *arriero*, thoroughly satisfied that he could wash his hands of the consequences, and whose good nature alone had induced him to attempt to prevent an explosion, saw that his mediation was looked upon with an unfavourable eye, so thought he had said his say; and, folding his arms, prepared to be, if not an indifferent, at least a disinterested spectator of the coming struggle.

It was, indeed, a singular and striking spectacle to see, in this dimly lighted room, amidst the crowd of strange costumes, these two girls, fiercely and resolutely standing two paces apart, ready to come to knife thrusts, while the music and the dance continued as if nothing was the matter, while the *aguardiente* was poured forth in floods, and while the merriest and maddest songs were shouted out around them.

"*¡Vaya pués!*" (now for the sport!) cried Clarita: "With how many inches do we fight, *querida?*" (my darling).

"With the whole length of the blade, *alma mía*" (my soul), answered Manonga; "I mean to leave my handwriting on your face!"

"Ah, *puñaladas!* We shall see. Are you ready, my dear?"

"As soon as you like, my pet!"

A ring was formed round the damsels, who, with bodies bent forward, left arms extended, and eye watching eye, waited, with feline impatience, for a propitious moment to rush upon each other.

They seemed well matched, both being young, active, and full of nerve. The *connoisseurs* in those matters, of whom there were many in the attentive crowd of bystanders, could form no opinion on the result of the combat, which threatened, for the matter of that, to be desperate, such flashes of ire sparkled from the wild eyes of the duellists.

After a moment or two of hesitation, or more properly speaking of gathering themselves up, Clarita and Manonga began to clack their tongues against their palates, producing a series of sharp smacking sounds; their blue gleaming knives glittered, and they darted upon each other.

But if the attack was lively, the defence and the parry was not less so. Both simultaneously bounded back, and fell into guard again. Each stroke had told; the battle had begun bravely, and either combatant had her face furrowed by a bleeding double cut. Neither one nor the other had predicted falsely: each bore the handwriting of the other on her countenance. The bystanders trembled with joy and admiration: never before had they been spectators of such a splendid *navajada*.

After taking breath for a while, the damsels were preparing to recommence the fight, this time with the determined purpose of making the bout decisive, when, all of a sudden, the ranks of the onlookers were shouldered right and left, and a man resolutely thrust himself between the two adversaries, and confronted them with a look of scorn.

"Hearken, *demonios!*" he cried in a sharp tone, and with accents of indescribable mockery.

The two women lowered their knives, and stood motionless, with eyes abashed, but head erect, their foreheads frowning, and preserving their attitude—the haughty expression of two foes who long to tear each other to pieces, and unwillingly succumb to commands, which they dare not disobey, though they curse them.

In spite of the deafening uproar the federalist lieutenant made with his guitar, he could not help hearing, at last, what was going on in the room. At the first impulse, he had placed his hand on the pistols which hung at his girdle; but an instant afterwards his anger grew, not calm, but cold and concentrated, instead of furious.

Don Torribio had risen from his seat, left the bench on which he sat enthroned, and furtively approached the combatants. He had attentively watched the different phases of the fight, and when he thought proper to interfere, had suddenly interposed between the duellists.

The soldiers had silently advanced behind their officer; they were now close at his heels, their hands on their weapons, ready for action at the first signal, foreseeing that Don Torribio's interference in this quarrel would speedily bring about another, in which they would have to take part.

Intuitively, the ring formed by the *arrieros* and wagoners had extended itself, and a large space was left open in the middle of the room. The two girls stood in the centre of the circle, knife in hand; and the lieutenant, with his arms crossed, amused himself by examining them narrowly, with a cynical sneer on his lips.

"Holloa, my chickens!" said he; "What! Are you ruffling your feathers for a cock? Is there only one on the perch? *¡Rayo de Dios!* What splendid St. Andrew's crosses you have dug in each other's faces! Are you both mad for love of this *pícaro?*" (ragamuffin).

Neither spoke; and the lieutenant continued his sarcastic speech:

"But where is this valiant champion, who lets the women fight for him? Does his modesty make him hide himself?"

Don Pablo came forward, looked the lieutenant straight in the face, and answered firmly: "Here I am."

"Aha!" said Don Torribio, staring at him for some time; "You are in truth a handsome fellow. I do not wonder at their passion for you."

The *arriero* remained mute, fully understanding the irony of the compliment.

"There, *niñas,*" the lieutenant went on speaking to the damsels, "which of you is the chosen one of this breaker of hearts? *¡Mil rayos!* Speak out!"

There was an interval of silence.

"Oh, that is it!" resumed Don Torribio; "You do not exactly know. Come, young fellow, do you speak, and tell me which of the two you prefer."

"I have no preference for either," said the *arriero* coolly.

"*¡Caramba!*" exclaimed the lieutenant, with pretended admiration; "*que gusto*" (what good taste.) "So I am to understand you love them both alike?"

"No; you are mistaken, señor. I love neither one nor the other."

"*¡Rayas pués!* That is a puzzler; and yet you let them fight for you. That is conduct worthy of chastisement, my master! As that is the case, I shall reconcile you two señoritas, and give a lesson to the discourteous *caballero* who flouts at the power of your black eyes. Upon my soul, such an insult calls for vengeance."

The spectators of the scene felt their hearts sink within them, while the soldiers laughed and jested among themselves.

On pronouncing his last words, the lieutenant drew a pistol from his belt, cocked it, and presented the muzzle at the breast of the *arriero*, who, motionless as ever, had made no gesture to escape the fate that threatened him.

But the two girls were roused. With the velocity of thought, they both at once threw themselves before him.

Manonga felt her breast pierced by the ball. "Alas!" she cried; "You despise me! What does it matter? I die for you! Clarita, I forgive you!"

Don Pablo bounded over the body of the luckless wretch, whose dying eyes still sought his, and threw himself, knife in hand, on the lieutenant. The latter hurled his heavy pistol at his head; but the *arriero* avoided the weapon, seized the officer round the body, and a deadly fray began. Clarita, with flaming eyes, eagerly watched the struggle between the two, ready to interfere as soon as an opportunity offered in favour of her beloved.

The bystanders were horrified; the dread inspired by the soldiers was so great, that although many more in number, and all armed, they dared not go to the assistance of their comrade.

In the meantime, the soldiers, more than half-drunk, seeing their officer struggling with a stranger, unsheathed their swords, and struck right and left among the crowd, shouting out their dreaded cry:

"*¡A degüello! ¡A degüello! los salvajes unitarios*" (Death, death to the savage Unitarians!)

Then ensued a scene of horror in the room, which was crowded with human beings.

The *arrieros*, pursued by the soldiers, who were pitilessly cutting them down, and calling to each other to slay, thronged towards the door to escape impending death. The disorder was at its height; all wanted to escape at once through the too narrow outlet. Made selfish by fear, and in the blind instinct of self-preservation, they stifled each other against the walls, crushed each other underfoot, and struck blindly with their knives, in order to hew themselves a passage through the human barrier that checked them.

Fear, when self-preservation is uppermost, makes man more cruel and cowardly than the wild beasts. That hideous egotism, which lurks at the bottom of the human heart, starts up when its bonds are suddenly broken. Man has then neither parents nor friends; he is deaf to every prayer; and, shutting his eyes, plunges forward with the blind and stupid ferocity of the maddened bull.

Blood soon flowed in torrents, and the victims increased in number, while the fury grew no less; nor did the assailed attempt to defend themselves.

At last the barrier gave way, and the wretches rushed out of doors, flying straight on, without knowing whither, in the sole thought of escaping from the butchery.

At this moment the corporal entered the room. A lamentable spectacle met his eyes: the floor was strewn with dead bodies, and wounded men weltering in their blood.

But he could not restrain a cry of horror when his eyes fell on Don Torribio. The lieutenant was tying the head of Don Pablo, which he had hacked off with his sword, to the long tresses of the fainting Clarita. The officer had been slightly wounded by the girl in the hip and arm, and blood was flowing from his garments.

"There," said he, having finished to his satisfaction the knot that bound Clarita's tresses to the long locks of the *arriero;* "since she loves him so dearly, when she comes to herself she can admire him at leisure, he is all her own now; no one will take him from her."

Then he looked for a time at the pale and fainting girl, with an expression of lust impossible to describe.

"Pooh!" said he, with a shrug of the shoulders; "Why should I? Let us wait till she opens her eyes. I shall have plenty of time to make love to her; and I want to enjoy her surprise when she wakes up."

And without another look at his victims, he set himself to help his soldiers in the massacre.

The first step he took, he encountered Luco.

"Halloa!" cried he; "where have you been, while we have been cutting up the *salvajes unitarios?* God take me! Here you come quietly; your sword in the sheath, and not a drop of blood on your clothes! What is the meaning of this conduct, comrade? Are you turned traitor, too, by chance?"

At this accusation the corporal feigned immense indignation. He frowned, bit his lip, and drew his sword, which he brandished menacingly.

"What words are those, lieutenant?" cried he. "Do you address such an insult to me? Do you call me, the most devoted partisan of our well-beloved General Rosas, a *salvaje unitario? ¡Vive Dios!*"

"Come, come; calm yourself," answered the lieutenant, who, like all men of his calibre, was as cowardly as he was cruel, and was intimidated by the pretended anger of the corporal; "I did not mean to insult you! I know you are to be trusted."

"It is well you say so," replied Luco; "for I have no mind to listen patiently to unjust reproach."

"Lose no more time in talking," said a soldier, interfering; "¡rayo de Dios! I have a capital idea."

"What is it?" asked Don Torribio. "Out with it, Eusebio, or it will blow you up."

The soldier laughed.

"This old hovel," said he, "is full of forage. Let us set fire to it, and roast in the flames all the salvajes unitarios who are here."

"¡Vive Dios!" cried Don Torribio, in high glee; "that is a capital idea. We will set about it at once. The general will be pleased enough when he knows we have rid him so expeditiously of a harbour for his enemies. Two of you arrange the straw properly, while we mount and chase those rascals back here. Not a soul of these malvados (malicious rogues) shall escape the punishment he richly deserves."

The lieutenant then signed to the soldiers to leave.

"I," said Luco, "will keep the door, so that no one inside can come out."

"That will do, my good fellow," answered Don Torribio. "Ah!" he added suddenly, as his eye fell on the poor girl extended on the floor, with the head of him she loved tied to her tresses; "here Eusebio! do not forget to place two or three bundles of straw under that sweet child. The dirty floor is a hard couch for her, and I want her to sleep sweetly."

He left the room, grinning like a demon.

He had scarcely got outside, before the corporal, without uttering a word, raised his sword, and, with one blow, cleft Eusebio to the chine. The wretch fell without a cry, like an ox that is slaughtered.

The second soldier who was present exhibited no signs of emotion.

"That was a pretty blow, Luco," said he, twisting his long gray moustache; "but are you not a little too precipitate?"

The corporal made him a sign to be silent, and, peering out of doors, listened attentively. A cry, low as the softest breath of the wind, met his ear.

"No Muñoz," he answered, "I am not too hasty; for there is the signal."

Then, putting the first finger of each hand into his mouth, he gave a whistle, so sharp and prolonged, that those present crouched against the walls, and trembled with fear, not knowing what new evil this portentous signal might bring upon them.

"*¡Sangre de Cristo!*" cried Luco, addressing the terrified *arrieros*, crouching on the floor, "Are you going to stay here and be massacred like stupid ostriches? Take courage *caray!* seize your weapons, and range yourselves by the side of those who have come to save you!"

The poor devils shook their heads in despair. Terror had deprived them of all energy, and they were incapable of organizing the least resistance.

The shouting of the soldiery was heard on every side, as they excited each other in their human chase; and each moment, wretches who had been hunted up from all corners, rushed in to seek a precarious refuge in the room whence they had escaped a few minutes previously.

Don Torribio, almost certain that he had driven all his game into the net, signalled to his soldiers to leave off, and ordered them to enter the *rancho*.

All of a sudden the galloping of several horses was heard; six cavaliers rode fiercely up, and ranged themselves in battle array before the door of the house.

The lieutenant started when he saw them, went to his horse, and made as if he would mount.

"Who are you, *caballeros?*" said he in menacing tones; "And how dare you dispute my passage?"

"You shall soon know, Don Torribio the Butcher," said a voice, whose mocking accent made the lieutenant turn pale.

# CHAPTER XVIII
# TREACHERY

There is one remark which has been often made. It is this: That, generally speaking, men who delight to dabble in gore—who unhesitatingly commit the most atrocious cruelties, and exercise their powers in exciting the terror they love to inspire—are cowards; and when they happen to meet with effective resistance, their cowardice falls to a baseness beyond comparison. Jackals and hyenas are ferocious and cowardly; men are jackals and hyenas—the thing is explained.

At the answer of the leader of the strangers, the *mashorqueras* became convulsed with terror. They comprehended that they were face to face with resolute foes, without having it in their power to retreat an inch. They crowded close to each other, and fixed their eyes in fright and amazement on the six men who, sitting calmly and impassively before them, bid them defiance.

Don Torribio alone felt no fear. The man was a savage brute, whom the smell of blood intoxicated, and who could only breathe freely in an atmosphere of carnage. Crossing his arms and raising his head defiantly, he answered the words of the unknown with a long laugh of contempt; then, turning to his terror-stricken soldiers:

"Will you suffer yourselves to be intimidated by six men?" he cried. "Come, my children; face about. *¡Vive Dios!* these *pícaros* dare not stand against us."

The soldiers, aroused by the tones of the voice they had so long obeyed, and ashamed of their hesitation, fell in as well as they could, and formed a line in front of the *rancho*. The lieutenant, putting spurs to his horse, made him execute a *demivolte*, and resolutely placed himself at the head of his troop. The strangers, notwithstanding the inequality of numbers, did not hesitate a moment, but charged the federalists sword and pistol in hand. Don Torribio received them bravely without retreating a foot. Having discharged their pistols, they took to the sword, and in an instant the *mêlée* grew terrible. In spite of their prodigies of valour and gigantic efforts, the strangers would, in all probability, have had the worst of it, when suddenly Corporal Luco, who had remained spectator of the fight, with four or five of his comrades, made his horse bound to the front, and, instead of ranging himself on the side of the federalists, attacked them vigorously in flank, and came with his comrades to place himself beside Don Leoncio.

This defection of a party of his soldiers raised Don Torribio's ire to seething point—the more so, as the *mashorqueras*, not knowing to what cause to attribute the strange conduct of the corporal and his comrades, began to suspect treason, to lose courage, and to reply but feebly to the blows of the assailants; who, seeing them falter, redoubled their efforts for victory.

The *arrieros* and wagoners, having in some measure recovered from their fright, and seeing the favourable opportunity of avenging the insults and villainies the hirelings of Rosas had so long heaped upon them, armed themselves with anything that fell in their way, and, burning to make up for lost time, rushed headforemost on their ferocious enemies.

But at this very moment loud cries reached their ears. Some forty mounted men entered at full gallop the zone of light proceeding from the post house, and, deploying with amazing dexterity and despatch, surrounded the *rancho* on all sides.

The riders who had galloped up so opportunely for the assailants and so inopportunely for the *colorados*, were Don Guzman de Ribera and his *peones*.

Having left Buenos Aires several hours ago, they ought long before this to have reached the *rancho*, which lay on the road they had to follow in order to get to the *hacienda* where Don Guzman hoped to meet his brother. But at a little distance from the town, Don Bernardo Pedrosa had managed somehow or other to cut his bonds; he slipped off the horse on which he had been placed, threw himself among the tall grasses, and disappeared before anyone suspected his flight.

Don Guzman had lost a good deal of time in marching for the fugitive, whose traces he could not find, and had only abandoned the pursuit when convinced that all his efforts to recover his prisoner were in vain. Recalling his *peones*, who were scattered right and left, he had resumed the road to the *hacienda*, feeling extremely uneasy for the consequences of his prisoner's escape; for he knew Don Bernardo too well to suppose for an instant that he would not strain every nerve to avenge the insult he had met with at his hands.

When Don Guzman was still about half a league from the *rancho*, some fugitives, escaped from the massacre, had run blindly among his men, and warned him of what was going on. Without suspecting how important these news might be to himself, his natural generosity excited the wish to assist, if possible, the persons engaged in this terrible affray; so Don Guzman, well acquainted with the ferocity of the Buenos-Airean tyrant ruffians, had increased the pace of his horses, and galloped in to aid the unfortunate people in their contest with the *mashorqueras*. His unexpected arrival decided the affair.

The lieutenant, finding flight impossible, retired step by step, fighting like a lion, and withdrew all his men into the *rancho*, himself remaining last in order to secure their retreat.

Don Torribio—the Butcher, as he was called—scorned to ask quarter. He himself had never granted it to a soul. The extremity to which he found himself reduced, far from diminishing his courage, had increased it tenfold. Feeling his last hour was come—that no human aid could save him—he resolved to fight to the last breath, and sell his life as dearly as possible.

The *mashorqueras*, following the example of their leader, drew fresh courage from the depths of their despair, and once within the *rancho*, busied themselves in fortifying it, so as to carry on the strife as long as they could, and to fall after an heroic resistance.

The doors and windows were barricaded with the utmost care; holes were knocked in the walls; and the ruffians, half-intoxicated with previous and still-continued libations, waited firmly for the attack, determined to die bravely in the assault their enemies would soon make on the *rancho*.

However contrary to their expectations, a long time elapsed without their adversaries commencing the attack. This suspension of hostilities, which was incomprehensible,—for they were ignorant of all that was going on outside,—gave them great uneasiness, and made the bravest of them tremble.

Man is so constituted that, however firmly he may have made up his mind to face death—however convinced he may be that his last hour is come—however prepared for the struggle, the consequences of which he knows and accepts beforehand—if that final struggle is delayed, his resolution fades, the fever that sustained him dies out, and he begins to fear, not death, for that he knows to be inevitable, but the agonies which he fancies may precede death. He creates a thousand sinister chimeras; and the unknown danger which threatens him, without his being able to divine how or whence it will come, appears to him a thousand times more terrible than that which he was prepared to face bravely and with a resolute heart.

The *mashorqueras* vainly sought, in copious draughts of *aguardiente*, a remedy for the wild terror which gradually overcame them. The mournful silence which reigned around them, the obscurity, wrapping them up as in a shroud, and the forced inaction to which they were condemned, concurred, in spite of their efforts, to increase the invincible terror that had seized upon them. The lieutenant alone preserved his ferocious energy, and awaited patiently the striking of the hour for his last battle.

Let us see what was passing among the assailants, and what had occasioned the delay in the assault.

Don Guzman de Ribera, as soon as the soldiers had shut themselves up in the *rancho*, wished to know, before he finished with the latter, who the persons were to whom his providential arrival had done such good service.

It was not long before his curiosity was satisfied; his brother Don Leoncio, who had recognised him from the first, rushed forward to offer his thanks.

The two brothers, who had been so long separated, threw themselves into each other's arms with tears of joy, and for some time forgot everything but themselves in the unexpected happiness of meeting.

When the first shock of their sudden reunion was over, Don Guzman took his brother's hand, and, leading him apart, uttered the single word, "Well?" with a smile which was intended to be gay.

"She is here," said Don Leoncio, trying to stifle a sigh.

"Did she consent to come?"

"It was she who wished it."

"That is indeed astonishing," said Don Guzman.

"Why so? Doña Antonia is one of those rare spirits who never recoil before an obligation, however hard it may be, when they know that honour binds them."

"True. Well, be it so; it is perhaps better as it is and that she is with you."

"Have you forgotten, brother, what occurred exactly a year ago today, at sunrise, between you and me, when, in a moment of folly, I confessed to you my love for Doña Antonia de Solis?"

"What is the good of recurring to it, brother? We are reconciled now, thank God; and I hope nothing may happen to separate us again."

"Do not hope so, brother," replied Don Leoncio in melancholy accents.

"What do you mean, brother? My wife—"

"Your wife has never ceased to be worthy of you; you will go and see her?"

Don Guzman hesitated.

"No," said he, at length; "not now; let us first finish with these rascals; then I will give myself up to happiness."

"Let it be so," said Don Leoncio, rejoiced.

Two persons now made their appearance; they were Don Diego de Solis, and Doña Antonia, his sister, and the wife of Don Guzman.

On seeing his wife, who had been compelled to withdraw from Buenos Aires in order to escape from the pursuit of Don Bernardo Pedrosa, Don Guzman, notwithstanding his resolve not to make himself known to her for the present, could not resist the temptation of pressing her to his heart.

The lady uttered a cry of joy on finding herself once more in her husband's arms.

Don Leoncio, a few months after the confession he had made to his brother, seemed to have forgotten his passion, and had espoused the second sister of Don Diego de Solis, four months prior to the day the events of which we are now recording.

So when Don Guzman was forced into a temporary separation from his wife, he had not hesitated to confide her to his brother, convinced that the latter's love for Doña Antonia had changed into honourable and lasting friendship.

"Why have you returned?" said Don Guzman, kissing his wife.

"It was necessary," she replied in a low voice, and suppressing a gesture of fear; "my sister herself recommended me to do so."

"It was very imprudent, my darling."

"Oh! I have no fears at your side. Will you not embrace your son, too?"

"Have you brought him with you?"

"I will not leave you again, whatever may happen." Then, bending to her husband's ear she whispered: "Your brother is as much in love with me as ever; his wife discovered his passion for me, and it is she and Don Diego who advised my return, as my position was growing intolerable."

Don Guzman's eyes flashed fire.

"They did well," said he; "but silence: my brother is watching us."

In fact, Don Leoncio, uneasy at this conversation apart, had guessed, with the intuition peculiar to the guilty, that he was the subject of their discussion, and exhibited signs of restlessness which all his efforts could not conceal. At last, unable to bear the suspense any longer, he approached his brother, and said to him curtly:

"What are we to do now?"

"Whatever you please," answered Don Guzman, who had been disagreeably affected by the sound of his voice after what his wife had told him.

Don Leoncio perceived the aversion his brother felt for him; he bit his lips, but dissembled his resentment.

"It is for you to decide," said he, "since it is you who have rescued us."

"I am at your service, brother. Don Diego," he continued, turning to the young man, "I trust my wife to your care. We shall most likely commence the assault at once. She and her infant must not be exposed to danger."

"Set your heart at rest: I will be answerable for them," said Diego, pressing his hand.

Before he left her, Doña Antonia threw herself once more on her husband's breast.

"Beware!" she whispered in his ear; "Don Leoncio is meditating treason against you."

"He would not dare!" firmly replied Don Guzman.

"Go; and fear not."

The lady, only half-consoled, followed her brother, and the two soon disappeared behind the bales and wagons.

The two brothers were left alone, and there was a long silence between them.

Don Guzman, with his arms crossed, and his head bent down, was in deep meditation.

Don Leoncio was watching his brother intently, with a strange expression on his countenance, and a sardonic smile on his lips.

At last Don Guzman raised his head.

"Enough of this," he said, "it has lasted too long." Don Leoncio started: he fancied these words were addressed to him; but his brother continued:

"Before attacking these ruffians we must summon them to surrender."

"Can you think of such a thing, brother. These men are *mashorqueras!*"

"So much the greater reason to prove to them that we are not rascals of their own kind, and that we practise the laws of warfare, which they glory in setting at nought."

"I submit, brother; although I know we are only losing valuable time."

Don Leoncio immediately ordered torches of resinous wood to be lighted, so that the besieged might clearly see him; and, tying his handkerchief to the point of his sword, resolutely advanced towards the *rancho*.

When Don Torribio saw the light of the torches, he comprehended that the assailants wished to enter into communication with him, and unbarred a window, holding himself in readiness for the parley.

As soon as Don Leoncio got within a pace or two of the door, he halted.

"Flag of truce!" said he.

A window was thrown open, at which the burly figure of the lieutenant made its appearance.

"What is it you want?" he replied, carelessly leaning his elbows on the windowsill.

"We demand that you surrender," said Don Leoncio.

"Do you, really?" said Don Torribio, bursting into a laugh; "And why do you want us to surrender?"

"Because all resistance is futile."

"You think so, do you?" replied the officer, with another laugh; "Try and dislodge us, and see what it will cost you!"

"Much less than you think."

"Pooh! I should be glad to know how."

"Enough! Will you surrender, or not?"

"It is ridiculous! May the devil embrace me, if you know with whom you have to deal! Do we ever demand quarter—we, *mashorqueras?* If we surrender, you will kill us, that is all. What is the good of it?"

"Then you are determined not to listen to terms?"

"Upon my soul, this is growing too tiresome!"

"You are resolved to defend yourself to the last?"

"*Canarios*, comrade! I should think so; tooth and nail. I will not stay any longer. Be off!"

"Well, we shall have you all soon."

"Try it, *compadre;* try it. In the meantime, as your conversation has little attraction for me, I shall take the liberty of breaking it off. Good luck!"

Saying this, he closed the window abruptly.

Don Leoncio turned to his brother, who had advanced to his side.

"Did I not tell you so?" said he, with a shrug; "Was I mistaken?"

"No; I admit it. Now, having saved our honour, we can act as we please."

Don Guzman leaned towards his brother, and spoke a few words in his ear; the latter smiled, and left him.

The *peones, arrieros,* and wagoners were posted behind the *galeras,* so as to be sheltered from the balls of the besieged. There they awaited the signal for the assault.

Don Leoncio busied himself during all this time in heaping dry grass and branches around the *rancho.* When sufficient had been collected, he set fire to it, and his men cast their burning torches on the roof.

The fire, fed by the wind, soon extended itself; and in a very short time the *rancho* was enveloped in flames.

The besieged gave vent to a cry of horror; the besiegers replied by a shout of triumph.

After all, the *mashorqueras* had no reason to complain; it was meted to them as they would have meted to others: they were undergoing the *lex talionis.*

In the meanwhile, the position of the besieged grew intolerable. Blinded by the smoke and scorched by the fire, which ran up the walls in long tongues of flame, calcining as they licked them, a sortie became inevitable, if they would not be burnt alive.

The lieutenant ordered the door to be unfastened: he opened it suddenly, and threw himself, followed by his men, into the thickest ranks of the assailants.

The latter opened their ranks to receive them, then closed in upon them, and surrounded them with a circle of steel.

At the moment when the last morsel of wall crashed into the fiery furnace, the last *mashorquera* fell, with his head cloven to the chine. All had fallen around Don Torribio, who had fought to the last moment with the desperate frenzy which makes a man almost invincible.

The sun rose in his majesty, illumining the savage depths of the Pampas.

The *arrieros* and wagoners, cowed by the night's work, and dreading the consequences, hastened to span the oxen to the heavy *galeras,* and load their mules. Anxious to quit the place, they were soon dispersing in all directions. Don Guzman and his *peones* remained masters of the field.

Soon after the attack commenced, Don Guzman was surprised that he did not see his brother near him; but he did not attach much importance to the fact, being more seriously occupied with other matters. Now, when the affray was over, he burned with desire to see his wife. He was amazed that Don Diego had not brought her to him as soon as all danger for her was over.

But he was not very anxious. Don Diego had probably not wished to expose the lady to the horror of crossing the field of battle, and soiling her feet with the blood in which the earth was soaked. He applauded his delicacy, and waited a few minutes, during which he repaired the disorder of his dress, and removed the traces of the combat.

At last he determined to look for his wife, whose long absence began to make him very uneasy.

Corporal Luco, as anxious as himself, undertook to guide him; he had a faint recollection of seeing Don Diego, accompanied by Doña Antonia, the nurse, and two or three more, going in the direction of a hollow in the ground at a little distance.

All of a sudden, the two men uttered a shout of sorrow, and recoiled in horror from the dreadful spectacle before their eyes.

Don Diego was lying on the ground, his chest pierced through and through. He was dead; and close to him Doña Antonia and the nurse were lying senseless. The nurse was Corporal Luco's wife.

Don Guzman fell on his knees beside his wife; he then perceived a paper, which she was clutching convulsively in her right hand.

The unhappy man had great difficulty in releasing it from her grasp; some words were written on it. Don Guzman cast his eyes over the lines, and threw himself on the ground with an agonising cry of despair.

The paper contained these words:

"Brother,—You have deprived me of the woman I love; I deprive you of your son: we are quits."

"DON LEONCIO DE RIBERA."

No doubts were possible after reading this: Don Leoncio was really the author of this odious abduction. He had contrived this horrible piece of treachery while his brother was coming, in all his confidence, to meet him. With an incredible refinement of wickedness, and in order to enjoy his revenge to the utmost, he had delayed the stroke, with the determination to make it fall on his brother's head like a thunderbolt.

For a long time, Don Guzman remained crouching on the Pampas, holding in his arms the lifeless body of his wife, whom he tried in vain to resuscitate. He lay there, absorbed in doubts, and trembling; seeing nothing; hearing nothing; lamenting the death of his wife; deprived of his child.

He was suddenly roused by a heavy stroke on his shoulder. He raised his head. A man was standing before him, with a smile on his lips.

"Don Guzman de Ribera," said he, with a mocking salutation, "you are my prisoner."

It was Don Bernardo Pedrosa, with a numerous escort of soldiers.

# CHAPTER XIX
# THE END OF THE STORY

Here Don Estevan paused in his recital.

"All this is frightful!" exclaimed Don Fernando, in accents of mingled anger and pity.

"It is not all," replied the other.

"But what connection has this horrible story with Don Pedro de Luna?"

"Did I not tell you when I first began that the history was his?"

"You did; but, carried away by the dreadful incidents of your narrative, I lost sight of the personages. My whole mind was so excited, that I fancied myself a spectator of the scenes that passed before me with such giddy rapidity, and did not recollect that one of the actors was so close to us. But how does it happen that you are so well acquainted with the details of this miserable tragedy?"

"I have heard them told many and many a day, from infancy till now that I am a man. My father was the Corporal Luco, whom you have seen so devoted to the Ribera family. My poor mother was the nurse, and I am foster brother to Don Guzman's child; for we were born about the same date, and my mother, who was brought up in the family, was very anxious to nurse us both, insisting that, in imbibing the same milk as my young master, my devotion to him would be endless. Alas! God has decided otherwise; he is dead."

"Who can tell?" said Don Fernando, with gentle pity; "Perhaps he may make his appearance again some day."

"Alas! We have no longer any hope. More than twenty years have elapsed since the frightful catastrophe, and during all that time no efforts, however active, have sufficed to lift a corner of the mysterious veil which conceals the fate of the poor child."

"His poor mother must have suffered dreadfully."

"She went mad. But the sun is rapidly sinking to the horizon, and night will be here before two hours have passed. Let me finish my tale, by telling you what happened after the arrest of Don Guzman."

"Go on, my friend; I am anxious to know the end of this dark story."

Don Guzman replied by a smile of contempt to the summons of Colonel Bernardo Pedrosa. He raised his wife in his arms, and prepared to follow his enemy. Notwithstanding his hatred of Don Guzman, Don Bernardo was a man of the world; the misery which overwhelmed the man he had so long persecuted touched his heart. His pity was aroused, and on his way back to Buenos Aires he showed the greatest consideration, treating him with all the respect his unhappy position demanded.

The Dictator was furious at the massacre of his hirelings. Rejoiced at finding a plausible pretext to free himself from a man whom, on account of his great reputation and influence amongst the highest classes of society, he had hitherto dreaded to attack, Rosas determined to make a terrible example of him. Rudely separated from his wife, the prisoner was cast into one of those horrible dungeons in which the tyrant's victims languished, awaiting the tortures he prepared for them.

But the Dictator's vengeance was not destined to be as complete as he hoped. The French and English consuls, moved by pity for the miserable state to which Doña Antonia was reduced, made energetic remonstrances to the tyrant, and even went several times to Palermo to hunt up the savage in his lair In short, by dint of prayers and menaces, they obtained the release of the poor woman, and her restoration to her family; Rosas gnashing his teeth and foaming with rage when he granted the favour. But he did not dare to brave the consuls, and felt his want of power to cope with them. Thanks to this beneficent intervention, and the mighty power they exercised in her behalf, Doña Antonia, at least, escaped the tortures the tyrant was preparing to inflict.

As to Don Guzman, all attempts in his favour were unsuccessful. Rosas not only refused to release him, but even to mitigate the terrible treatment to which he was ordered to be subjected in prison.

Unfortunately, Don Guzman was guilty in the eye of the law. The consuls could take no official steps and were obliged to desist, for fear of exasperating the tiger to heap greater injuries on the man in whom they took such lively interest.

Six months had elapsed since Don Guzman was arrested. Thanks to the care with which Doña Antonia was surrounded, she recovered her reason. But her position was thereby rendered worse; for she was now able to appreciate her calamity to its fullest extent. She comprehended how great was her misfortune; and her despair reduced her to such utter prostration, that her life was in danger.

While this was going on, the rumour was spread abroad that Don Guzman, who had seemed forgotten in his dungeon, was to be brought up for judgment, and shortly to appear before a court martial.

Rosas eagerly seized the opportunity of giving all publicity to a trial for high treason, hoping to make men forget the murders committed in his name, in the interest of the discussion which would arise concerning the trial.

The report was soon officially confirmed; the day was named on which Don Guzman was to appear before his judges.

But there is one person of whom we have not spoken for some time, and to whom we must now recur, —no other than Corporal Luco.

The worthy corporal, when he saw the *arrieros* and wagoners go off, and that Don Leoncio had abandoned his brother with the greater number of *peones*, did not attempt to deceive himself as to his own position. A traitor and deserter, the least that could happen to him would be to be shot. So when, by the first rays of the rising sun, he saw a cloud of dust rising afar off in the Pampas, he concluded that soldiers must be hidden by it; that these soldiers were coming to avenge their comrades, whom he, Luco, had helped to slay with so much good will; and that if they caught him, they would instantly shoot him. The prospect was not pleasant to the corporal; at the same time he loved his master, and could not resolve to leave him. He was thus in great perplexity, and unable to come to a decision, though time pressed.

Luckily his wife came to the rescue, and made him comprehend that any attempt, in Don Guzman's present state, to induce him to fly must fail; that, after all, it was better to preserve his freedom, in order to use it hereafter to obtain his master's; and lastly, that he too, Luco, was a father, who ought to save his life for his child's sake.

All these reasons conquered the corporal's hesitation. He seized one horse, his wife another; and both vanished on one side, while the soldiers came up on the other.

When he arrived at Buenos Aires, a bright idea struck him. Excepting Muñoz and three other soldiers who had taken his part and fought with him against their former comrades, all the *mashorqueras* had been slain. Not one remained to accuse the corporal of the treason of which he felt himself guilty. Muñoz, whom he encountered strutting before the gates of Buenos Aires waiting for his arrival, banished all his scruples.

Taking up his part directly, the worthy corporal accompanied by his confederates, went straight to his colonel, to whom he told his own version of what had happened at the *rancho*, launching out in invectives and threats of vengeance against Don Guzman, for whom he expressed the utmost abhorrence.

His artifice succeeded beyond his expectations. The colonel charmed with his conduct, and trusting to his tale, made him a sergeant, and gave the corporal's stripe to Muñoz. The brave *colorados* overwhelmed the colonel with thanks and protestations of devotion to Rosas, and retired, laughing in their sleeve.

Luco managed so well during the six months before Don Guzman's trial, and gave such convincing proofs of his attachment to the cause of the Dictator, that the latter, deceived in turn, although, like all other tyrants, he made a virtue of distrust, reposed the greatest confidence in him; and when the sergeant asked to command the guard which was to take charge of Don Guzman during the trial, not the least objection was made. This was exactly what the sergeant wanted: all his machinations during these six months tended to this one aim; so, when the day for the trial was named, he prepared his batteries, and kept himself ready for action when the critical moment should come. Luco had sworn to save his master; and what the sergeant once resolved, he carried out, let the consequences be what they would.

Unhappily, the greatest obstacles in the way of the sergeant under these circumstances came from Don Guzman himself. The prisoner wished to die. For a long time Luco racked his brain in vain attempts at finding some means to persuade him to relinquish the feeling. To all his arguments Don Guzman replied, that his cup was full; that life was a burden to him; and that death was the only good he could henceforth look for.

The sergeant shook his head, and retired, perfectly convinced of the fallacy of the arguments. At length he arrived one day at the dungeon, and opened the door with a countenance so radiant with joy, that his master could not help remarking it, and asking what had made him so happy.

"Ah," replied the sergeant, "at last I have found out the way to convince you."

"You are dreadfully tenacious of your plan to save me," said Don Guzman, with a mournful smile.

"More so than ever, ¡canarios! This time there will be no doubt about your compliance. In two days you shall judge for yourself."

"So much the better," said Don Guzman, sighing; "it will be over the sooner."

"Good! We are not so badly off for friends as you think, señor—amongst others, the French and English consuls. There is a fine French schooner in the harbour, which only waits for your presence on board to sail directly."

"Then she runs the risk of never leaving Buenos Aires."

"Pooh! pooh! I am of a different opinion—I think quite the contrary. I have come to an understanding with the French consul. The day after tomorrow the schooner will set sail: she will send a boat to fetch you, and will hug the coast till you come. Once under the protection of the French flag, who will dare to touch you?"

"For the last time, listen to me, Luco," said Don Guzman firmly: "I will not—understand me—I will not be saved. I intend that the infamy of my death shall cover the Dictator with confusion. I thank you for your devotion, my good old servant; but I demand that you cease to compromise yourself by your efforts for me. Let us speak no more of it."

"Then," said the sergeant, "your mind is quite made up? Nothing can change your determination?"

"Alas! One single person might have that influence over me; but that person is in ignorance of all that happens around her. Happily for her, she has lost her reason, and with reason her memory—that incurable cancer of a broken heart."

The sergeant smiled, and, opening his uniform produced a letter from his breast, and, without a word, handed it to Don Guzman.

"What is this, Luco?" said the latter, as he hesitated to take the letter.

"Read it, mi amo," replied the sergeant. "I wanted to give you a complete surprise; but you are so obstinate, I am obliged to deploy my forces."

Don Guzman opened the letter with trembling hands, and rapidly ran through it.

"Almighty Father!" he exclaimed, "Is it possible? Doña Antonia has recovered her reason, and bids me live!"

"Will you obey this time, mi amo?"

"Do what you will, Luco; I will obey you in all things. Oh, how I wish to live now!"

"¡*Cuerpo de Cristo!* You shall live, *mi amo*. I swear it to you."

With this consoling promise, Luco quitted the prison.

The day of Guzman's trial arrived at last. The Dictator, who knew how much sympathy the prisoner excited, considered it prudent to make a grand military display on the occasion. The city was literally crammed with troops, the precautions being taken more for the purpose of intimidating the friends of the prisoner, than as precautionary measures against an escape, which he deemed impossible.

The French schooner, as Luco had predicted, sent a boat's crew ashore, on the pretence of closing the agent's accounts; she then weighed anchor, and stood on and off in the river expecting her boat.

The detachment detailed to escort the prisoner was strong, and composed entirely of *colorados*, Rosa's most devoted troops. It was placed under the command of Colonel Don Bernardo de Pedrosa; the special platoon in charge of the prisoner was under the orders of Sergeant Luco and Corporal Muñoz.

Twenty minutes before the specified time for commencing the march to the court, Luco entered his master's dungeon, and had a final conversation with him. He then gave him two pairs of pistols and a poniard, and left him, saying;

"Remember *mi amo*, to keep quite quiet till you hear the words, never mind from whom: 'To the devil with the sun! It blinds one!'—that is your signal."

"Make yourself easy; I will not forget. Remember your promise to kill me, rather than to let me fall again into the hands of the tyrant."

"Enough, *mi amo*. Pray God to help us; we stand in great need of Him."

"Farewell, Luco: you are right; I will pray."

The two men parted, not to meet again till the decisive moment.

However, the sergeant grew more anxious as that moment approached. The formidable preparations of the Dictator raised his secret apprehensions. But he gave no signs of his perturbation, for fear of discouraging his accomplices; on the contrary, he affected an air of perfect confidence, though he kept grumbling under his moustache: "Never mind, it will be a hard tussle; we shall have plenty of firing."

Soon after, the clock of the cabildo (court of justice) struck ten. The drum called the soldiers to arms; the gossips in the street stretched their heads forward, murmuring an "Ah!" of satisfaction: all eyes were fixed on the prison.

They had not long to wait. At the close of a few minutes, the prison door opened, and the prisoner came forth. His face was pale, calm, and stamped with indomitable resolution. He marched quietly in the middle of a dozen soldiers commanded by Sergeant Luco. The latter, as if wishing to be specially careful of his prisoner, strode on his right, Muñoz on his left, almost side by side with Don Guzman.

The platoon was preceded by a strong detachment of *colorados*, at the head of which curveted Colonel Don Bernardo de Pedrosa on a magnificent coal-black stallion; in rear of the prisoner there was a second detachment, as strong as the one in advance. The procession advanced slowly between two mournful and silent crowds of people, who were with difficulty kept down by two lines of sentries.

It was one of those magnificent spring mornings which South America alone has the privilege of producing. The fresh breeze from the Pampas, laden with odoriferous scents, rustled in the leaves and branches of the gardens attached to the houses, and cooled the air heated by the beams of the tropical sun.

The procession still continued its march. In spite of the danger which lay in any exhibition of sympathy for the prisoner, the crowd respectfully uncovered as he passed. He, calm and dignified as at the moment he quitted the prison, marched on, his hat in his hand, saluting, right and left, the people who were not afraid of testifying their respect.

Two-thirds of the road had already been travelled; a few minutes more, and the prisoner would reach the tribunal, when, in the Calle de la Federación, several spectators, no doubt too rudely pushed back by the soldiers lining the road, resisted the pressure to which they were subjected, drove back the sentries, and, for a moment, almost broke their line. As the procession approached, this tumult gradually increased: cries, recriminations, and threats were bandied about with the vivacity and rapidity peculiar to the races of the South, until what seemed at first sight to be a squabble of no importance, began to assume the dimensions of a veritable riot.

Don Bernardo, uneasy at the noise he heard, left the head of the escort, and came galloping back to ascertain what was going on, and to pacify the tumult.

Unluckily, the popular feeling had risen with so much rapidity, that at several points the ranks had been broken, the soldiers isolated, and—how it happened no one could say—disarmed, with unexampled celerity, by persons of whom they had no knowledge. In short the procession was cut in two.

Don Bernardo saw at a glance the gravity of the situation. Making way, with considerable difficulty, through the crowd, he rode up to the sergeant, who, cool and imperturbable, still stuck to his prisoner.

"Aha!" said the colonel, with a sigh of satisfaction, "Take me good care of the prisoner. Close up! I fear you will be obliged to open a passage by main force."

"We will open one, do not you be alarmed, colonel. But to the devil with the sun! It blinds one."

The moment he uttered these words, a soldier who was close at hand seized the colonel's leg, and threw him from his horse on the ground. In the same instant, Luco caught hold of the bridle, while Don Guzman, rapid as thought vaulted into the saddle.

What we have related took place so suddenly, and the whole was done so adroitly, that Don Bernardo, completely confounded, was nailed to the ground by a bayonet before he could comprehend what was happening: it is even probable that he died without guessing the cause of the riot.

In the meantime, the twelve riders of the platoon had closed around their ex-prisoner, and started at full speed through the thickest of the throng.

Then a curious thing occurred: these inquisitive gapers, who were an instant before so crowded and compact that they had broken through the line of soldiery, open right and left before the fugitives, shouted their joy at their success, and, the moment they had passed, closed up the breach they had themselves made, and again presented an impassable human barrier to the rearguard, which vainly strove to break it.

Armed men seemed to start suddenly out of the ground, gave the soldiers back blow for blow, and offered a resistance sufficiently energetic to allow time for the fugitives to secure their safety.

Then, suddenly as if by enchantment, these menacing crowds, which had so lately disputed the ground, retreated, melted away, in some manner or another; and that so speedily, that when the soldiers, recovered from

206 | The Bee Hunters

their surprise, were prepared for a vigoro·
front of them: the insurgents had disa᷑
behind them.

This audacious affray might ᴠ
that, on one side, the prisoner had ᴠ
Pedrosa, and five or six soldiers, lay w
proving the reality of the daring *coup-de-ι.*
such remarkable audacity and success.

Don Guzman and his companions found ι
waiting for them. Five minutes later, they were ᴠ
and when pursuit was ordered, the schooner cou.
horizon, like a halcyon's wing balanced on the breeze.

On board the schooner Don Guzman found his w᷑
sailed for Veracruz.

We have already related the decision which Don Guzmaɴ
and in what manner he carried it out.

In order to insure the success of the researches he was about to mᴠ
find his son, and to secure his own tranquillity, Don Guzman, on setting ι
in Mexico, resigned his own name for that of Don Pedro de Luna, to whicι
he had a right, and under which we shall still continue to designate him.
[1] He hoped by these means to escape the persecutions of Don Leoncio,
whose hatred, still unsatiated by the abduction of the child, might possibly
lead him to attempt to add his brother as another victim.

Don Guzman's calculations were correct, or seemed so. Since his
departure from Buenos Aires, he had never heard of his brother: no one
knew what had become of him, nor whether he were alive or dead.

Five years after his arrival at the *hacienda*, a fresh misfortune overtook
the poor exile. Doña Antonia, who had never completely recovered the
shock to her mind, the consequences of the terrible occurrences in the
Pampas, and whose health had always languished since, had expired in his
arms, after giving birth to a daughter.

This daughter was the charming girl whom we have presented to our
readers under the name of Doña Hermosa.

From that time forth, Don Pedro concentrated his affections on this
delicate creature, the only bond which attached him to an existence which

ppy, and which, struck by the cold breath of adversity,
ne so miserable.

no had accompanied him into exile, he alone remained.
dead: he had seen them sink, one after another, into the
Luco's wife, the confidante of her master's sorrows, was
ne education of his daughter; a charge she executed with care
beyond praise.

s the tale related by the *major-domo*. In order that the reader may
stand the events recorded in subsequent chapters, it is necessary
him that Doña Hermosa was sixteen at the commencement of our
d that four years intervened between the retirement of Don Pedro
acienda de las Norias and the birth of his daughter. Consequently
years had elapsed since the occurrence of the circumstances narrated
n Estevan Diaz.

[1] See "Stoneheart," the companion volume.